Modesty Blaise

Peter O'Donnell began writing at the age of sixteen when he sold his first story. He has lost count since then but thinks the tally reaches over a thousand short stories and novels. He also writes television and film scripts.

Born in 1921, he spent two years working on juvenile periodicals and served in the Royal Corps Signals during World War II. He began writing strip cartoons – the best known of these are probably 'Garth' in the *Daily Mirror* and 'Tug Transom' in the *Daily Sketch*. 'Modesty Blaise' took him a year to create and in 1962 she was presented as a strip-cartoon character in the *Evening Standard*. The cartoon was an immediate success, soon syndicating in over forty countries, and the 'Modesty Blaise' series of novels followed.

D1341537

Also by Peter O'Donnell in Pan Books

Sabre-tooth
A Taste for Death
Pieces of Modesty
The Impossible Virgin
I, Lucifer
The Silver Mistress
The Night of Morningstar

Peter O'Donnell
Modesty Blaise

Pan Books London and Sydney

First published in Great Britain in 1965
by Souvenir Press Ltd
This edition published 1966 by Pan Books Ltd,
Cavaye Place, London SW10 9PG
19 18 17 16 15 14 13 12 11 10
ISBN 0 330 10474 8
© Peter O'Donnell 1965
Printed in Great Britain by
Richard Clay (The Chaucer Press) Ltd, Bungay, Suffolk

This book is sold subject to the condition that it
shall not, by way of trade or otherwise, be lent, re-sold,
hired out or otherwise circulated without the publisher's prior
consent in any form of binding or cover other than that in which
it is published and without a similar condition including this
condition being imposed on the subsequent purchaser

For Constance

ONE

FRASER adjusted his spectacles to the angle which he knew would produce the effect of prim stupidity he favoured most. Running a finger down his nose, he stared obtusely at the open dossier in his hands.

'I would suppose, sir,' he said cautiously, 'that Modesty Blaise might be a person awfully difficult for us—er—actually to get.' He blinked towards the big, grey-haired man who stood by the window, looking down at the night traffic hurrying along Whitehall.

'For a moment,' Tarrant said, turning from the window, 'I hoped you might split that infinitive, Fraser.'

'I'm sorry, Sir Gerald.' Fraser registered contrition. 'Another time, perhaps.'

Tarrant moved to the big desk across one corner of the room. Settling in his chair, he opened a polished wooden box, took out a cigar, and addressed himself to lighting it.

'A remarkable woman, Fraser,' he said, watching the heavy smoke coiling up in the warm fluorescent light. 'If you had been a child, on your own, in a Middle East D.P. camp in '45, do you think you could have managed to retire at twenty-six with well over half a million sterling? A small female child, of course.'

Fraser quickly reviewed his selection of expressions, and chose the slightly offended one with pursed lips. Tarrant studied the look, then nodded his approval.

'The point is,' he went on, 'that we're hardly likely to get her for money. Not on the Civil Service scale of two thousand a year, anyway.'

Fraser lifted a hand with middle finger delicately bent, and scratched minutely at the scalp beneath his thinning hair. 'Some of our people have a vocation for the work,' he said diffidently.

'Yes. She seems to have a feeling for this country.' Tarrant frowned at his cigar. 'After all, she chose to settle here. But I don't feel that a clarion call to service is the way to get her, either.'

'Blackmail?' Fraser tried to combine furtiveness, daring and distaste in one expression. He fell short, and received a sympathetic wag of the head from Tarrant.

'No . . . not blackmail. I don't think we really have the levers for it, Fraser. And we need much more than reluctant co-operation.'

'I wonder if . . . ?' Fraser let the sentence hang while he carefully selected a buff half-sheet from the dossier and peered at it unnecessarily for several seconds. 'I wonder if this might do?'

Tarrant took the slip and read the short message through twice. 'The hesitant but hopeful look,' he thought, and looked up at Fraser to find that he was right.

Briefly he wondered why a man with Jack Fraser's field record should take such pains to project himself as an ineffectual dolt, now that he was safely behind a desk. Sheer habit, probably. The pose had served him handsomely in the past and might be hard to put aside now. Tarrant had no objection to the game. The two men were old friends and Fraser could speak with earthy bluntness on the brief occasions when he laid the pose aside. In any case it was a harmless game, sometimes useful and frequently amusing.

'The message only came up from Cipher an hour ago,' Fraser said with a vague, apologetic gesture. 'They wouldn't attach any importance to it, of course. Just part of a general routine report. But it did occur to me that perhaps . . . ?'

'I think it might do very well indeed.' Tarrant passed the half-sheet back and glanced at his watch. 'Ten o'clock. Do you think she might see us tonight?'

'No time like the present.' Fraser rolled out the phrase sententiously, not quite able to hide his delight at the opportunity. 'Shall I try her number, sir?'

There was a pleasant warmth in the night air as Fraser drove his old Bentley down Constitution Hill and swung with bland belligerence through the traffic at Hyde Park Corner.

Rightly drawing an outraged cry from a taxi-driver, he responded with an apologetic simper, immediately followed by a bellowed oath of such horrific imagination that Tarrant was hard put to conceal his admiration.

'Your conversation with Modesty Blaise was very brief,' Tarrant said as they drove through the park. 'Did she ask no questions?'

'None, Sir Gerald.' Fraser hunched over the wheel and blinked worriedly through the windscreen. 'When I asked if you might call she just said: "Yes. Now if you wish." She seemed to know your name.'

'She does. On two occasions she sent Willie Garvin over from Tangier to sell me rather valuable items of information. Some Nasser stuff, and a very useful thing on the Russian organisation in The Lebanon.'

'What impression did you have of Garvin, sir?'

'A rough diamond, but remarkably well polished in parts. His speech is Bethnal Green—though I believe his French and Arabic are very good. His manners are impeccable; I lunched him at Rand's Club to over-awe him, but he might have been born to it. His bargaining was cheerful but ruthless. And he had the relaxed superiority of ... well, of a plenipotentiary sent by a reigning empress.'

'Not of a consort?' Fraser asked diffidently.

'Definitely not that. As courtier to queen. No more.'

'A pity, really.' Fraser sighed, and shouldered an Austin Mini aside. 'If that *had* been the relationship, it might have made your position stronger. I mean, now that Garvin's in trouble.'

'Yes. But on the other hand ... ?' Tarrant made it a question inviting completion.

'That's true.' Fraser nodded solemnly several times. 'With a consort relationship, Garvin probably wouldn't be in trouble. And you'd have no position at all, sir.'

The tall block looking out over the park had been designed by a disciple of Le Corbusier and completed little more than a year ago, a triumph of simple elegance. Below ground-level lay a private swimming-pool, squash courts and a gymnasium, for use of the residents and their guests. The facade was of rubbed stone, the roof-line broken by receding planes with balconies. At the summit, the pent house faced south and was bounded on two sides by a covered terrace of concrete flags with grass-grown joints.

The pent house had sold for seventy thousand pounds.

At the desk in the large foyer a uniformed commissionaire inclined his head politely in response to Tarrant's enquiry.

'Yes, sir. Miss Blaise rang down that she was expecting you.'

Beyond a field of soft maroon carpeting stood the solid doors of a private lift. The commissionaire touched a button and they slid quietly open.

'Yes, here we are. She's sent the lift down for you. If you gentlemen would step in, please? It'll take you direct to the top—doesn't serve any other floors.'

'Thank you.' Tarrant pressed the button and the doors slid shut. The lift started with slow courtesy, then accelerated smoothly. At the top, the doors slid back and the two men stepped out.

They were in a broad open foyer floored with ceramic tiles in charcoal-grey. Beyond lay a large room extending some fifty feet to the far wall, where a floor-to-ceiling window looked out over the park. The room was contiguous with the foyer but on a lower level, three steps down from a slender wrought-iron balustrade which edged the foyer across the width of the room.

Throughout there was the imprint of a strong personality, and the immediate impression was of warmth and simplicity. But then the eye began to find strange enigmas in that simplicity, a curious mingling of styles which should have clashed but astonishingly blended.

The foyer was furnished with two chairs, Louis XVI bergère, and a drum table. To one side was an alcove for coats, behind a maize velvet curtain. The floor of the room proper was set with plain octagonal tiles, dull ivory in colour. On it were scattered seven or eight rugs of varying size, glowing with the rich colours of Isfahan.

The middle of one wall was broken by a run of masonry in natural stone, with a hole-in-the-wall fireplace. The remaining walls were of golden cedar strip. They bore half a dozen pictures and a François Boucher tapestry. Of the pictures, Tarrant recognised a Miro, a Braque still life, and a Modigliani. The others were unknown to him.

All doors leading from the room, and the two leading off from the foyer, were of teak veneer. They extended from floor to ceiling, and were sliding doors.

In one corner of the room, broad curving shelves held a scattering of ornaments—a porcelain-mounted lion clock after Caffieri, backed by a pair of Sèvres plates; a jade dragon bowl of the Chia Ch'ing period, and a silver vinaigrette; three superb ivories, a Clodion statuette, and an antique mahogany knife-urn.

The lighting was superb, and the larger pieces of furniture were in plain colours against the rich patterns of the rugs. Tarrant noted the deep-buttoned chesterfield in black hide, the two Barcelona chairs in mellow tan, and a long, low table tiled in white and gold.

Built-in shelves along part of one wall held books and records, with the satisfactory, slightly untidy look of usage. There was a hi-fi towards the end of the shelves, partly hidden by a Coromandel screen.

But it was to the rugs that Tarrant's eyes kept returning. They touched him with the same pleasurable melancholy as certain music, *Les Préludes* of Liszt, perhaps.

Beside him he heard a long, reverent sigh from his companion.

'Hannibal's piles,' breathed Fraser, who found relief from emotion in coarseness. 'What a bloody cracker.'

Together they moved to the steps dividing the low wrought-iron balustrade. Fraser, himself again now, hugged his briefcase awkwardly and darted suspicious glances about him. From an open doorway on the right of the room there came the faint greenish glow of daylight fluorescent, and the soft hum of a small machine.

Tarrant put down his bowler hat and umbrella on a chair.

'I think you'd better cough, Fraser,' he suggested.

'Don't trouble yourself, Mr. Fraser.' The voice held a mellow timbre with a slight foreign inflexion. The intonation was cool but not unfriendly. She stood in the open doorway with the fluorescent light behind her. The face was smooth and calm, with high cheekbones under dark, contemplative eyes. She would be five foot six, Tarrant thought, but with the black hair drawn up into a chignon on the crown of her head she appeared taller.

Her skin held a soft, matt tan that would have made a fortune for any man who could get it into a bottle. Her mouth baffled Tarrant. Studied in isolation it was a touch too wide, but in the totality of her features a smaller mouth would have been wrong. Her neck, he decided, though magnificent, was definitely too long ... but then again that wonderful poise of the head would have been marred by a shorter neck. Her legs——

No, dammit, they weren't too long. He wasn't going to fall into the same trap again. This girl was made to be looked at as a whole—and as often as possible, for preference. He was surprised to find that he had an urgent wish to see her smile.

She wore a cling sweater in winter-white with a polo neck. The sleeves were pushed carelessly back almost to her elbows. It was tucked into a wine-red skirt of fine tweed, with pleats at each side and pocket flaps. The skirt was held by a broad black leather belt with a double ring, and fell just to the middle of the knee. Her legs, of that same matt tan, were bare. She wore dull gold open sandals with set-back heels, and the touch of coral red on the toenails matched her lips.

'Miss Blaise...' Tarrant moved down the steps, extending his hand. 'I'm Tarrant. And may I introduce my colleague, John Fraser.'

Her hand was cool, and he felt the play of wiry sinews in the long fingers. She turned a little to greet Fraser, and Tarrant saw her eyes strip the man of his obtuseness, label him 'not-to-be-underestimated', and file him away in her mind.

'Forgive us for calling so late, Miss Blaise.' Tarrant let no more than a hint of apology colour his words. 'Are we disturbing you?'

'Not very much. I'm interested to see you.' The directness of the answer disposed of formality. 'But there's something I'd like to get finished. It will only take three or four minutes—please come in.'

12

She turned back into the room, and they followed. Tarrant had been in a lapidary's workshop before, but had never seen one as tidy as this. There were three separate benches, each with a tall stool. One bench held a bed of three horizontal wheels connected to a motor at the end. The lead wheel was some distance from the other two, and behind it stood a jar of carborundum. There was a tin of finest emery flour behind the wooden wheel, and a small jar of putty powder behind the felt wheel.

On the second bench stood a small, watchmaker's lathe fitted with a slitting-saw—a four-inch vertical disc of phosphor-bronze, its edge impregnated with diamond dust.

Modesty Blaise seated herself at the third bench, and gestured for the men to take the other two stools. She picked up a dopstick with a sapphire cemented on its broad head. At a long glance, Tarrant estimated the gem at forty carats. It had been cut *en cabochon,* and now she was working on it with a point carver. She switched on, and the running spindle began to turn.

Her face grew absorbed. Holding the dopstick in two hands, the butts of her palms resting on the angle plate, she slid the gem towards the cutting bit.

Tarrant looked about him. A large wall-safe stood open. Several drawers of varying sizes had been taken from a rack in the safe and lay on the bench at his elbow. One drawer was filled with a dozen or more gems in the rough—diamonds and rubies, emeralds and sapphires. Another held smaller gems, cut, faceted and polished.

Then, in a larger drawer, he saw the carved semi-precious stones, and caught his breath. There were tiny jars and bottles carved from jade and agate, a satanic head in gold sheen obsidian, and a rose in pink alabaster. He saw an eight-armed goddess in white chalcedony, and a huge flat oval of intricately chased jet.

For three minutes there was no sound in the room except for the whine of the motor. Fraser, his mask forgotten, watched intently.

Modesty Blaise switched off the motor and stood up. She screwed a jeweller's glass into one eye and studied the sapphire

13

for ten seconds, then lifted her head, allowing the glass to drop into her hand.

'May I see it, please?' Tarrant asked with a hint of genuine diffidence.

'Of course. There's still some polishing to be done.' She passed him the glass and the dopstick.

The head of a girl was cameo-sculpted on the sapphire in semi-profile, long hair drawn back, shoulders bare. Incredibly, the tiny face was alive. Tarrant tried to see how it had been achieved by those simple outlines and hollows, but it was beyond analysis. In silence he passed the dopstick and glass to Fraser, then looked at Modesty Blaise.

'This is your hobby, carving gemstones?' he asked.

'Yes.' She met his eyes. 'I don't handle them professionally any more.' Her face was suddenly illumined by a surge of silent laughter. Here was the smile he had wanted to see. It was rich with delight, completely without restraint, and holding a gamine touch of mischief. Tarrant found himself grinning back at her.

'Not professionally,' he said, and inclined his head in agreement. 'We know you're retired, Miss Blaise. And naturally you need a hobby to occupy you.'

Her smile had gone now, leaving only a memory of it in the eyes. With Tarrant's last words the memory vanished and she looked at him thoughtfully.

'Of course.' Her voice was neutral. 'Now, what will you drink?'

They followed her into the big room, and she moved to a small bar, jutting from an alcove, which held shelves of bottles and glasses.

'Please sit down. Sir Gerald?'

'A small brandy, please.'

'And you, Mr. Fraser?'

'Oh—er ...' Fraser drew a finger down his nose. 'A large one, please,' he said with nervous bravado, then shrank back into his chair. Fumbling busily, he took two folders from his briefcase and rested them on his lap.

Tarrant watched with approval the economy of movement she brought to the business of fixing the drinks. The brandies were placed on a small table between the two men. She poured a glass of red wine for herself, a vin ordinaire he noticed, then settled at one end of the chesterfield and drew her feet up.

'It's interesting to meet you, Sir Gerald,' she said, lifting the glass slightly in acknowledgment. 'I used to have a dossier on you before I retired.'

'Oh, I'm a dull old stick, Miss Blaise.' He sipped the brandy, and felt the Midas touch that turned the throat to gold. 'You have a much more fascinating biography.'

'How much do you know of it?'

'Ah. Fraser would be terribly upset if I claimed that we *knew* anything. Most of it is a series of guesses and deductions.'

'May I hear them?'

'Of course.'

Tarrant nodded to Fraser, who opened a folder and frowned at the typescript within.

'Well—er—briefly, Miss Blaise,' he said uneasily, 'we first have you on record at *about* the age of seventeen. We believe you came from a D.P. camp in the Middle East, and there was no way to check your exact age.'

'I can't help you there, Mr. Fraser,' she said gravely. 'I've never been able to check it myself.'

'I see. Well, to summarise, you were a stateless person, and at this approximate age of seventeen we have you working in a small gambling establishment in Tangier. It was controlled by the Louche group—Henri Louche being a man who headed a small criminal organisation. On his death at the hands of rivals one year later, you took control and there followed a remarkable expansion.'

Fraser looked up from the dossier owlishly.

'I am not,' he said, 'at this stage differentiating between items of fact and items of supposition, you understand?'

'That's very wise, Mr. Fraser.' She rose, picked up a silver cigarette box and offered it to Fraser. The cigarettes were Perfecto Finos. When he declined, she took one herself and set a humidor of cigars at Tarrant's elbow.

'I wasn't expecting you,' she said. 'I'm afraid there's only a choice of Burma cheroots and Petit Coronas.'

'I shall enjoy a Petit Corona, thank you. But what if you had been expecting me, Miss Blaise?'

'You smoke a Punch-Punch claro, I believe.'

'I do.' He rolled the cigar gently between his fingers, watching her as she returned to her seat. 'Willie Garvin has an eye for detail. Your dossier on me must be quite exhaustive.'

'It was. But it wasn't dull. Please go on, Mr. Fraser.'

'The group,' said Fraser, turning a page, 'under the—ah—new management, became known in due course as The Network and operated on an international scale. The crimes included art and jewel thefts; smuggling; currency and gold manipulations; and an espionage service.'

'My own information,' she said, exhaling a feather of smoke, 'is that The Network at no time traded in secrets belonging to Her Majesty's Government.'

'We have wondered about that,' Tarrant said reflectively. 'Can you suggest a reason?'

'It might be that the responsible person wanted to settle here eventually, and had no wish to be considered undesirable.'

'Why here?'

'That could be a long story. I don't think it's important.'

'We also note,' Fraser said dubiously, 'that The Network abstained completely from two profitable fields of crime—drugs and vice. On two occasions it gave valuable help to the United States Bureau of Narcotics.'

She nodded. 'So I believe. I suppose if one takes a point of view one must act positively when opportunity offers.'

'In 1962,' said Fraser, 'we have as a fact that you married and divorced a derelict Englishman in Beirut. We believe this was a purely financial arrangement for gaining British nationality.'

'Yes. Very purely.' Again the sudden smile briefly lit her face. Fraser cleared his throat, looked embarrassed, and stared down at the typescript.

'So,' he went on, 'we now go back to the time two or three years after you started The Network, when you were joined by William Garvin. We have his personal dossier as an appendix here.' He fluttered some pages. 'He was in an approved school in England, and later served two short prison sentences before disappearing abroad. There, for a number of years, he was in many kinds of trouble in different parts of the world. I will omit what details we have, but we believe you found him in Saigon, soon after he was discharged from the Foreign Legion. From that point on, we—ah—move into the field of speculation again.'

Fraser paused and drank some brandy. Fraser was a brandy man, and Tarrant watched with interest his struggle to suppress a look of astonished pleasure. Bravely, after a frozen moment, Fraser put down the glass and wrinkled his nose noncommittally.

'It would seem,' he said, returning to the dossier, 'that Garvin was a close associate of yours for six or seven years, Miss Blaise—until last year, in fact, when The Network was split up among its various—er—branch-managers in different countries.'

He closed the folder and looked up archly. 'We know that you both came to this country eleven months ago, Miss Blaise, and we know that Garvin bought a public house called *The Treadmill*, on the river. We also know that you are both extremely wealthy, which may explain why there has been no hint,' he paused and gave a furtive leer, 'of any—um—illegal activities since that time.'

'Very good,' said Tarrant. 'Beautifully articulated, Fraser. You have delightful vowels.' He received the expected simper of demurral, and glanced across at Modesty Blaise enquiringly.

'It's interesting,' she said slowly, 'but as you say, mainly speculation. I don't feel you can use it for any drastic move.'

'I've no thought of using it.' Tarrant paused, and there was silence. One good thing about this girl was that silence didn't worry her. She allowed time to think, without rushing to fill the gaps.

Tarrant was thinking now, and he was conscious of disappointment. This girl fascinated him. She was beautiful and stimulating. Her serenity, against the strange dark background of her life, was enormously exciting. But so far there was something missing—a quality he had learned to sense in his

17

agents as he could sense the quality of a fine cigar before smoking it.

This was a thing hard to define. More of a potential than a quality, perhaps. The potential for cold ferocity joined to an inflexible will. Good God, she must have had it once. Could she have lost it now? So far he had caught no hint of it in Modesty Blaise. She was perfectly relaxed, perfectly controlled, and that was right. But he could detect nothing of the vital potential to turn tiger. Was the core of steel rusted and the flame of will dead?

'Far from using our suspicions against you in any way,' he said amiably, 'we rather hoped you might be useful to us.'

She drank from the glass of red wine, not taking her eyes from him.

'Nobody uses me, Sir Gerald,' she answered very quietly. 'Nobody. I made up my mind about that long ago—before that dossier begins.'

'I understand. But I hoped to persuade you.'

'How?' She looked at him curiously. Tarrant studied the tip of his cigar and glanced casually across at Fraser, who sat with one hand resting on his knee. The fingers and thumb were straight, and close together; the hand was palm down. Fraser's opinion was that this should be played straight. Tarrant agreed.

'We realise it would be pointless to offer you money, Miss Blaise,' he said. 'But we can offer you Willie Garvin.'

'Willie?' The dark eyebrows arched upwards.

'Yes. Have you been in touch with him recently?'

'Not for about six weeks. Then he was in town for a couple of nights and spent them here. We went back to *The Treadmill* together for the weekend to try his new speedboat. After that I spent a month with some friends in Capri, and got back a week ago. I haven't been in touch again yet.'

'You won't find him at *The Treadmill*.'

'That doesn't surprise me. Willie's dream of running his own little pub has palled rather quickly. He moves around quite a lot—and he has a wonderfully varied list of girl-friends. From *premier cru* to honest *vin du pays*.'

'Garvin isn't indulging his romantic palate. He's a very long way away, on the other side of the world. And he's in prison, Miss Blaise. Not under his own name, I may say. But I suppose it hardly matters what name a man is hanged under.'

Then it came, and Tarrant savoured it with infinite joy. Modesty Blaise had not changed her expression or posture by a hair's-breadth. She still sat with legs drawn up at one end of the couch, the glass of wine in her hand. Nothing had altered. Yet suddenly the whole room seemed charged with the crackling emanation of force from that still figure.

To Tarrant it came as the briny scent of a storm, when the static potential builds up to breaking point before discharging to earth in a savage explosion of energy.

'Hanged?' Her voice was still mellow. As mellow, thought Tarrant, as the martial call of Roland's horn.

'Or shot,' he answered with a slight gesture. 'It's not exactly imminent because the situation in ... in the place where Garvin finds himself is still a little confused. I feel there might just be time for somebody to do something—if they managed it within the next eight or nine days.'

Modesty Blaise crushed out the half-smoked Perfecto Fino and drew a jar of Sèvres porcelain towards her. From it she took thick black tobacco and a yellow paper. Absently, with practised ease, she spread tobacco along the paper, rolled and lit it.

'This is all a little cryptic, Sir Gerald,' she said.

'Yes. Intentionally so, of course.'

'You want to use me for——?'

'For one operation,' he broke in quickly. 'One special job, my dear. That's all. It's something you're uniquely fitted for, and it may prove to be no more than a watching brief.'

'In return, you'll tell me where Willie Garvin is now?'

Her question hung on the air. Tarrant drank and put down his glass. Fraser's hand, still resting on his knee, had turned and was loosely curled. Opinion—put the screw on hard. Tarrant reviewed the advice and rejected it.

'No,' he said, rising. 'We'll make it a gift, Miss Blaise. And we'll go now, since I'm sure you'll have a lot to arrange in a very short time. Fraser, pass Miss Blaise the copy of that message, please.'

19

For an instant Fraser's eyes widened in genuine surprise, then he recovered and ducked his head obsequiously, fumbling in his briefcase. She took the buff half-sheet from him and paced slowly across to the huge window, reading it, the cigarette clipped between her fingers.

'Thank you.' She returned to where the two men stood waiting, and handed the slip to Fraser, her eyes on Tarrant. 'I take it this job of yours isn't too immediate, Sir Gerald. I shall be out of the country for the next ten days or so.'

'If I might talk to you when you return, it would be very satisfactory.' He took her hand. 'Goodbye, and I hope your trip goes well.'

'Thank you again.' She walked with them to the raised foyer and the lift. The doors slid back as she pressed two buttons on the control-panel.

'You're a clever man, Sir Gerald.' She looked at him with frank interest. 'How did you know?'

'I'm sorry. Know what?'

'That I hate blackmail. But that I'm a compulsive payer of debts. I'm sure that isn't in my dossier.'

'No.' Tarrant picked up his hat and umbrella. 'But I've met your Willie Garvin.'

'He wouldn't have discussed me.'

'Indeed not. But he's not an enigma—I found him easy to read. And I felt he must reflect you. After all, you created him.'

Fraser seized the opening.

'Like master, like man,' he said portentously and with hidden delight.

When the two men had gone she stood by the window looking out across the dark park while she finished her cigarette. Once she half smiled and shook her head.

'Should have seen it coming,' she murmured. 'Hard to blame you, Willie. My God, I know just how you felt.'

She stubbed out the cigarette and went to the telephone. For the next hour she was busy making several calls, one to a startled man eight thousand miles away. When this was done she went through into her bedroom, of pale green, ivory and silver-grey. The wall was panelled, and the panel to the right of the big double bed was of painted steel. It opened by the setting of the dressing-table drawers in a particular order and position, and it moved on soundless bearings.

Beyond lay a tall cubby-hole, six feet square, originally intended as a walk-in wardrobe. For a moment she stood looking at the three heavy trunks which stood on the floor, and at the variety of smaller boxes on the side-shelves. There was a glint of amused resignation in her eyes.

'I wonder why we kept all our gear, Willie love?' she said aloud.

Bending, she began to open one of the trunks.

In the parked car, Fraser sat behind the wheel and spoke with the pinched approval of the loser congratulating the winner.

'I feel you handled that with great success, Sir Gerald, if I may say so. I didn't dare to hope that putting her in debt would be effective.'

'You may say so, Fraser. You may. But I take it you realise that putting her in our debt was almost irrelevant?'

'I beg your pardon?'

'She's lived on a dangerous tight-rope for the best part of twenty-six years. How easy do you think it is to stop?'

'But she has achieved her ambition, sir. Half a million or so, and a life to match.'

'Meaningless. Or tragic, perhaps. Danger can be a drug, and she's hooked by it. Dammit man, you were still hooked by it yourself at nearly twice her age. I had to *drag* you behind a desk. This girl doesn't show it, of course. She's totally controlled. But the withdrawal pains must be there.' His voice grew dry. 'They didn't show with Willie Garvin until now.'

'I'm sorry.' Fraser swallowed miserably and shot him a hunted look. 'I haven't taken your point yet, sir. You seem to be saying that putting her in debt over Garvin isn't the *real* reason that we were able to get her.'

'It's the excuse,' Tarrant said softly. 'She needed an excuse, whether she knows it or not. I wasn't looking for a way to force her. I was looking for the right way to *let* her do this job for us, Jack.'

21

The use of the first name called a halt to the game Fraser loved, and signalled that for the time being play was suspended. Fraser relaxed and rested his arms on the wheel, a slow grin spreading over his face.

'Well stuff me standing load,' he said admiringly. 'You bloody old fox.'

TWO

MODESTY BLAISE stood with her flank against the trunk of a palm, some ten feet from the thinning fringe of trees. Night had long since fallen. The bellbirds and parrots were silent, and from behind her there came only the rustle and murmur of the living forest. From a star-splashed sky a waning moon glinted down upon the metalled road which wound between the forest and the savanna.

The prison stood in a half-circle of beaten earth where the ground had been cleared in a wide curve reaching back from the road. It was a temporary prison, converted from a barracks, a long single-storied building of adobe, shaped like a letter T. The cross of the T faced the road, the upright jutted back towards the trees, with a wide door at its base. Immediately beyond the door lay the guard-room.

Modesty had stood there, motionless, for two hours now. Every ten minutes a ragged sentry with a slung Garand rifle passed within thirty feet of her on his beat. A useless sentry, she thought. You could hear him coming and going, catch the clink of rifle on bandolier, and see the red glow of his cigarette a hundred yards away.

Six weeks ago he had been a rebel. Now he and the rest of his friends were Government troops. The ex-Government troops were now the rebels, but not for much longer. General Kalzaro's coup had succeeded beyond the point of reverse, beyond the point where he needed to be prudent about disposing of those who had fought on the losing side.

Six days had passed since her meeting with Tarrant, and she knew now that his assessment of the situation had been a shrewd one. Santos, in Buenos Aires, had confirmed that assessment only forty-eight hours ago. If Willie Garvin was to be brought out alive it would have to be very soon.

She wore black denim slacks, loose enough in the leg for free movement, the bottoms tucked into thick-soled combat boots. A thin black polo-neck sweater covered her body, neck and arms. Her hands and face were dark with camouflage cream. The high chignon of her hair was now a short, tightly-bound club hanging at the nape of her neck.

She watched a ramshackle truck pull away from the prison and out on to the road. Its grass-stuffed tyres squealed as it jolted away round the bend, carrying the day-guards who supervised working-parties of prisoners repairing the road two miles north. Fifteen minutes later the sentry patrolling this rear beat of the unfenced perimeter was relieved.

Soon now she could begin. The tingling warmth within her spread in a glow of curious happiness through every part of her being. She resented it, tried to quell it, then yielded in the wry knowledge of wasted energy.

You couldn't make yourself over again at twenty-six. She had learned that lesson over the past twelve months. Willie must have learned it too, and studiously hidden it from her as she had hidden it from him.

In the dark years long gone, almost from the first dawnings of memory, each night and each day had held fear and danger for the lone child moving like some small wild creature through the war-turmoil of the Balkans and the Levant. But later, with puberty, there came a time when fear was trans-muted into stimulus, and the moments of danger which had once brought terror now brought only a keener sense of being alive.

It was a pity. There were so many better ways of living fully. But it was too late now, and she had long ago learned not to cry for the unattainable.

The new sentry was starting his return beat from the west. Modesty flexed her fingers round the little object in her right hand. It was a kongo, or yawara-stick, a thing of hard smooth wood, shaped like an elongated dumb-bell so that the shaft fitted into the palm with the mushroom-shaped ends protruding from the clenched fist.

Placing her feet carefully, she moved forward. There was no sound, for the ground was covered with a thick moist carpet of rotting leaves.

The sentry was thinking about women, specifically about a

girl in the village they had taken a week ago. That had been a night. He grinned at the memory, his blood stirring.

She was about eighteen, and completely new to it, but obedient as a cowed bitch once Sergeant Alvarez had explained how it would be for her otherwise. It was Alvarez, too, who had produced the amusing idea of offering a bottle of whisky to whichever of the six men could devise the most imaginative position.

Ricco had won, of course. The sentry chuckled admiringly at the memory. It was a miracle the old sod hadn't pulled a leg muscle, or suffocated the girl——

Something white lay on the ground ahead and to one side, near the bole of a tree. He moved forward, peering. It was a square piece of paper, but with something resting on it. He bent closer. A coin. A *gold* coin . . .

Modesty moved out behind the bent form. One hand darted out to grip him by the hair, the other came down like a hammer, the lower butt of the kongo striking precisely below the ear.

He slumped bonelessly, and she caught the rifle, lowering it with him. From the small pocket on her left thigh she took a slender metal tube and uncapped it. Into her palm she tipped two little white cylinders of compressed cotton-wool, about the size of cigarette-tips. She sniffed them warily, catching the faint, sickly-sweet smell, then knelt and slid them into the man's nostrils.

Her feet made no sound as she moved swiftly across the open stretch of beaten earth towards the pool of light which spread from the lamp above the open door. Here, to one side of the door, a man leaned against the wall looking at a tattered girlie magazine, his rifle propped beside him. She circled a little to approach him from the side, edging along the wall, her back flat against it.

When she was six feet away he lifted his head. Even as shock widened his eyes she took one long pace and twisted to bring her leg swinging in an arc. The booted foot took him full in the groin. For an instant the unconscious body was rigid with paralysis, then it melted slowly to the ground. No need for the anaesthetic nose-plugs.

She stepped over him and went through the doorway. Now the kongo was in her left hand, and in her right was the little MAB Brevete automatic, drawn from the soft leather holster belted beneath her sweater. The gun was no stopper, unless you were very accurate. Modesty Blaise was very accurate. And the advantage lay in the gun's comparative quietness.

Ahead of her was a long, broad corridor with steel-barred cell doors on either side. From it came the stench of unwashed humanity, the wailing of a man broken by fear, and the shrill, gasping cries of one in a nightmare.

On her right, the heavy door of the guard-room stood half open. Within, a radio was blaring martial music interspersed by news bulletins gabbled at a high pitch of excitement.

Modesty spent two seconds reviewing alternatives. She would have liked to push on, but had learned the hard way that nothing was more vital than to secure the line of retreat. There was a white bullet-scar on her flank, just below the buttock, to remind her of the penalty for neglect.

She slipped the kongo into its squeeze-pouch in the ribbing at the bottom of her sweater. From the stretch-pocket on the front of her right thigh she drew out a curious object consisting of a nose-clip and a mouthpiece, with a small drum, one inch deep, connecting the two. A miniature gas-mask.

For a moment she hesitated over whether to use The Nailer. This meant taking off her sweater and bra, and going into the room stripped to the waist. She felt no reticence about the idea, for it was a highly practical one, first improvised on a life-and-death occasion with Willie Garvin in Agrigento five years ago, and she had proved it twice since. The technique was guaranteed to nail a roomful of men, holding them frozen for at least two or three vital seconds.

She decided that it was unnecessary here. With the guards relaxed and unsuspecting, The Nailer was superfluous. Quickly she fixed the gas-mask on, the clip gripping her nose, her lips holding the rubbery mouthpiece firmly against her gums.

She pushed open the door and moved in, eyes sweeping the whole room on the instant of entry. Four soldiers sat round an upturned crate playing cards. The window beyond them was shuttered. Good. The men were grouped in a limited target. Better still. They sat frozen, eight eyes staring towards her, a hand rigid in the act of gathering scattered cards for the deal.

The man facing her was burly and wore sergeant's stripes on his grubby jacket He was the first to recover, and as she kicked the door shut behind her she tabbed him as the danger-man. A slow grin began to spread across the stubbly face as his eyes moved from the strangely obscured features to the thrust of her breasts and curves of her body.

She moved the gun slightly, drawing his eyes so that he stared straight at the round black eye of the automatic, as steady as if held in a clamp. The grin faded and the eyes narrowed watchfully.

From the other thigh-pocket she drew out a black, domed metal cylinder. It was like a pepper-pot. She moved forward and reached out to place it on the crate. For that moment her gun hand was no more than a foot from the shoulder of one of the men. She sensed the inward tensing of his muscles for sudden movement, but she kept the gun aimed unwaveringly at the middle of the sergeant's face. A bead of sweat trickled down his brow, and he rapped out a savage whisper of command in Spanish. *'Don't move, you son of a pig!'*

The man hesitated. She put down the squat pepper-pot and heard the faint click of the mechanism at its base as she stepped back two paces. A soft hissing came from the pepper-pot, barely audible under the blaring radio.

The sergeant stared, sniffed in renewed alarm, then looked at her with vicious eyes. His left hand still lay splayed on the crate, over some cards. His right began to creep slowly round his belt to the holstered revolver there.

For an instant she altered her aim, and the gun yapped sharply. A bullet drilled into the crate between two of his spread fingers, throwing up a little crater of splinters. The olive face grew grey, and he sat like a statue, eyes fixed on the hissing cylinder like the eyes of a hypnotised rabbit.

One man lurched sideways and crumpled to the floor. The sergeant and another fell only five seconds later. With an inward wave of laughter she saw that the fourth man was

27

holding his breath. His face was growing darker and his eyes bulged in hopeless desperation.

There came an explosive huff of exhaled air and the long sighing sob of helplessly indrawn breath. Still glaring stonily, the eyes closed and he keeled over.

Modesty turned to the two things she had marked on the wall in that first photographic survey of the room—a bunch of large keys on a ring, hanging on a hook; and beneath them, on the same hook, a curious harness of black elasticised webbing, a chest harness. Attached to it were two slim black sheaths of hard leather, each bearing a flat, black-handled throwing knife.

Later, when danger was past and she could unblock her mind to feeling again, this moment would bring a strange mixture of emotions. There was the warmth of happening upon a souvenir of times past. There was the sadness of seeing a symbol that marked a vain pipe-dream, never to be realised. And there was the touch of something like fear in seeing this thing alone, separate from the man of whom it was a part.

She took down the keys and the harness, moved quickly out of the room, and closed the door. Quietly she began to move down the broad corridor between the cells, taking the gas-mask off as she went.

Willie Garvin lay on the splintered boards of a narrow bunk, hands behind his head, staring dully at a lizard on the cracked ceiling of the cell. A wedge of light from the passage threw the bars of the door in broad black shadows across the stone floor.

He was a big man, an inch or two over six feet, thirty-four years old, with tousled fair hair and blue eyes set in a face made up of small flat planes. His hands were large, with square-tipped fingers, and his body was hard and well-muscled, particularly the powerful deltoids running from neck to shoulder.

On the back of his right hand was a big scar, shaped like an uncompleted S. It had been made with a red-hot knife-blade, wielded carefully by a man called Suleiman, and it was uncompleted because Modesty Blaise had come into that room beneath the warehouse and killed Suleiman by breaking his neck, using the man's own considerable weight to do it.

Alone in the tiny cell, Willie Garvin lay with a grey lethargy blanketing his mind. It was like the old days, the grimy, pointless and hated days, which stretched back from a time seven years ago through the whole of his life; the days before Modesty Blaise, who had suddenly and magically turned his world upside down and made everything All Right.

But now the light that had been turned on in his head throughout those seven years was no longer there. The old groping obscurity was back.

Willie Garvin knew that he should be doing something. A crummy load of ragged-arsed soldiers had caught him and put him in gaol and were going to shoot him soon. If this had been a couple of years back, and on a caper for The Princess, it would have been a dawdle. His mind would have been buzzing with ideas. Given two hours he could have figured six different capers for walking out of this stinking hole.

But a couple of years back he would never have got himself into this anyway—not against such half-hard opposition.

He felt sickened by himself, but there was nothing to be done now because the light had gone out and the wheels in his head had stopped turning. After seven years in which he had walked like a man ten feet tall, he was back in the void again, without anchor or purpose or hope. And soon he would be dead.

'Christ, she'll be mad at me when she hears,' Willie thought vaguely.

Something clinked gently against the bars of the door. He turned his head and saw the black figure half-crouched in the wedge of light.

There was no instant of delay in recognition. Willie Garvin sat up unhurriedly, swung his feet to the ground, and walked quietly to the door. In that time, smoothly and quite un-dramatically, the light in his head was there again and the wheels were turning. The recent past fell away like a fading dream.

She looked at him carefully, gave a little nod, then passed the knife-harness through the bars and began methodically to

29

try the six keys. Willie stripped off his grimy shirt, slipped the harness in place, with the hilts of the knives lying snugly in echelon against his left breast, and put on the shirt again, leaving it unbuttoned from the top to a few inches above the waist.

A key turned and the door swung open. Across the flagged corridor a huddle of four gaunt prisoners in a small cell stared with dull, incurious eyes. Modesty put the keys down on the floor, a bare arm's-reach from them, and saw hope spark in their faces. She nodded to Willie. A knife was in his hand now, held by the point between two fingers and thumb.

They walked side by side along the middle of the corridor at an unhurried pace, and turned at the T-junction along the shorter stretch which led to the guardroom at the end.

Modesty felt the comforting glow of familiarity expanding within her, and sensed the same in Willie. She was moving half-turned to watch the rear and left, so she could not look at him, but she knew that his eyes would be scanning front and right, calmly alert for the first hint of trouble. There was no point in telling him to use minimum force. He would know.

They were ten yards from the open doorway when there came a startled exclamation from outside, and she knew the unconscious soldier there had been found. A man appeared in the doorway, hurriedly bringing his rifle round from the slung position. They moved on without change of pace under his shaken stare.

The rifle came to bear, and they split to either side of the broad corridor, offering separate targets. The soldier swung his rifle uncertainly from one to the other as he fumbled with the bolt.

Modesty lifted her automatic, and like a magnet it drew the rifle-barrel towards her as the bolt snicked back.

Willie's move.

He dived, somersaulting, and the rifle swung frantically back to cover him. But one foot hooked behind the soldier's ankle, the other drove for his knee, and the man went down flat on his back as if drawn by a coiled spring attached to the back of his neck. As the breath exploded from his lungs

30

Modesty's boot swung with controlled force to the side of his head.

Willie was on his feet, coming up with that flickering shoulder-spring—the one move she had never been able to learn for all his patient teaching.

They moved on, easing warily round the stone uprights of the doorway, and facing opposite ways.

All clear. Modesty turned and nodded. Together they ran hard for the trees.

As the thick layer of decaying vegetation sank underfoot there came an outbreak of shouting from the prison. Scattered shots began to sound from the road which formed the front of the perimeter. Some of the prisoners were out, and confusion was beginning.

Modesty slowed to a steady pace. They ran on through vine-hung trees and small clearings. Dappled moonlight touched them as it filtered through the trees. Every fifty yards a scrap of white paper pinned to a tree-trunk charted their route. After half a mile they emerged on to a narrow dirt road.

The car, a black Chrysler, was parked behind a clump of shoulder-high grass. Willie held the door open for Modesty to take the wheel, then ran round to the passenger seat. With dipped headlights the car lifted from the bumpy verge and on to the road. Modesty held the speed at fifty in third until they reached the junction with the metalled road, then slipped into top and pressed the accelerator hard down.

There was a long silence, broken only by the smooth purr of the engine and the drumming of tyres. She was aware that Willie, beside her, was no longer at ease as he had been throughout the action. He sat very upright, tense and awkward. A quick glance at the mirror showed her the sheepish apprehension on his brown face.

Hesitantly he felt in the glove-compartment, found cigarettes, and lit two of them, passing one to her. She took it and inhaled, keeping her eyes on the dark road.

'Over the border in half-an-hour,' she said quietly. 'No problem there. I spread a gold carpet on the way in.'

'I'm sorry, Princess.' Willie Garvin shifted uneasily. 'You didn't ought to 've come.'

'No?' She snapped a glance at him. 'They were all set to top you, Willie, you damn fool. And I wouldn't even have known if Tarrant hadn't told me.'

'Tarrant?'

'The same one.'

'That was decent of 'im.' He frowned. 'But there'll be a pay-off?'

She made no answer, letting him sweat. This was the first time in many years that she had needed to jolt Willie, but he had asked for it and he knew it.

'How d'you get here, Princess?' he asked after a while.

'I heard about you from Tarrant a week ago, booked a flight, and rang Santos in B.A. Asked him to set up a quick in-and-out job for me—the layout, the bribes, everything.'

'You *asked* 'im?' There was a touch of indignation in Willie's voice.

'I couldn't tell him. Santos doesn't work for me any longer. Remember?'

'But he played ball, anyway?'

'He knew I'd break his arms if he didn't.' Her tone sharpened. 'What the hell got into you, Willie? We quit, didn't we? No more crime. We made our pile, split up the organisation, and quit.'

'I wasn't going bent again, Princess——'

'Be quiet and listen, Willie love.' She felt the swift relief in him at her use of the old familiar term. 'You've got a bankful of money and a nice little pub on the river. All you ever wanted. So why come out here and get tangled up as a mercenary in a banana-state revolution?'

Willie sighed. 'My manager runs the pub better'n I could,' he said with a touch of bitterness. 'I was going bonkers, Princess, honest. Up the wall. I 'ad to 'ave a break.'

'Did you have to get caught? And my God, *stay* caught? Willie, it's humiliating. You've gone solo for me often enough before.'

'Yes—for you. It's always been easy when you told me to go an' do it.' He ran a hand through his hair. 'I just couldn't get me 'eart into this lot, Princess. Being on me tod, everything just seemed to shut down. I was scared it might ... but I 'ad to do *something*.' He inhaled broodingly on his cigarette. 'It's no good. Retirement don't suit me some'ow. I dunno 'ow you stick it,' he ended respectfully.

Modesty swung the car off the main road and on to another track, following Santos's careful instructions to the letter.

'Neither do I,' she said in a neutral voice. 'This is the first time I've come alive in a year.'

Willie sat up straight and turned to stare at her.

'Well, then,' he said softly. 'Look, suppose we went back on the old caper, Princess? Start fresh and build up a new Network——?'

'It wouldn't have any point now. We've got all we wanted. And without a point, we'd soon lose out.'

He nodded bleakly. The light was full and clear in his head now, the wheels meshing smoothly, and he knew that her words were true.

'Then what we going to do?' he asked helplessly. 'I mean, just for a break now an' then! *You* know how it is, Princess. The bits between capers are good, but only because they're in between. Without the capers it's all just ... just stale beer.'

'Tarrant's pay-off,' she said slowly. 'It's a job he wants done. But I don't know anything about it yet.'

'Us working under Tarrant?' There was mingled hope and annoyance in Willie's voice.

'Not under. For him. On a particular job. And he didn't pressure me, Willie. But I don't know about "us". This latest effort of yours won't have impressed him.'

'Ah, look Princess! That's different. You can tell Tarrant. I mean, I never laid an egg like this before, all the time I worked for you, did I?'

'No. But that's over now, Willie. I can't bring you in just because I might need help. It means you taking orders from me again. And you're a big boy now. I want you to be your own man.'

'I don't.' He spoke with flat desperation. 'If you don't take me back, I'm a goner.'

'Oh, Willie ... I don't know.' She was troubled. 'Look, we'll see what Tarrant brings. But I hate taking you for granted, and I won't have Tarrant do it, either. Just leave it with me and keep your nose clean. I don't want you in any more trouble.'

'Don't worry, Princess. I've been a right burk. I'm sorry.'

'I won't worry.' The lights of the small border-post showed ahead, and she lifted her foot, turning to look full at him for a moment. Willie saw the rare smile that suddenly lit her face, the smile worth waiting a week for. 'All I'm worrying about now is flight schedules, Willie. I've got a date at Covent Garden on Tuesday.'

THREE

TCHAIKOVSKY'S music swelled and faded. The swans floated away. Siegfried moved in pursuit with his guests, leaving the drunken figure of Wolfgang alone on the stage.

The curtain swept down on Act One of *Swan Lake*, and the devotees thundered their applause.

When Modesty Blaise entered the big, richly decorated bar, it was already crowded. She wore an evening dress of palest apple-green, with an embroidered bodice and a floating panel. Long white gloves reached to her elbows. Her only jewellery was a massive amethyst pendant, superbly carved.

Men shot keen, furtive glances at her and women stared more openly, but she was unaware of it. Her eyes were warm with enjoyment of the last hour.

Her escort was a well-tanned man of about thirty, in a dinner jacket of midnight blue. His name was David Whitstone.

'. . . so all being well,' he was saying, 'Ronnie hopes to have the yacht ready at Cannes by the first week in June.'

'And he's invited you?'

'Us.' His eyes dwelt on her with satisfaction, missing the quick flash of coldness in her expression. 'You and me. Together. For two or three months, down through the Greek Islands.'

'Very romantic. I'd like a drink, please—a glass of red wine.'

'I'm not too sure they actually have any wine, but——' He broke off to stare at the man who stood smiling benevolently at him, with a glass of red wine in one hand and a whisky in the other.

'Modesty, my dear.' Tarrant bowed his head to her. 'Senile though I am, my powers of anticipation are unblunted. Red wine?'

'Sir Gerald. How kind.' She took the glass. 'Do you know David Whitstone? David, this is Sir Gerald Tarrant.'

'How do you do?' The automatic and never-answered question was asked in unison.

'Now if only I'd had another hand, my dear boy,' said Tarrant regretfully, 'and if only I'd known your taste . . .'

'Never mind.' Modesty put a hand on David's arm. 'Go and get yourself a drink.'

'I don't think I'll bother.' He was frowning slightly. 'There's rather a scrum.'

'I'd like some cigarettes, please. No, not yours. Some Gauloises.'

'I'm damn sure they won't have them.' He met her gaze and shrugged. 'Oh, all right.'

She watched him go, and spoke quietly to Tarrant: 'So soon, for your pound of flesh?'

'It doesn't arise,' he said carefully. 'But if you could see your way to lending me some assistance, I'd be most grateful. Unfortunately the matter has become urgent—even to the point of interrupting your evening. Please feel free to decline.'

'What do you want me to do?'

'See my Minister. He's at the House now.'

'Pompous Percy?'

'You possess trade secrets. Have you met the Right Honourable Percival Thornton?'

'No. But I know his collection of pictures. One of my subgroups removed a Cezanne from it when he was ambassador in Paris a few years back.'

'You delight me, Modesty. But I should let auld acquaintance be forgot in this instance. If you intend to see him, that is.'

She looked towards the manoeuvring scrum at the bar.

'Yes.' She finished her drink and handed him the glass. 'Shall we go now?'

'A word to your escort first, perhaps?'

'I'd rather be discourteous. He took me for granted.'

'Ah. I shall bear that in mind.'

They drove down the Strand and Whitehall in Modesty's Daimler Dart. It was ivory in colour, and the engine held no esoteric mysteries of adaptation. Over her evening dress she wore a Dior-designed mink coat in emba tourmaline, three-quarter length, with bishop type sleeves and a high mandarin collar.

'Congratulations on bringing Willie Garvin back alive,' Tarrant remarked as they waited at the lights. 'A pity he's lost his touch.' With satisfaction he sensed the slightest stiffening of her body.

'He hasn't,' she said briefly.

'But you weren't thinking of co-opting him for this job, I take it?'

'I don't know what the job is yet.' She left it there, and Tarrant was content for the moment.

If the job really existed, as he believed, then it would hardly be the kind to send Modesty Blaise into without her right arm. But he had a strong hunch that she was reluctant to bring Willie Garvin in—not because she didn't want him, but because she felt she had no entitlement to involve him. Tarrant hoped that the right kind of prodding would do the trick.

In a room overlooking New Palace Yard, the Minister put aside a file and rose behind his desk.

'Delighted, Miss Blaise. 'Evening, Tarrant.' He shook hands. His voice was fruity and booming. The Right Honourable Percy Thornton had come to politics from the Bar. He was a reliable man, very methodical, with the virtue of not being too clever and the greater virtue of having a flair for doing the right thing, even if sometimes it was for the wrong reasons.

Tarrant, as he seated Modesty, saw her take in the fact that despite what the Minister must know of her he remained completely incurious about her. A spark of amusement touched her eyes.

'Now,' said Thornton, leaning back with a profound stare. 'The Sheikdom of Malaurak. I doubt if you know of the place, Miss Blaise?'

'It's a small patch of rock and sand between Syria and Iraq. Recognised by the Treaty of '56. Oil was found there recently.'

'Quite so.' Pompous Percy was unruffled. 'Now the ruler of this little country is Sheik Abu-Tahir. Not a cultured man, I fear.' He jerked his eyebrows up and down, looking dubious. 'Until now, he's been a penurious, tent-dwelling fellow. Something of a brigand, I suspect. However, we must be charitable, h'mm?'

'Yes. If you want his oil.' Modesty's voice held no inflexion. Tarrant sat back, enjoying himself.

'I think it's fair to say,' Thornton began judicially, 'or rather, it would not be *un*fair to say, that we've been working to reach a mutually beneficial arrangement. His Highness, as he likes to be called, is in this country now, and we've completed secret negotiations for the oil concession. But the arrangement is rather quaint. He's a difficult chap, eh, Tarrant?'

'I only saw him briefly at your office two days ago, Minister.'

'Yes.' Thornton linked his fingers and rested his chin on them, looking at Modesty. 'Well, our friend has no time for foreign credits, pieces of paper, anything of that nature, Miss Blaise. We've paid him half a million sterling for—ah—current expenses, and the rest of the down payment is to be ten million pounds. In diamonds.'

He waited for a reaction, received none, and continued with no sign of disappointment.

'This chap isn't terribly sophisticated, you understand, and he wants the kind of wealth he can see and touch. To be delivered to the strongroom of the Anglo-Levant Bank in Beirut. Are you with me so far, Miss Blaise?'

Modesty inclined her head. 'Yes. I have been listening.'

Tarrant treasured the answer for later retailing to Fraser, but the Right Honourable Percival Thornton merely nodded satisfaction.

'Good,' he boomed briskly. 'The diamonds are being amassed in Cape Town and will shortly be carried to Beirut in the strongroom of *The Tyboria*—one of the passenger-ships used for carrying gold consignments.'

Tarrant coughed. 'I did suggest recommending to His Highness that the diamonds should go by air, Minister. They'll only occupy a few cubic feet. Say one large crate or two smaller ones.'

'Rejected,' Thornton answered with a wave of his hand. 'In

March '63 King Saud's private Comet IV crashed in the Italian Alps near Monte Matto. It was carrying jewels, gold and currency to the tune of about four million pounds. And the scattered wreckage was only found after six weeks of searching. Just one small valise of gold was recovered. Now I won't say Sheik Abu-Tahir read of this, because he doesn't actually read. But he knows of it. And he's not going to trust his diamonds to any damned infidel flying machine.'

Tarrant gestured acceptance, and the Minister looked at Modesty again.

'There it is, Miss Blaise. Nominally the Sheik is responsible for the diamonds as soon as they're sealed in the ship's strong-room at Cape Town. But we want to ensure safe delivery. If anything went wrong, His Highness might get a little—ah ...' He sought judiciously for the right word.

'Stroppy?' Modesty offered politely, and Tarrant closed his eyes with pleasure.

'Exactly. Stroppy,' nodded Thornton. 'And one can't enforce contracts with minor powers these days. If he did default, and if we happened to have a gunboat within five hundred miles, we'd have to shift it out damn quick before somebody accused us of naked aggression.'

'Why should anything go wrong with the diamond-delivery?' Modesty asked, and the Minister's glance passed the question to Tarrant.

'There's been a leak,' Tarrant said. 'This was all top secret, but one of my people in the South of France reported a whisper about an enormous quantity of diamonds being shipped. I told him to trace the source of the whisper, and he died.'

'Could be coincidence, of course,' Thornton said, frowning. 'We all have to shuffle off this mortal coil sooner or later.'

'With respect, Minister ...' Tarrant weighed the lengths to which he might go, 'I feel that piano-wire drawn tightly round the throat suggests that in this instance somebody took time by the forelock.'

'You have a point there,' Thornton nodded, and looked at Modesty. 'It's Tarrant's job to start at shadows, and he has this unlikely idea that there's a plot to steal the diamonds. We shall have armed guards on the strongroom, and His Highness has insisted on supplying his own guards as well. So the thing can't be done, short of piracy, and *The Tyboria* will be armed against that.'

'You're taking expensive precautions which you believe to be wasted?' she asked with a slight lift of the eyebrows.

'Not quite. I'm giving Tarrant *carte blanche* for any precautions *he* thinks necessary, because it's most important to make a good impression on Sheik Abu-Tahir. We've had to mention Tarrant's suspicions to him, of course, and he's somewhat alarmed. Therefore I've instructed Tarrant to give his full personal attention to the matter. Question of goodwill, Miss Blaise, that's all.'

'How do I come into the picture?' Modesty asked. She opened her handbag and took out a thin gold case, but Tarrant was before her with a box of the same Perfecto Finos he had seen her smoking at the pent house.

'You're a part of Tarrant's *carte blanche*,' Thornton said with a slight shrug. 'He tells me you have profound knowledge of the Continental and Middle Eastern underworlds, and assures me that you are uniquely equipped, in experience and in contacts, to discover if there *is* a plot, and if so, who's behind it and how it's supposed to work.'

'I see. But you don't believe in it?'

Thornton leaned forward and grimaced. It was a moment before she realised that this was a smile. The man was trying to be gallantly reassuring.

'I'm quite sure Tarrant is imagining things,' he said. 'I don't think you need have any worries that you might be running into danger, Miss Blaise.'

'Thank you, Minister. That's very comforting for me.'

'Not at all.' Thornton waved a gracious hand. 'Well, Tarrant, you must take this young lady along to see Sheik Abu-Tahir and tell him all about her before she starts—ah—doing whatever it is. Make a big thing of it with the chap, and keep him right in the picture.'

'Yes, Minister. I'm lunching with him at his suite in The Ritz tomorrow, so I'll take Miss Blaise along with me. There is just one point I ought to mention, perhaps—concerning the probability of this plot.'

'Yes?' There was a touch of impatience in Thornton's query.

'At the first rumour I put a local man in to investigate it, and he was garrotted, as you know. But then I sent a man out to follow up. A very good man—Ivor Grant. He handled that rather nasty Czech business, you remember?'

'Naturally I remember. Well?'

'Ivor Grant has failed to report on four scheduled times over the past forty-eight hours, Minister. I think we've lost him.'

FOUR

Ivor Grant was quite certain now that he was going to die. He was a tall, thin, very wiry man of thirty-eight, with black hair sleeked back, though it was untidy now.

In the past ten years Grant had walked many dark and devious paths for Tarrant. Some had been dangerous, a few very dangerous. But even at the worst times he had always been able to see a way out—at short odds, perhaps, but nevertheless a possible way.

This time it was different. From the moment he had woken from unconsciousness on the ship, shackled to a bunk in the dark cabin, he had felt a growing sense of being in hands which gripped once and for all.

That feeling had increased when they brought him ashore under a cloudy, moonless sky, marching him along the mile and a half of rough track which ran the length of the narrow island to the beginning of a rocky slope leading up to the monastery. The men were professional and assured. Grant knew that they could only serve a ruthlessly efficient master. They were of several nationalities, and spoke little, but the common language seemed to be English of varying quality.

The handcuffs on his wrists chinked slightly as he stirred on the solid oak settle which stood against one wall of the small room. On a chair by the open door a swarthy man in a dark T-shirt and denim trousers sat with a gun resting on his knee, watching impassively.

Grant judged men by their eyes; and these eyes, disinterested, lacking all tension, told him that if he made a sudden move he would get a carefully placed bullet—through the leg, probably. The exact placing depended on the man's orders.

Flexing his thighs to ease the cramp in them, Grant sat still and began automatically to arrange facts in his head, as if for a report.

An island. Very small. Somewhere in the Mediterranean. Two miles long, and tapering from half a mile wide to an elongated point; rocky, barren, with a thin fringe of scrubby beach. But at the western end the island threw up a miniature mountain two hundred feet high, with the great stone monastery perched upon it.

Number of monks in the monastery—uncertain. There were three at work when he was brought through the big kitchen. They were evidently a silent order, communicating by sign-language, and they ignored the fair-haired chunky man with a burp-gun who watched over them. But their eyes followed Grant with troubled melancholy.

He recalled that there were at least another thirty monks kneeling in prayer in the small chapel when he was shepherded along the gallery above and through a heavy wooden door at the end. On a lower level he had passed a row of small, bare cells. In one of them was a body lying roughly stitched in a coarse blanket.

The man who questioned him was called McWhirter, a lean-faced Scot with a jerky walk and the manner of a hired clown. The questioning was a strange affair, with McWhirter by turns laughing, confidential, persuasive.

There was no violence. Grant produced frightened indignation and his cover story. McWhirter chuckled delightedly.

'Och, I wish he'd tell me to break ye doon, Grant laddie,' he beamed, rubbing dry hands together. 'We'd have a rare bit o' fun, eh?' His smile invited Grant to join him in the pleasurable speculation.

'Who—who's *He*?' Grant mumbled, trying to give the impression of a terrified and bewildered man clutching at the straw of appeal to higher authority.

'Ah! An' who's *your* "he"?' countered McWhirter with a boyish hoot of laughter. 'Eh? Boulter, is it? Or Dicky Spellman? Or Tarrant, mebbe? It's a rare gaggle o' departments ye have in London!'

Grant's uncomprehending stare did not alter, but each name hit him like a club. He had worked for Boulter in Military Intelligence before being seconded to Tarrant's department. And Spellman was the recent appointment on the naval side.

43

'I don't get any of this,' he said doggedly. 'What are you all doing here anyway? I mean—*guns* and everything. And I saw a body in one of those cells!'

'A man o' God,' McWhirter said reassuringly. 'Freed from the base clay at last. It's not that these clerical fellers made any trouble, exactly, but——' He looked sideways at Grant and his eyes twinkled. 'Weel, they greeted us wi' a sort of passive resistance, d'ye see, an' it seemed best if we made a wee example. A scapegoat, ye might say.' He frowned sternly. 'Och, there's scriptural precedent for it, laddie. Scriptural precedent.'

'You ... killed one of the monks?' Grant knew with sick distaste that there was little acting in his show of fear.

'Aye.' McWhirter spread his hands in a wide, sincere gesture. 'It was the simplest way for everyone. By far the simplest.'

'You're crazy!' Grant said with sudden vigour. 'I want to see your boss, whoever he is!'

'So ye shall,' McWhirter nodded, rising blithely. 'But ye have to be patient for a wee while. He has a couple o' fillums to watch. Carlos here will keep ye company.' He indicated the silent man with the gun.

'*Films?*' Grant spoke like a man doubting his own sanity. The habit of years made him probe for information, even though he would never be able to report it. 'You mean ... sort of *blue* films or something?'

McWhirter stared, all humour fading from the long-jawed face. His eyes held frigid disdain.

'Ye disgust me, man,' he said coldly, and turned away.

'Well never mind that, just hold on!' Grant let belligerence creep into his tone. 'I don't care what your boss is doing—I bloody well want to see him! Who does he think he is, anyway?'

'He's called Gabriel,' said McWhirter, and went out.

It was then that Ivor Grant became quite certain that he was going to die. His only concern now, as he sat slumped on the rubbed wooden settle, was the manner of his dying.

Twenty minutes later McWhirter reappeared, spritely and jocular again. With him was the heavy man with short-cropped fair hair, the man Grant had seen in the monastery kitchen. He spoke slow English with a Nordic accent.

'Twenty-three thirty hours,' said McWhirter, consulting his wristwatch. 'Time all good bairns were in bed, heh? Come along, laddie, Borg will take ye in tow. Wi' Gabriel, it's important to watch the timing. Ye mustn't hustle him, but ye mustn't keep him waiting, either.'

Handcuffed to Borg, Grant was led up stone steps, through an empty refectory, and along a broad corridor where saintly statues looked down from niches in the wall. McWhirter paced ahead, long-legged and bouncy, talking continuously.

'D'ye know *The Yeomen of The Guard*, Grant laddie? Fairfax's song.' He burst into a toneless fragment of melody. ' "*I-i-is l-i-ife a boo-oon . . .*" Ah, it's a logical bit o' philosophy. A man canna complain if he dies in July, since he's lucky not to ha' died in June, d'ye see? But on the other hand——' McWhirter, striding past a man with an automatic pistol who sat on a wide window-ledge, wagged a meaningless finger at the man and winked broadly. The man ignored him.

'On the other hand,' McWhirter repeated, 'ye have the converse in the second stanza. "*I-iis l-i-ife a tho-o-rn?*" Well in that case a feller can't complain about dying now when he might have had to live another dawn, heh? Now hush, for God's sake.' The last words were spoken in a quite different tone.

McWhirter's hand was on a studded oak door. He opened it quietly on to a large, carpeted room, and tiptoed in, beckoning Borg to follow with Grant. As soon as they had entered he closed the door.

The room was dark except for the flicker of a projector throwing a coloured film on a screen which hung on the wall to the right. As Grant's eyes grew accustomed to the darkness he saw a big desk across the far corner, a wall lined with books, and a number of religious pictures and statuettes. Cigarette-smoke drifted in the air, and on a polished wooden table with godrooned legs stood a dozen bottles of various drinks.

From the size and the lack of austerity in the furnishing, Grant decided that this must be the abbot's sanctum. And perhaps, he thought bleakly, the abbot was lying stitched in that blanket below.

There were four men in the room. One sat in an armchair of carved oak. The other three were ranged behind him on plain chairs, and from their attitudes they were bored. But not the man in the armchair. He sat with chin resting on folded hands, leaning back, absorbed in the picture. And every few seconds he would give a sudden, tittering giggle.

Grant looked at the screen. The film was a Tom and Jerry cartoon. Tom, the cat, was crouched by the open door of a room, his face set in a diabolical leer, a baseball bat poised as he waited for Jerry. But the mouse was emerging from a small cupboard behind Tom, on the far side of the room, pushing a roller-skate with a flaring blow-lamp tied to it.

The man in the armchair gave a snigger of anticipation. On the screen, Jerry set the skate rolling. It whizzed across the floor, and Tom shot to the ceiling with a shriek as his buttocks turned cherry-red. He landed, legs moving in a blur, and shot like a rocket through the window. Seconds later the picture dwindled in a decreasing circle and the credits began to roll.

A man stopped the projector and switched on the lights. As Grant had noted earlier, the monastery had a small power-plant of its own. Now he was trying to make a guess at the number of men in occupation here, excluding those who had brought him from the ship and who had presumably gone aboard again. There were six in the room with him, the swarthy man who had guarded him, and in his perambulations through the monastery he had seen armed men in the chapel and at strategic points in the corridors. Thirty at least, he decided. It was another fact to add to his useless store of information.

The man in the armchair got up, the last remnants of a grin fading from the thin lips. When he looked at Grant the face held nothing at all. Its emptiness was almost a positive thing. The flesh was putty-coloured and looked spongy. Black hair, rather long, was brushed straight back over the pointed ears. The eyes were hooded, and set unnaturally wide, but it was their colour that held Grant's gaze. The irises were like small discs of bleached khaki, almost white, so that at first impression they seemed to be completely absent, leaving only the black pupils centred in the white expanse of eyeball.

'I want to go over the latest figures, McWhirter,' Gabriel said, and the voice was as colourless as the eyes. 'Who's this?'

'Feller called Grant.' McWhirter's manner was as blithe as ever, but Grant noticed that he wasted no words. 'Ye'll recall that before we left Antibes, the group we retained to cover security in the South o' France sprang a leak.'

'Pacco's group. Yes. A British agent began to snoop. He was dealt with.'

'Aye. Borg played him a fugue wi' the piano wire.' McWhirter's head jerked in acknowledgment towards the big man handcuffed to Grant. 'But they followed up. Sent another feller over. This one.'

'Who picked him up?'

'Kalonides. Aye, he'd got that far. Kalonides brought him in tonight on the scheduled run. He thought maybe ye'd want to open the laddie up, Gabriel.' McWhirter looked hopeful.

Gabriel moved to the big desk, where several files and a clipboard of papers were neatly arranged.

'No,' he said briefly. 'See to him.'

McWhirter smiled at Grant with rueful congratulation, then looked at Gabriel again. 'It would be a little something for Mrs. Fothergill, perhaps?' he suggested diffidently.

'Where is she now?' Gabriel was absorbed in the file he had picked up, and was giving only half his attention to McWhirter.

'On the terrace below.' McWhirter nodded towards the tall, curtained windows. There was a stir of interest among the other men.

'All right.' Gabriel put down the folder. A man in slacks and a heavy sweater moved to draw back the curtains.

'Come along, laddie, I'll introduce ye.' McWhirter turned to the door with his spring-heeled walk. Borg jerked at the handcuffs and Grant moved with him.

In the corridor they passed a monk carrying a tray of food, a guard pacing behind him.

'Strange thing, a life o' meditation,' said McWhirter, hands

47

in pockets, head thrust forward as he walked energetically ahead. 'I've never felt the call to it mysel', but I'd think an order vowed to silence would have certain disadvantages. I'm a student o' the dying art o' conversation, d'ye see, and when ye consider . . .'

Grant closed his mind to the voice, blurring it into the background. His nerves were tense now, and he was very frightened, but his mind remained coldly clear.

Mrs. Fothergill? The name meant nothing to him. She was presumably to be concerned in killing him, but he rejected pointless speculation about details.

Grant focused his mind on the idea that, with luck, he might take somebody with him. Borg, perhaps, but McWhirter for preference. It was a matter of choosing the best moment. Grant knew how to kill a man quickly, but he had only one hand free; the other was shackled to Borg's wrist, and Borg was a heavy, powerful man. Still, if he went for the eyes first, stiff-fingered, then swung a knee to the groin, he might just have time to——

They stopped by an open door, crossed the room beyond it, and halted by tall windows which opened on to a flagged terrace, broad and semi-circular with a low stone parapet. It seemed to Grant, as McWhirter opened the windows, that beyond the parapet the ground dropped away at a steep slope. He could hear the murmur of the sea below.

Borg took out a key and unlocked the cuff on Grant's wrist. It came as a surprise, and before Grant could take advantage of it the thrust of a powerful arm sent him staggering out across the terrace. The heavy windows closed.

Grant regained his balance and stared about him, nerves crawling. The half-moon of the terrace swelled from the centre of a cloister running almost the full length of this side of the monastery.

There came a sound of voices, and Grant looked up. Thirty feet above was a long balcony which he realised must extend from the sanctum where he had seen Gabriel. There were figures on the balcony—four or five men, shadowy in the light of the room behind them. The one standing a little apart was Gabriel. They were all looking down, waiting.

Grant backed warily to the centre of the terrace. Something like hope sparked within him. If he could get down the rocky slope to the sea, and hide somewhere on the island ... finding him would take time, a full day maybe. And in a full day anything could happen——

A red glow flickered across the edge of his vision and he turned sharply. Vaguely, from above, he heard the sound of a familiar, chuckling voice. McWhirter had joined the men on the balcony.

Grant's eyes were on the red glow. It hovered in the air against a curious patch of darkness. The patch of darkness moved, and resolved itself into a figure seated on the low coping of the terrace at its widest point, about twenty-five feet away.

A man smoking a cigar. Walking slowly towards him now— no, by God, a woman!

She wore a grey shirt with long sleeves and dark, rumpled trousers held by a leather belt. Her feet, in grubby plimsolls, were curiously small. She might have been forty. The face was heavy-jowled and devoid of make-up except for a gash of carelessly applied lipstick. Inexpertly dyed blonde hair rose in a short fuzzy crop from her head. Her neck seemed to slope out almost directly from below the jaws to the broad shoulders. Her breasts were large but tightly confined; there was little movement beneath the shirt.

Mrs. Fothergill, thought Grant, and felt his stomach twist with a stab of nameless fear.

She took the butt of the cigar from her lips and flicked it over the parapet in a thin trail of sparks. Her mouth widened in the shape of a grin but the lips remained tight over the teeth, so that the grin showed only as a dark, curving ellipse. She flicked both hands in a slight beckoning motion.

'All right, sonnyboy.' The voice was husky with a trace of adenoidal twang. 'Let's get on with it.' On the last words her body seemed to flicker forward, and a muscular hand smashed in a contemptuous backstroke across Grant's face.

The shock of it was more stunning than the blow itself. He reeled back, twisted to regain his balance, and dropped into a crouch, staring incredulously. By instinct he had fallen into the ready position of the judoka, and Mrs. Fothergill surveyed him with approval.

'That's better,' she grunted, and began to edge in, thistledown light on the small feet.

Grant's brain checked factors at racing speed. A woman. A hermaphrodite more likely. Very tough, very experienced, very fast. But half a woman, anyway. He should have enough edge to put her out of action. Then over the parapet and a quick scramble down——

She swung a lazy blow with clenched fist towards his head. He moved his forearm to block it, saw the feint too late, and only half-rode the savagely swung foot to his kidneys.

Grant heard himself give an animal grunt as he twisted away, staggering. She was coming in again. Desperately now he whirled and flung himself forward in a surprise recovery, watching for the lash of a foot as he lunged at her throat with the bunched tips of his fingers.

She caught his wrist with a loud slap, gripping it hard, and for a long moment they stood unmoving. In that time all hope drained from Grant. He knew, with sick disgust, that she was stronger and faster than he was.

Closing his mind to the knowledge, he tensed to drive in with the knee—and knew that she had sensed the move in the same instant that he had planned it. Her other hand clamped on his arm. He was jerked forward like a rag doll, and a hard shoulder slammed brutally against his heart.

He went down, sprawling, and heard her chuckle as she stepped back. Somewhere through the mists of dizziness and despair he heard a murmur of voices from the watchers above.

Doggedly Grant got to his feet, heart thumping, breath hissing as he gulped air. Again he moved in, and this time she swayed aside and chopped with the edge of her hand to his bicep. It was like being hit with a blunt axe.

He staggered past her, turning. His right arm hung limp, and he wondered dully if the bone was broken.

Now there was new excitement in her face, and the small dark eyes were glittering with pleasure. Grant stood swaying, waiting for her, hoping that over-confidence might give him one last chance of a counter—a kick to the stomach. There was little else he was capable of now.

She came in, curving her body past the kick like a matador, and took his good arm as he clawed for her face. She locked it under her armpit and jerked suddenly. Grant screamed as the bone snapped. His face was close to hers, and nausea swept him at the almost orgiastic stare of pleasure in her eyes.

Mrs. Fothergill let him go and swung a casually brutal backhand across his face. A foot caught behind his ankle, and he fell back on the flags. Blackness eddied about him as his head jarred against the hard stone. Desperately he tried to move, but the muscles would no longer respond.

Mrs. Fothergill drew in a long, contented breath, and exhaled it. She glanced up at the balcony, then straddled Grant's supine form. Hitching up the knees of her trousers, she knelt astride him. Carefully she adjusted her hands round his throat, thumbs on the larynx, and began to squeeze.

Gabriel watched Grant die, then turned back into the sanctum. The others followed.

'Have ye ever wondered,' McWhirter said musingly, 'about *Mister* Fothergill?' One man laughed. Another spoke questioningly in Spanish, and a third began a pidgin-English translation of McWhirter's remark. Gabriel cut him short.

'Get that mess on the terrace cleaned up,' he said, jerking his head towards the door in dismissal. 'I want to talk to McWhirter.'

He sat down behind the big, mellow desk as the men filed out. McWhirter linked his hands behind his back and began to pace across the room with a precise, measured gait, brow wrinkled in concentration as he waited for Gabriel to speak.

'Is this accurate and up to the minute?' Gabriel said, picking up a sheet of foolscap.

'Aye. If it's what I gave Crevier to type. We can run a quick check.' He halted and screwed up his eyes. 'Hire of Lamelle organisation in Lebanon, fifty-two thousand. Ditto for Pacco group in South of France. Retainer fees: Singerman in Amsterdam, De Groot in Cape Town, Mashari in Port Said,

51

and Zweif in Haifa—four thousand five hundred each. Lapos Island take-over, twelve thousand.'

Still with eyes closed, McWhirter tugged thoughtfully at his ear, then continued in the same rapid monotone.

'Shipping and special equipment, sixty thousand seven hundred. Bribes, payments for information, and commission to sub-agents, eight thousand three-fifty. Internal salaries and overheads, fifteen thousand four hundred. Estimated future expenses, forty thousand.'

He opened his eyes and looked at Gabriel. 'All figures in sterling. Total of £258,450. Estimated gross revenue £10,000,000, less distribution costs of £2,000,000. Net profit of £7,741,550.'

Gabriel put the sheet of figures down and nodded. 'Have you worked out how to handle the receipts?'

'The usual way. This is just bigger. You've fifteen legitimate companies operating in various fields an' in different parts of the world. They'll absorb the revenue between them. I've drafted out a skeleton arrangement involving purchase o' shares through nominees, and certain take-over arrangements. It's verra complex, but if ye'd like to see it——?'

'No.' The colourless eyes rested on McWhirter. 'I don't imagine you'd do anything stupid.'

McWhirter's lean face lost a little of its colour. 'I'm no' that kind o' fool, Gabriel,' he said dourly.

There was a thump on the door and it opened. Mrs. Fothergill came in, wiping her hands on a large, grubby handkerchief. There was a lazy repleteness in her heavy face.

'Ah, dear lady!' McWhirter strode jerkily to greet her, glowing with admiration. 'D'ye know I envy you, Mrs. Fothergill? Happy the lad or lass whose needs are simple.' He took her hand and patted it gently, hovering over it. 'No lust for riches, eh? No romantic problems. Just a jug of wine, a book of muscle-building, and a wee killing now and then——'

'Knock it off, McWhirter,' Mrs. Fothergill said good-humouredly, pushing him away. 'I wouldn't mind a drink though, now you mention it.'

A nod from Gabriel, and McWhirter poured an inch of whisky from the array of bottles on the side-table.

'Your health, dear Mrs. Fothergill,' he said, handing her the tumbler with a winning smile. 'You won five pounds for me. I laid evens wi' Borg that ye'd strangle yon feller, an' Borg was sure ye'd do that wee neck-snapping trick, like wi' the good abbot.'

'I thought about it,' Mrs. Fothergill admitted. 'But it's all over a bit too quick that way.' She ruminated for a moment. 'He was an abbot then, that other one?' She drank, ruminated again, then lifted the glass and drained it. 'And you took five pounds off Borg for this one? I'll have that off you at poker tomorrow, sonnyboy.'

She looked across at Gabriel with something appallingly like a shy simper.

'Thanks, Gabriel. I mean, you know—for the bit of fun.'

'All right, Mrs. Fothergill. Send Mendoza in, will you?'

She nodded, wiped her mouth on the handkerchief, stuffed it in her trouser pocket, and went out.

Grinning, McWhirter started to speak. He saw Gabriel absorbed in the sheet of figures, and remained silent. Two minutes later a dark-faced man in shirt-sleeves entered. Gabriel got up.

'Run that last film again, Mendoza. The blow-lamp one. You haven't seen that yet, McWhirter?'

'Er ... no. No, I've not. Kalonides only brought the print in tonight.'

'All right. You can stay.' It was a favour.

The lights went out and Mendoza set the projector going. McWhirter stiffened his jaws to hold back a yawn. Gabriel settled himself in the big wooden armchair. As the titles rolled his face came alive and he began to grin.

FIVE

'IT's a classic example,' said Tarrant. 'Our Right Honourable friend is doing the right thing for the wrong reason.' He hooked his heels over the rail of the high stool and watched Modesty Blaise pour boiling water over fresh-ground coffee in an earthenware jug.

They had driven from Westminster direct to Modesty's pent house and were in the big kitchen, a place of ice-blue and white with the gleam of chrome. She made no answer to his comment. Tarrant noted with satisfaction that her thoughts were elsewhere and that there was a slight frown of annoyance between her eyes.

'It may be his method, of course,' Tarrant went on. 'If a thing works, he's not called to account, and if it doesn't work he can defend it on the wrong grounds and confuse the Opposition.'

'You mentioned Willie Garvin earlier.' Modesty leaned back against a unit bearing shelves of spices, and lit a cigarette.

'Yes.' Tarrant's manner was amiably dismissive. 'He's a pleasant enough chap, of course. But basically he's an uneducated criminal with a record as long as your arm.'

She looked at him with hostile eyes. 'Mine's longer—except that it's not on record. And Willie's clean for the last seven years. What's more, in the only way that matters to you he's infinitely better educated than any man you care to name.'

'I admit he has certain curious skills,' Tarrant conceded. 'But this is surely a job calling for finesse.'

'I back Willie to out-think any man you can put up. And that's only part of it. You need more than finesse to cope with piano-wire round your throat.'

'You don't agree with Pompous Percy that this was a coincidence?'

She made a gesture of impatience. 'Of course not. Ten

million poundsworth of diamonds is a big, big job, and that narrows the field to the big, big boys. There are just three who might tackle it—but only one of them is a probable.'

'Yes?'

'That piano-wire killing sounds like Borg to me. And he's a Gabriel man.' She set out two cups and saucers and began to pour the coffee.

'Gabriel,' Tarrant said quietly, watching her hands. He was silent for several seconds, then asked inconsequentially: 'Who looks after you here?'

'I have a houseboy called Weng. He's Indo-Chinese, and at the moment he's down at Benildon, in Wiltshire, where I have a small cottage and a few acres of woodland. Weng's there because I keep three horses and the groom is on holiday. He'll be returning tomorrow. Why did you change the subject when I spoke of Gabriel?'

'To gain time. No cream or milk, thank you. I've been trying to collect what I know of Gabriel from the dusty shelves of my memory.'

'I doubt if you'll find very much there.'

'You're right, my dear. Our file and the Interpol file on Gabriel are both slim and inconclusive. In theory he's a very rich, very respectable gentleman, with many diverse interests, of Latvian origin but a naturalised Venezuelan—or is it Bolivian?'

'The second, but it's not important. What's important is that Gabriel, in practice not theory, is a criminal heavyweight. The biggest there is, from Lisbon to Hong Kong. His resources are enormous.'

'You've met him?'

'Once, briefly. I crossed swords with him by accident. We'd planned a big job, lifting a consignment of gold at Calcutta. And so had Gabriel. He sent for me and told me to back down. I didn't argue—I backed.'

She picked up the cups of coffee, set them on a tray, and carried the tray through into the spacious living-room. Tarrant followed.

'Very wise,' he commended. 'You ran The Network for profit, and a gang war is always costly. But this affair is

55

different. I'll provide all the backing you want—far better support than Willie Garvin can give you.'

She stood very still and looked at him searchingly. 'You're not a fool, Sir Gerald. I wonder why you're talking like one?'

He started to speak, knowing he had prodded too hard, but she stopped him with a quick shake of her head.

'No. Sit down and have your coffee. And listen to me.' She waited while he obeyed. 'I found Willie Garvin in a Saigon gaol, and I bought him out. He was nasty and he was dumb, but he was lethal. I had reason to think I could do something about the nastiness and the dumbness. No, not reason—just a feeling.'

She sat down on the black hide chesterfield facing Tarrant, and slowly stirred her coffee.

'I was right,' she said. 'Much more so than I'd imagined. The first thing Willie gave me was total loyalty. You can only guess at what that meant to me in my kind of business. I also discovered that Willie could think—very clearly and very fast. It must always have been there, but it was latent; perhaps because he'd never had an aim or goal before.'

'And what goal did you give him?'

'I didn't.' She hesitated. 'Working for me seemed to be enough; and the way he developed was astonishing. You know, I've learned a great deal from Willie Garvin. And even better than being able to think, he has instinct.'

She looked up at Tarrant and smiled suddenly. 'You won't believe this, but he can sense trouble coming. His ears prickle.'

Tarrant stared. 'You're joking.'

'No. It's saved my life twice. I don't know how many times it's saved his. Another instinct is that he knows my mind without being told. When you're up the sharp end, as Willie calls it, that's something money can't buy. And finally, he's in a class of his own when it comes to action. I've seen him——'
She broke off with a little shrug and picked up her cup of coffee. 'Never mind. Seven years is a long time, Sir Gerald, and Willie Garvin's is a long story. I'm not going to tell it now.'

'I do take your point,' Tarrant said slowly. He put doubt into his tone, feeling that the critical point was at hand. 'But all this is in the past, and it's a full year since Garvin worked for you. I would feel he's gone down-hill badly, and I'm bound to insist that you don't bring him into this. I'm sorry...' He let his voice trail uncomfortably into silence. It was a silence that lasted a full minute.

Modesty finished her coffee, put down the cup, and stood up. Tarrant rose with her.

'Then it ends here,' she said coolly.

'I beg your pardon?' Tarrant's manner was as frosty as her own. 'I feel that at this stage you're already committed.'

'No. I agreed to do a certain job for you. But I'm not an employee, Sir Gerald. If I do the job, I'll supply my own tools.'

Tarrant held his face rigid for five seconds, then let it relax in resignation and gave a faint sigh. 'Well ... if that's your ultimatum, I can only yield. When will you speak to Garvin?'

'It's for you to speak to him.' There was no concession in her face. 'Willie doesn't belong to me. But I need him. And I think if you ask him very nicely to help me, he'll probably agree.'

Right through the guts, Tarrant thought with wry admiration. 'I'll ask Willie nicely,' he said. 'Where and when?'

'You're taking me to lunch with Sheik Abu-Tahir tomorrow.' Her voice was friendly again. 'Can you spare time to run out with me to *The Treadmill* that evening?'

'You heard what my master said. I'm to give my full personal attention to this.'

'Tomorrow evening, then. And perhaps in the meantime you can find out where Gabriel is now and what he's doing— or supposed to be doing.'

'I'll get Fraser busy on it. He's duty officer tonight. Will it be all right if I pick you up here at twelve forty-five tomorrow?'

'I'll be ready. And I take it there's no time to be lost in starting this job?'

'None. The diamonds go aboard *The Tyboria* in two weeks' time, and come into Beirut three weeks later. It doesn't allow you a lot of leeway for getting a line on the operation.'

'No.' She sat on the arm of a chair and looked at him

curiously. 'Have you made any guesses on what shape it might take?'

'I would have thought any attempt must be made at one end or the other—Cape Town or Beirut. The South African authorities are responsible at Cape Town. Beirut's a little more vague. But I can take care of the two ends through official channels.'

'You're concerned about in between?'

Tarrant shrugged uneasily. 'I suppose so, though it hardly seems to work. The fact is, I'm playing a hunch. If I were Willie Garvin, my ears would be prickling.' He smiled at her. 'But I'm uncertain all along the line. That's why I want you coming up from underneath. If you can find the shape of the operation, I shall know where to concentrate my efforts.'

Modesty fingered the splendid amethyst pendant that lay against her flesh just above the curving line of the dress. Her eyes were distant. Looking at her, seeing her wholly as a woman, Tarrant felt a sudden dreamlike sense of unreality. It was absurd, out of all reason, that he should be talking of these things to this warm and beautiful female creature. She was never made to walk with death and violence at her shoulder. Looking at the long smooth column of her neck, he thought of piano-wire, and his stomach constricted.

'How fast I can move,' she said, 'depends very much on the kind of reaction I get from my old contacts. They tend to wear their mouths shut. But it's possible that for me . . .' She stood up and shrugged. 'They may speak out of one corner.'

'What will you ask?'

'About diamonds. And about Gabriel. If he shows up clean I'll have to think again. But I'm picking Gabriel to start with, so please find out all you can about him.'

'Very well.' The momentary sense of unreality had passed, and Tarrant was professional again. 'Thank you for the coffee, my dear. I'll say goodnight.'

When the lift doors had closed on Tarrant she went out on to the terrace and smoked a cigarette. Her thoughts were turned inward and she was watching herself vigilantly. With satisfaction she noted that there was no tension, only a sense of warm exhilaration.

She stubbed out the cigarette and went back into the pent house. The panelled walls of her bedroom were ivory, the fitted carpet was pale green, and the bedspread and curtains silver-grey. A door led off to a large bathroom with a sunken bath and a shower cubicle. Here the walls were of very light pink tile, and the floor was laid with large black composition tiles, soft and warm to the foot.

She adjusted the mixer on the bath and let the water gush while she undressed in the bedroom. Beneath the lined evening dress she wore no slip, only plain black pants over gossamer sheer tights and a black bra. Her underwear was opaque and without trimmings, yet wholly feminine in cut and style. She had never in her life worn a girdle or needed to.

In the bathroom she stood naked before the full-length wall-mirror and studied her body with a careful appraisal that was devoid of conceit.

No sign of fat. She hadn't gone soft in this last year. There had been plenty of exercise—a daily swim, the long rides at Benildon, and the occasional work-outs with Willie Garvin, for old time's sake. Or had it been just for old time's sake . . . ?

She ran probing fingers down the muscles of her thighs and calves, then straightened and drummed gently against the flat stomach with the sides of her fists.

Muscle-tone good.

Smoothly she arched her body right back until her palms touched the floor behind her; she brought one leg up straight, with the toe pointing to the ceiling, then followed with the other leg, and brought them down together in a controlled movement to complete the slow-motion back-flip.

Her mind searched her body carefully for any hint of stiffness or strain, but there was none, and she gave a little nod of satisfaction.

The bath was three-quarters full now. She turned off the water and sank into it, pulling a bath-cap over her hair. A telephone stood in a recess near the head of the bath. She lifted the receiver and began to dial.

Willie Garvin muttered an oath as the phone rang persistently.

'Leave it,' whispered the blonde girl, propped on an elbow and hovering over him, her face close to his. 'They can't ring for ever.' She dipped her head to bite his ear.

Her voice held the well-bred county drawl. She was twenty-three, the daughter of a gentleman farmer, and engaged to the son of another gentleman farmer. Willie hoped the lucky man didn't bruise easily. This girl was all teeth; still, if you could take it while she warmed up, it was worth it in the end.

'Lay off a sec, Carol,' he said, and rolled on to his side, his back towards her, picking up the phone from the bedside table.

''Allo?'

'It's me, Willie. Are you on an extension?'

''Allo, Princess.' His voice was warm with pleasure. 'No, I'm on the main phone, by the bed. The extensions are switched off.'

'Anybody with you?'

'Yes. Nobody important, though. Just passing the time.'

'My God, Willie, she'll love that bit.' He heard laughter in her voice. 'All right, I'll talk and you acknowledge, right?'

'Sure, Princess. Go ahead.'

She spoke quietly for several minutes, and he listened with complete absorption. To anybody who might have overheard, her words would have been cryptic, for she used a mixture of argot from French, Arabic and English, but to Willie Garvin the inwardness of every sentence was plain.

At one point he gave a low whistle and grinned without humour. ''Ope you're right, Princess. Be nice to get that one by the shorts. It always stuck in my craw when we 'ad to back down that time.'

Later he said: 'Sure. You bring 'im along about eight, then. 'Ow d'you want it played?'

He listened again, and chuckled. 'Okay, Princess. No, you didn't disturb me a bit. So long for now, then.'

He put down the phone and lay back with hands behind his head, smiling up at the ceiling with euphoric content. It was as he reached for cigarettes on the bedside table that he had an abrupt sense of something missing.

His mind raced back over the last few minutes, picking up the sounds and movements which had barely penetrated his consciousness—the sudden bouncing of the bed, and the flutter of stockings and underwear; the flouncing and muttering; the snap of an overnight case and the slam of the door, followed by the fading click of heels marching purposefully away along the passage.

Willie Garvin sat bolt upright and stared about the empty room in hurt astonishment.

'Carol?' he said indignantly. 'Carol!'

SIX

TARRANT'S cab drew up outside the pent house block behind an open Rolls-Royce in two tones of blue, a Mulliner-Park Ward convertible. A uniformed chauffeur sat at the wheel.

'Keep the meter going,' Tarrant said to the taxi-driver, and glanced at his watch. 'I don't think we'll need to wait more than a minute or so.'

As he got out of the taxi, Modesty Blaise came down the steps from the entrance. She wore a two-piece of pure silk jersey in steel blue, the skirt slim, the overblouse pouched and with a deep cowl collar. Her gloves were of white kid, matching her handbag, and she wore no hat.

Tarrant, who knew his jewellery, priced the single strand of pearls at her throat at seven thousand pounds. She was very beautiful, and he felt a pang of deep melancholy at the knowledge that he was putting her in hazard.

She greeted him, smiling, and said: 'We won't need the cab. Weng will drive us.'

Tarrant looked at the Rolls. Now he saw that the chauffeur was a young Asiatic, about nineteen years old, who sat at the wheel with folded arms and an air of calm superiority.

'You needn't worry,' Modesty said. 'Weng's taken the advanced driving course.'

'I've every confidence.' Tarrant paid off the taxi. 'But I'm not used to such a regal transport.'

'I only bought it in a mad moment,' she confessed as Tarrant opened the door and handed her in. 'But Weng loves it, and it's the right thing for the occasion. When you go to visit a Sheik, you do it in a style that honours him.'

Glancing sharply at her as he settled beside her, Tarrant saw that she spoke quite seriously.

'I'm obliged,' he said. 'It hadn't occurred to me.'

The Rolls glided silently into the stream of traffic heading for Park Lane.

'Have you anything on Gabriel?' Modesty asked.

'A little. But we're expecting more reports during the afternoon. I'll go over it with you this evening at Willie Garvin's place.' Tarrant looked about him and lifted an eyebrow. 'Does our advanced driver know the way to the Ritz?'

'Yes. But I have to make a call first. It won't delay us more than two minutes.'

The car wound through side-streets north of Oxford Street and halted at a small parade of shops. Modesty got out quickly and went into a shop with a narrow, peeling facade. Above it Tarrant could just make out the word 'Antiques' in faded lettering. Weng alighted and stood by the door, waiting.

Within two minutes Modesty returned. Weng held the car door for her, then resumed his seat. A hundred yards on they were halted by a long double line of traffic, jammed on the right turn at the lights ahead. Tarrant, who liked to move unobtrusively through life, was conscious of the stares drawn by the open Rolls and its occupants. But his unease was tinged with pride at being in the company of the woman who sat beside him.

'Oh, my God,' he thought suddenly. 'I must look like her sugar daddy.' He turned his head to glance furtively at her, and found that she was looking past him, absorbed in something on the nearside, where area railings guarded a row of basements. A small boy, with cowboy hat and belt, crouched on the steps and peered through the railings, an alloy-cast gun in his hand. Another small boy, also with a gun, and wearing a sheriff's badge, hugged a pillar-box and looked out from behind it warily. For the moment their game was suspended as they gazed at the Rolls.

The boy behind the railings lifted his gun, pointed it at Tarrant, cried *'Pow!'*, and ducked out of sight.

'Pow! Pow!' This time it was from the pillar-box. A small head emerged warily to observe the damage.

'When I was young,' Tarrant mused as the car edged forward a few yards, 'we always said "*Bang!*" Not very onomatopoeic, I suppose, now one considers it——' He broke off, startled. Modesty had turned and was kneeling in a crouch

63

on the seat. Her right hand was clenched with two fingers extended to imitate a gun.

She lifted her head, aiming at the small figure peering round the pillar-box. '*Pow!*'

The face lit up in a grin of astonished delight, then vanished. '*Pow!*' from the railings. Another from the other side of the pillar-box, and a quick response from Modesty. Tarrant swallowed hard. He saw with bleak satisfaction that a tinge of red was creeping up the back of Weng's neck and that he was fidgeting with the wheel, anxious to move.

'*Pow!*' Modesty fired and ducked. A fusillade came from the railings and the pillar-box. Tarrant turned a basilisk glare upon two young women with shopping baskets and a middle-aged man with a briefcase who had stopped to watch the battle.

The car ahead moved, and on a final '*Pow!*' from the railings Modesty jerked up and spun round to crumple out of sight on the seat. Looking back, Tarrant saw the two miniature cowboys standing on the pavement and gazing after the Rolls with worshipful awe.

When the car had turned the corner Modesty sat up and pushed a wisp of hair into place. Her eyes were sparkling with enjoyment. 'I hadn't really thought about it,' she said, 'but it's more like a ricochet, I suppose.'

'I'm sorry.' Tarrant eased a finger round his collar. 'What is?'

'Pow. You were talking about Bang and Pow.'

'So I was. I'm afraid you made your chauffeur blush for you.'

'I don't doubt it.' She gave a sudden urchin grin. Leaning forward she tapped Weng's shoulder. 'The trouble with you, Weng my boy, is that you're a snob.'

'Thank you, Miss Blaise.' The voice was accented but cultured. 'I try to be.'

'Then why don't you do as I ask and train for a career?'

'You put me to school in Hong Kong, and then three years at the University there, Miss Blaise. It is enough.'

'It's only a beginning. Do you want to be my houseboy all your life?'

'Yes, thank you, Miss Blaise.'

Tarrant made a mental note that one day, if the chance came, he would ask about Weng. He sensed a story which might yield yet another fresh aspect of Modesty Blaise; and he was becoming increasingly intrigued by the many-sided nature of her character.

At the Ritz, the commissionaire saluted as he opened the car door. Tarrant handed Modesty out and they went inside. The chief receptionist came forward to greet them.

'Miss Blaise, Sir Gerald. His Highness is on the second floor. Lunch has just been served in his suite.'

'Served?' Tarrant raised his eyebrows. 'We're surely not late, Mr. Manetta?'

'Not at all, sir. But His Highness wished for everything to be ready. Will you come this way?'

'No—ah—problems with our host and his entourage?' Tarrant asked as they moved towards the lift.

'We don't have problems at the Ritz, sir,' Mr. Manetta said with gentle reproof. 'Only moments of unusual interest.'

'Any of those?'

'The question of arms had to be discussed. Most of His Highness's gentlemen feel lost without their rifles. They sleep with them at home, I understand.'

'It could disconcert your other guests,' Tarrant conceded as the lift doors opened. Modesty stepped in and the two men followed.

'We arranged that two rifles should be retained for the personal guards,' said Mr. Manetta. 'They're not loaded, of course. We pointed out that Her Majesty's guards at Buckingham Palace don't carry ammunition.'

Tarrant looked mildly surprised. 'Don't they?'

'We were careful not to enquire, sir.'

Modesty smiled. 'I'm wondering about food. Have there been any moments of interest over the menus?'

'Providing freshly-slaughtered goats was a slightly complex administrative exercise, Miss Blaise. But apart from that——'

'*Goats?*' said Tarrant, staring. 'Good God, you don't mean that Jacques Viney was asked to cook *goat*!'

'A lesser chef might have objected,' said Mr. Manetta

calmly, and stood aside as the doors slid open. Following Modesty and Tarrant out, he led the way along a broad corridor. 'Our M. Viney is an artiste,' he went on, 'who rose to the challenge as one would expect of him. His goat's-meat *ragoût* has been a tremendous success.'

'I'm very glad,' said Tarrant. 'We want His Highness to be happy here.'

'I can reassure you on that, Sir Gerald. In fact, he asked if M. Viney would return to Malaurak with him. There was the suggestion of building a palace with very excellent kitchens.'

Tarrant closed his eyes for a moment. 'And?' he asked.

'M. Viney was most courteous in his thanks, but felt bound to decline.'

Tarrant dabbed his brow with a folded handkerchief. 'Do give M. Viney my warmest compliments,' he said fervently.

The connecting doors of the suites along one corridor on the Park side had been opened to make a huge suite sufficient for the complete entourage. Outside the central door of the corridor two tall Arabs stood on guard. Their robes had the brilliance of newness, but their chins were bristly and the slung rifles on their shoulders held the patina that comes from many years of constant handling. One was a short model Lee Enfield, the other an old French Lebel.

'His Highness waits you,' said one of the Arabs, and opened the door. Tarrant saw a look pass between the man and Modesty, a look of warm greeting restrained by formality. It startled him, but there was no time to speculate about it.

'I'll leave you now,' said Mr. Manetta, and sketched a courteous bow.

The large drawing room was in the Louis XVI style that held throughout the Ritz. There were a dozen or more Arabs, one or two in chairs, but most of them squatting on the floor. Again, the new robes and colourful trimmings seemed oddly out of place against the dark, desert-weathered faces.

A big white cloth was spread on the floor, with cushions scattered around it. On the cloth were fine bowls and silver flagons, baskets of coarse black bread, platters of cheese, and a variety of fruit. In the middle stood a large hot-plate of glowing charcoal, bearing an earthenware vat in which a dark brown stew simmered gently.

All the Arabs rose, Sheik Abu-Tahir from a chair on the far side of the white cloth. He wore a white burnous with a red and gold headband. The ruler of Malaurak was a man of middle height, in his early fifties, with a short greying beard, little more than a stubble reaching up his cheekbones to his ears. The face was seamed and craggy, with small shrewd eyes. 'A tent-dwelling brigand...' the Right Hon. Percival Thornton had called him, and Tarrant found little to quarrel with in the description.

'Your Highness,' Tarrant said with a slight bow. 'Allow me to present Modesty Blaise.'

Abu-Tahir's eyes rested on Modesty, twinkling. He touched a hand to his forehead and to his heart.

'Salam alêkum, sayyide.'

Modesty's hand moved in the same gesture. 'Nehârkum sa'îd we-mubârek.'

'Awhashtena.'

Tarrant knew that one. 'You have made us lonely.' Again he was puzzled.

'Allâh ma yûhishek,' said Modesty.

The gravely-spoken formal greetings were over. And then Abu-Tahir stepped forward with outflung arms and hugged Modesty like a bear. 'Modestee!' he cried joyously.

As she returned the embrace one of the men shouted: 'Fatet el sayyide!'

Abu-Tahir turned, an arm still about her shoulders. 'Yes!' he rumbled. 'It is the Princess—she is with us again.' The men crowded about her, dark faces split in smiles of welcome, all talking at the same time.

Abu-Tahir lifted a hand for silence and looked at Tarrant.

'I have sorrow,' he said laboriously, 'that my men not speak English good. I speak many words. I say sorrow for them that they make poor welcome for you, Sir Tarrant. But they have much happy to meet again El Sayyide—the Princess. Come now, sit please.'

Holding Modesty's arm he amiably shouldered two men aside and kicked cushions into position in front of the chair.

Sinking down, he drew Modesty down beside him on his right. She hitched her skirt above the knees and sat with practised ease, legs drawn up and to one side. Tarrant sighed inwardly and took the cushion on the Sheik's left. Abu-Tahir clapped his hands and began to give orders.

'Not with your knees up like that,' Modesty said to Tarrant as the bustle of serving began. 'Cross-legged, knees out, and relax. Like His Highness.'

'Thank you.' Tarrant manoeuvred his limbs awkwardly. 'I only wish we had Fraser here, it would open up a whole new range of facial expression for him. He'd love it. You know, when I recall Pompous Percy saying you'd probably never heard of the Sheikdom of Malaurak...' He shook his head reproachfully. 'I think you might have told me, my dear.'

Bowls had been filled from the vat of stew, and now a large bowl was placed in front of Abu-Tahir and his guests. With a gesture he invited Tarrant and Modesty to begin.

'Right hand,' she said quietly, reaching forward. 'Thumb and two fingers only. And no business yet.' Tarrant watched her, then hitched up his cuff and groped in the bowl. He found a piece of meat, shook it free of surplus gravy, and put it in his mouth. It was astonishingly good.

As the meal progressed Tarrant found himself with a growing liking for Abu-Tahir. The man was rough-hewn but had a natural courtesy. Though he was clearly longing to talk to Modesty he devoted most of his time to Tarrant, speaking in slow, ungrammatical English.

With dignity he enquired after the health of as many of the Royal Family as he could remember, and then began to work his way through a curious collection of English names which he had evidently picked up over the years. There was a disconcerting moment over the health of Lord George, whom Tarrant identified after several tense seconds as the late Lloyd George; but much pleasure was shown at Tarrant's assurance that the great footballer, Stanelli Matthews, was in good strength.

'And this lady my west,' said Abu-Tahir. 'I see her in film when we pass at Baghdad. Very beautiful and very nice chess. She is well, Sir Tarrant?'

Baffled, Tarrant tried to catch Modesty's eye. She was engaged in a lively flow of question and answer with half a dozen of the Arabs squatting round the big cloth, and he gathered from their guffaws that there was no lack of salt in her conversation. But she must have had an ear open for Tarrant, for without looking round she said: 'Mae West,' and quickly patted her breast.

'Ah yes, Your Highness,' Tarrant said, relieved. 'I can't speak with authority on my west, I'm afraid. She is an American lady. But I believe she's very well.'

'I hope is so,' Abu-Tahir nodded soberly. 'She has very nice chess.'

Tarrant was mildly surprised when wine was served, but assumed that Abu-Tahir and his people were not strict Muslims. He was again surprised when after the cheese and fruit there came, not coffee, but very strong tea, brought to a vigorous boil three times on an electric hotplate before being poured into small cups.

Modesty burped noisily, and Abu-Tahir beamed with pleasure and satisfaction. Remembering his manners, Tarrant tried gallantly, but the eructation eluded him. He uttered an imitation and hoped that it would pass.

'Ahh!' said Abu-Tahir, and clapped Tarrant heartily on the shoulder. 'Sir Tarrant is cunning. He brings *El Sayyide* to destroy these bad dogs who wish for taking my diamonds! It is good!'

Tarrant understood that business could now be discussed. He said: 'Thank you, Your Highness. I felt that Modesty Blaise could well help to discover these bad dogs. But I did not know that you and she were old friends.'

'Ah...' Abu-Tahir lifted a hand, and his men fell silent. 'I will tell you, Sir Tarrant. Long, long back, there is a small girl-child. She passes through Malaurak. It is a hard land. She is alone. Her wearing is rags, and she has hunger. But not fear. She is very...' he groped for the word, 'very *fierce*, like small wild animal. She not asking help—but I give. I take her into our tents. Tell women to give food.'

He rested a hand on Modesty's and she roused from a reverie, smiling at him.

'I stayed for half of one year,' she said. 'And I was the best goat-herd of all your people, Abu-Tahir.'

'Is true,' he nodded, and there was a murmur of assent from the squatting men. Abu-Tahir turned back to Tarrant.

'The child grows flesh on bone,' he said. 'We are sorrow when she leave us. Many years pass, ten year perhaps, and she is forgotten.' He shrugged. 'In Malaurak each day is hard; man forget the yesterday. But then come bad people who wishing to take my country. Greedy Arab. There is much trouble and we have not good strength.'

He slapped his hands together with a loud clap and his men stirred eagerly, like children listening to a favourite and oft-told story.

'But now Modestee has good strength!' he said with a harsh chuckle. 'And *she* does not forget, Sir Tarrant. From far away, she hear. Now is she *El Sayyide*, the Princess, and all things come to her ear. She remember she has eaten my salt. And so *El Sayyide* comes, with much money, with many guns for my people ... and with Willee Garvin. Ha, that one!'

A fierce grin curved the bearded lips, and there was much head-wagging and guffawing among the men. Abu-Tahir spread his hands in a crushing movement, jabbing them downwards, and made a noise with his mouth. '*Phwwt!* Six week, and trouble is finish Sir Tarrant.' He threw back his head and suddenly bellowed with laughter, nudging Modesty with his elbow.

'You remember Kassim, Modestee? In the wadi that night? His face, just when you kill him. Is very making us laugh! Oh-ho-ho-ho-ho ... !'

'He did look surprised,' she said, and added something in Arabic. The Arabs rolled about, bellowing with mirth.

'Ahhh ...' Abu-Tahir wagged his head and wiped his eyes on his sleeve. Becoming serious again, he put a hand on Modesty's arm. 'From then you are not forgotten in Malaurak. Now there comes oil from the sand, and I am much rich. You will make safe my diamonds, *El Sayyide*, and I will make you fine presents. What you wish. Is bargain, ha?'

Modesty spat lightly on her palm. Abu-Tahir grinned and followed suit. The two palms were slapped together.

'Is bargain,' she said. 'You are generous, old friend. And as you speak of presents, I tell you that Sir Tarrant has brought you a gift—a small thing only, from guest to host.'

Tarrant stared at her.

'I believe you put it in your inside pocket, Sir Gerald.'

The antique shop, Tarrant thought. When she came out and got into the car. But he hadn't felt a damn thing. He put a hand to his inside pocket. Next to the wallet lay a small flat packet. He brought it out and handed it to Abu-Tahir.

The Sheik broke the sealing wax and unfolded the stiff white cartridge paper. Inside was a pad of cotton-wool surrounding an oval watch, incredibly slim, with a case of hand-chased gold. On the inside of the case, when Abu-Tahir sprang it open, was a Limoges enamel panel in rich colours, showing the head of the Queen.

For long seconds Abu-Tahir gazed down at the watch, holding it delicately in his rough, powerful fingers. Then he looked up with wonder and awe in his face. 'This will not leave me ever, Sir Tarrant,' he said slowly. 'And when time is finish for me, it shall lie with me beneath the sand.'

'Sir Tarrant is happy to have chosen so well,' Modesty said gravely.

'I am indeed. Very happy, Your Highness. And I'm grateful to Modesty for reminding me of it.' Tarrant inclined his head courteously to her as he spoke.

One of the men was asking a question, repeating it, but Abu-Tahir was too entranced by the watch to pay attention. In the question, Tarrant caught the name of Willie Garvin.

'Your Highness...' Modesty touched the Sheik's arm and he came out of his trance with a little start.

'Ah, yes! Rashid asks well, Modestee. Where is our good Willee Garvin? To make safe my diamonds you will bring him also?'

'He has retired,' she said. 'To his own small caravanserai in the country. I spoke with him by telephone, and he asked that I give you good greeting from him, Your Highness.'

Abu-Tahir stared at her anxiously. 'But he must be with you, *El Sayyide*! If you go to find these bad dogs, you must take him also!'

Her eyes rested on Tarrant. 'Willie Garvin is no longer my man to command, and it is not for me to ask him, Your Highness. For this we must rely upon Sir Tarrant.'

The Treadmill stood a hundred yards from the river and a few miles from Maidenhead, as it had stood for nearly two centuries. At the rear, a brick path wound between trees to the water's edge and a boat-house. A narrow creek bounded one side of the grounds, and against the trees bordering the creek was a very long low building of brick. There were no windows in the building, only a heavy door at one end.

It was ten minutes to eight when Modesty turned into the small car-park at the front and edged her Daimler Dart into a space marked 'Reserved'. She wore a black skirt and a blouse of dark red Thai-silk with a light camel coat thrown over her shoulders.

Tarrant held the door and handed her out.

'Reserved for you?' he asked, glancing at the parking space.

'I'm afraid so.' There was no apology in her smile. 'Willie does that sort of thing for me. It's outrageous, of course, and I love it.'

The pub was full but not crowded. Mostly regulars, Tarrant judged, looking about him. He had put on a quiet sports jacket with dark trousers, and felt comfortably at home. The dress here was casual and sporty, the people mostly young to middle-aged. There was a small group playing darts and another round two pin-tables at the far end.

A heavily built man of fifty and two young women were behind the long bar. Willie Garvin would be popular here, Tarrant thought. A character.

'Hallo, Mr. Spurling.' Modesty was speaking to the heavily built man. 'How's the knee?'

'Lot easier thanks, Miss Blaise. They've done some special heat treatment on it. And how are you keeping?'

'Fine, thank you. Is Willie here?'

'Out the back, Miss. He said you'd be along. Just carry on through. And look in to have a drink with us before you go.'

'We'd like that, Mr. Spurling.'

She took Tarrant's arm and went past the end of the bar,

through a swing door which led to a passage running right through to the rear of the pub.

'Does Willie live on the premises?' Tarrant asked as they emerged into the open and paused for their eyes to adjust to the darkness.

'Yes. Very comfortably. He had the whole upper floor modernised.'

'Who looks after him?'

'I made him take on a housekeeper. She comes in daily and cooks for him and the staff.'

'But he lives alone?'

Tarrant caught the gleam of her smile in the darkness. 'Off and on,' she said gently. 'Willie's a good mixer.'

She took his arm again and guided him along the brick path, branching off halfway to head for the long, windowless building. At the door she paused and took a key from her handbag. When she opened the door, Tarrant noted the thickness of it and the safe-like fit. Beyond lay a small square space and another door. Beside it was a grid in the wall and a push-button. Modesty thumbed the button and spoke into the grid.

'It's me, Willie. And Sir Gerald.'

A moment of silence, then a click, and Willie's voice sounded metallically through the speaker. 'Right, Princess, come on in.' Tarrant heard another and more solid click, this time from the inner door. Modesty turned the handle, swung the door open, and gestured for Tarrant to precede her.

Beyond, between white-painted walls, the dark cork-tiled floor stretched for almost forty yards. The place was brilliantly lit. In the centre was a mat twenty feet square, of sponge-rubber covered by canvas. To the left of it, at the far end of the long hall, the wall was recessed for an archery target. A parallel range on the other side of the mat ended in a sandbagged wall.

One corner, to the left of the door, was partitioned off, and above the partition Tarrant could see twin showers emerging from the ceiling. On both walls were racks carrying an extraordinary collection of weapons, ancient and modern. There were a dozen bows, ranging from the short Mongol recurve to the long English yew and the giant eight-foot laminated wood bow of the Japanese; there was a bow of steel, another of laminated plastic, and one of impossible slimness which appeared to be made from tapering tubes of jointed steel.

Another rack carried rifles, and another hand-guns. Tarrant ran a professional eye over the rifles, noting the new Ruger 10/22 carbine with the rotary magazine. Most of the hand-guns were small and lightweight. There was a hammerless Smith & Wesson Centennial and a .38 Special Colt Cobra. Among the automatics Tarrant saw an Astra Firecat, a very small Browning he could not name, and a MAB Brevete.

'Don't ask about licences,' Modesty said, and moved to a panel mounted beside the gun-rest at the firing point. 'Willie's fixed a moving-target gadget for me.' She tripped a switch, then pressed a button. Tarrant saw a white clay-pigeon disc float at head-height across the sand-bagged wall at the target-end of the range.

'Very nice,' Tarrant said. 'I take it this place is sound-proof?'

'Yes.'

'I also take it that Willie is something of a marksman.'

She shook her head and smiled. 'He couldn't hit a barn standing inside it. Not with a hand-gun. And he doesn't like them anyway. But he's good with a rifle—anything you can really sight with.'

'This range is just for you, then?'

'Yes. I've told you, Willie's very thoughtful. I come here to practise sometimes.'

'On the archery range as well?'

'I like that best.'

'It's a great sport, I understand. But rather impractical, surely? You can't carry a bow and arrows around with you.'

She said nothing, but gave the sudden grin that he was beginning to recognise and look for. Its cause eluded him on this occasion. Slowly he moved with her along the racks.

'What gun do you prefer for business, my dear?'

'I seldom carry one. I've used one even more seldom. It's only necessary when things go really wrong.'

'I would agree. You seem to take the art of usage very seri-ously, though.'

74

'One must,' she said simply. 'However rarely you use a gun, when the moment does come you're either ready or you're dead.'

'And which gun do you prefer?'

'It depends. If I'm not likely to need it in a hurry I prefer the Brevete.'

'A toy, surely?

'It's adequate—if you are. Willie doesn't approve because he hates automatics. They can jam too easily.'

'And what if you're likely to need the gun in a hurry?'

'The Colt .32.'

'From a shoulder holster?'

'No. They don't go with having breasts. I use a snap-holster Willie designed, belted at the back of the hip. It means wearing a short jacket to cover it, or course.'

'And isn't that a hindrance?'

'Not with the F.B.I. draw. You clear the coat with the movement.'

Tarrant nodded. 'Willie must be very skilled to design these various items for you.'

'He is. He makes up special bullets for me. Very little noise.'

'Most useful.' Tarrant looked around him. 'I understood we should find Willie here.'

'He'll be in his workroom, beyond that door at the end. But don't worry. He'll expect you to stop and look at his collection.'

'I'm fascinated by it. Is this actually a quarter-staff I'm looking at now?'

'Don't be superior.' She touched the thick blackthorn staff which hung at an angle in two loops of leather. 'Willie says this is the finest non-explosive hand-weapon ever devised. He can make that piece of timber spin so fast you can't see it.'

'Not an item one can easily carry around in this day and age, though.'

'I know. Willie's very sad about that. He's a natural artist, really, and he looks on fighting with guns the way Rembrandt would look on painting by numbers.'

'He's very good with a throwing-knife, I believe.'

Modesty looked at Tarrant. 'If you ever see him at work with his knives,' she said quietly, 'you'll stop calling him "very good".'

Tarrant smiled an apology and they moved on past a rack of strange, barbaric-looking weapons. He recognised a Samurai sword and a Japanese cross-spear, but others were unknown to him. He touched an object like a butcher's steel, the hilt covered with sharkskin. From the base-guard of the hilt a short metal tine curved out and then ran parallel with the blade.

'Another super-weapon?' he asked.

'Far from it.' Modesty took the weapon down. 'It's an old Japanese *jitte*. This tine makes a fork with the blade, and you were supposed to catch your opponent's sword in the fork and disarm him with a sharp twist of the wrist. You should hear Willie on it.' Her voice dropped two tones and she produced a gravelly Cockney, devoid of her usual trace of accent. 'My life, Princess, you'd 'ave to be dead lucky.'

Tarrant laughed and watched her put the *jitte* back, thinking that her mimicry had been remarkable and hoping that he would never be a victim of it. 'The dojo,' he said, nodding towards the mat in the middle of the hall. 'Who does Willie work-out with? I can't imagine he allows many people in here.'

'None,' she said. 'You're the first. Willie and I work-out together.'

Tarrant kept his face impassive. 'Hardly a fair match, I would think. I'm sure you're very good, but on weight alone...'

'Willie always takes a handicap on a real session.'

'I'd be interested to watch a real session sometime.'

She smiled. 'You might be shocked. We play very hard.'

They moved on to the door at the far end, between the sandbagged wall and the archery target. Modesty opened the door, and Tarrant followed her in. Willie Garvin, in slacks and a T-shirt, was using a micrometer to measure a tiny piece of metal which he held in tweezers. The room extended across the full width of the building and was lit by daylight fluorescent tubes. It was the cleanest workshop Tarrant had ever seen.

A metal-topped bench ran from wall to wall, thirty feet long, carrying a large vice, a smaller one, and a watchmaker's lathe. At one end stood a modified high-speed dental drill. On the wall at the back of the bench were narrow shelves and two nests of small wooden drawers. In a rack at one end was a wide variety of metal-working tools, and at the other end, behind glass, a set of watchmaker's tools. A bunsen burner stood beside a tray of sand, and on a small separate bench there was an Emerson micro-manipulator. To Tarrant's right on a draughtsman's table, lay some rough sketches and a finished blue-print of what appeared to be an electronic device.

Willie Garvin put down the micrometer and the piece of metal carefully, and grinned in welcome at Modesty.

'Nice to see you, Princess.' He pulled out a tall stool for her to sit on. When she was seated he turned to Tarrant, extending a hand. ''Allo, Sir G. How's the Department?'

'Short on the right staff as usual,' Tarrant answered wrily, shaking hands. 'I expect Modesty has told you that I've persuaded her to help me out on a special job?'

'On condition,' said Modesty. Then—'Oh, Willie, you've finished it!' She picked up a silver statuette, about four inches high, mounted on a round, inch-deep base. The goddess was naked, standing on the tip of one foot with the other leg extended behind her, body arched, head thrown back and arms extended a little behind her, as if she were running into the wind.

Modesty pressed a small button on the base, and a short tongue of flame leapt from the smiling mouth of the goddess.

'Look, Sir Gerald, isn't that beautiful?' She picked up a magnifying glass and studied the curving side of the base, then handed the lighter and the glass to him. Under magnification Tarrant saw the line of engraving in cursive script. *Yrs. faithfully—Willie.*

'It's superb,' said Tarrant, and looked up. 'I'm here because I'm interested in your less delicate talents, Willie. Can I persuade you to go on this job?'

Willie leaned back against the bench and rubbed his chin dubiously. 'No 'ard feelings, Sir G., but I know your kind of caper. Can't really see meself putting on a false nose and passing messages to a bloke in a fag-shop in Trieste or somewhere. Here, 'ow d'you like this, Princess?'

He opened a drawer and took out a red suede tie. It was already knotted, and was made to fasten by a clip at the back. On the front of the tie was an imitation diamond the size of an olive, set in a long and heavy silver mounting.

'Nice, eh?'

'Isn't it a little loud for you, Willie love?'

'Not meant to be all that quiet.' He grinned suddenly. 'It's lined with plastic explosive. Enough to make a hole where the lock used to be, anyway. Detonates on a ten second delay after you've unscrewed the stone from the mounting. Easy to carry, and there's a safety-catch be'ind the mounting——'

He began to go into technical details. Tarrant drew in a long quiet breath. So they were going to twist his tail for a while. Well, it would be worth it, he hoped. If his anti-Garvin line had stung Modesty sufficiently to overcome her qualms about bringing Willie in, then the side-effects would have to be accepted stoically.

'Returning to our muttons,' he said, when Willie paused, 'I'm sure you must know that this isn't a routine intelligence job. Modesty will have told you——'

'Modesty is curious,' she broke in, staring at something on the bench. 'I thought I was the only woman allowed in your workshop, Willie.' She pointed to a lipstick case lying on the bench, but did not touch it.

'I expect,' said Tarrant heavily, 'that it's another gadget, my dear.'

'Sir G. my old darling, you're right,' Willie said, and watched Tarrant wince. 'Look, you'll like this, Princess.' He took off the top of the case, pushed the button up the curved groove to extrude the lipstick, and drew it across his palm, leaving a red line. 'Now that's normal. But when you give the base a couple of turns like this . . .'

He capped the lipstick, reversed it, and flicked the button again. There was a sudden violent hiss, and the papers on the drawing-board fluttered.

'That was only compressed air,' Willie said. 'But you can shoot a burst of tear-gas—enough to disable a bloke at six feet.

It's your colour, Princess. I'll load it properly before you go.'

'It's a good one, Willie. Thanks.'

'Is there anything else?' Tarrant asked mildly, and Willie frowned.

'There's several things I'm working on, Sir G.,' he said with a touch of severity, 'but I'd rather get down to business if you don't mind.'

'Do forgive me.' Tarrant sketched a gesture of apology. 'To business, then. The guess is that we're up against Gabriel. Will you take the job?'

Willie hitched himself on to the bench. His lightness of manner had gone now. 'Sure,' he said. 'I'm in. What did you get on Gabriel through your Department?'

'Not much, I'm afraid. Until ten days ago he was at his villa between Cannes and Antibes. Now he's disappeared. But his yacht's lying at Haifa with full crew. That's only a short hop from Beirut, where the diamonds will be coming in.'

Willie looked a query at Modesty.

'I'd say the planning and admin were done in the South of France,' she said. 'That's where Sir Gerald has had one man killed and another gone missing.'

Willie nodded. 'And now they've moved out to advance base, wherever that is. No line on Borg or McWhirter or any of the others, Sir G.?'

'I'm sorry. We don't even have them listed. You know more about Gabriel's set-up than we do.'

'Not enough.' Modesty lit a cigarette and slid her case along the bench to Willie. 'The only place to start digging is around the Cannes-Antibes area.'

'So I thought.' Tarrant put his hands in his pockets and began to pace slowly. 'I've a man there to handle communications—and anything else you might want him to do. I mean anything. He's very good.'

Modesty said: 'What's his cover?'

'He's an artist, with a studio in the old quarter of Cannes. Fluent French. His mother was American and he spent half his life there, but prefers Europe. He has dual nationality and passes as American, British, or French—the first two legally. I'm sure you'll find Paul Hagan satisfactory.'

'I'm sure.' There was an odd quality in Modesty's voice, and a hint of suppressed laughter. Tarrant looked up quickly, sensing that something had passed between Modesty and Willie, but she was studying the tip of her cigarette and Willie was looking blandly at the ceiling.

'Does the Deuxième Bureau know about him?' Modesty asked.

'That's the point. We use him jointly. It's an unusual arrangement, but it works. I've got a clearance from Léon Vaubois to use him on this. Hagan rather likes to do things in his own way, but I've sent instructions that he takes orders from you.'

'As long as he remembers that.'

'I'm sure you'll manage to keep his memory fresh on it, Modesty. My feeling is that he'll fit in with you very well.'

'Yes.' Modesty slipped down from the stool and carefully stubbed out her cigarette in an ashtray. There was a sparkle of wicked humour in her face as she glanced at Tarrant. 'I'm sure he'll do that if he can, Sir Gerald.'

SEVEN

PAUL HAGAN took careful aim and swung his arm. The stainless steel boule arced through the air and cracked sharply against Perrier's boule, to send it skidding away from the jack. There were grunts of approval from the other players.

'*Ça y est.*' Hagan picked up his boules, shook hands all round, and moved off the dusty patch of ground on to the hot pavement. He left the boules with the lady who ran the *tabac*, and walked past the busy market to the steep slope which led up to the old quarter.

He was a lean, compact man in his late thirties, a fraction under six feet, and with quiet, appraising eyes. When he spoke English it was with a very slight southern drawl. Hagan had two vocations—to paint pictures and to live dangerously. Men tended to be a little wary of him. Women liked him, liked the unusual blend of hardness and sensitivity, the combination of artist and pirate.

Five minutes brought him to the two-storey house where he leased a three-room apartment on the upper floor. He went up the stairway, feeling in the pocket of his slacks for the front-door key.

The door opened direct on to the big room he used as a studio. It had a good light, and was cluttered with canvases stacked round the walls. Half of the room did duty as a dining-room, and an oval gatelegged table stood against the wall. A door led off into the kitchen, and on the far side of the studio was a short passage serving the two bedrooms and the bathroom.

Hagan looked round the studio. It was a mess, he thought, but attempts to tidy up were a waste of time. You picked something up and hunted for somewhere else to put it down. In the end all you got was a re-arrangement of the mess. At least the place was clean.

On an easel near the window stood a large blank canvas. He

81

had planned to start a new painting this week. The form of it had been growing within him. It might be quite a while before he got around to that now, he thought.

He looked at his watch. Only a couple of hours to wait. The taut excitement he had felt in his stomach for the last thirty-six hours quickened suddenly, and his throat felt dry.

He went into the kitchen and took a bottle of coke from the fridge. Opening it, he poured two fingers of vodka into a tumbler and half filled the glass with coke. The drink was cool and fresh. He looked round the kitchen. Fresh bread, fruit, plenty of meat in the deep-freeze, and a variety of canned foods; milk, butter, cheese. Hagan didn't think he had forgotten anything.

He went back into the studio, glass in hand, and stopped dead. The blank canvas had gone, and in its place on the easel stood a painting of a girl. She was nude, and sat in the middle of a bed, a rumpled counterpane of pale blue candlewick spread around her. The pose was entirely natural. She leaned sideways, propped on one straight arm, her legs partly curled, in a half-sitting, half-lying position. Her head was slightly turned to look straight out of the picture. She had black hair, drawn up into a chignon at the back. Her face was composed, the dark eyes warm and intelligent. The flesh firm, the breasts round and full. Her shoulders were wide for a girl but right for her body, and curved superbly up into a long, smooth neck.

The picture was not quite finished. The left arm, and the hand which rested lightly on her thigh, were incomplete. More than once Hagan had stood with brush poised to finish the painting, but always he had laid the brush aside.

The quality that came from the girl, the quality he had been so excited at capturing, was the complete unawareness of her nudity. There was no hint of shyness, neither was there any hint of boldness. She might have been clothed, or she might not; it seemed not to have occurred to her as a matter of any importance.

Hagan let out his breath slowly and put down the glass. His eyes still on the painting, he said; 'Come out, wherever you are.'

Her voice came softly from where the passage joined the

studio. 'I'm sorry. I'm sorry I had to run out on you before you'd finished it, Paul.'

He turned to look at her, and felt the old excitement flare through his body. She wore a white blouse and a grey skirt; both were cheap but smart. Her chignon was coiled loosely at the nape of her neck. Her shoes were white, with a high vamp and small heels. She was dressed as a thousand other French girls here might be dressed—not the holiday-makers but the residents.

Hagan looked at the picture, then back at the living girl. There was no expression on his face.

'I was pretty sorry myself,' he said. 'And kind of knocked out at first. Until I found that the girl I'd been entertaining for that couple of weeks in Paris wasn't Lucille Bouchier—but Modesty Blaise.'

'And then how did you feel?' She came towards him as she spoke, looking up at the strong-boned face.

'I'll tell you. I felt mad as a wet hen. That lasted five minutes. Then I laughed. I mean I really laughed. I told myself, "What the hell, Hagan, son—it was worth it, wasn't it?"'

Abruptly the impassive look was wiped away by a grin. He relaxed, and Modesty relaxed with him.

'No hard feelings, then?' she asked.

'Not from me. My boss didn't laugh, though. Maybe you remember I was working for International Diamond Security at the time?'

'That was the whole point, darling,' she said with a hint of apology touching her smile. She slipped a hand through his arm, and together they stood looking at the picture.

'The whole point,' he said slowly. 'That's what I've wondered about since. You had a big parcel of gems being smuggled out of Sierra Leone and into the pipe-line. So the main idea was to dig information out of me on counter-measures.' He took her by the shoulders and turned her gently to face him. 'But was that the whole point? Were you conning me *all* the time?'

She put her arms up between his, and linked her hands behind his neck, looking up into his face.

'Well ... I'm not smuggling anything today,' she said softly. 'You can search me, officer.'

He slid his hands down to her waist, then brought them up slowly until his palms rested against her breasts, watching her eyes, trying to read them.

'You realise we have to be very thorough, ma'am?' His voice was as quiet as her own, his body suddenly taut. 'I must ask you to step into the search-room.'

'Of course, officer. I want you to be completely satisfied ...'

In love, she used her splendid body to give joyously and without restraint, ranging from glad submission to urgent demand. The happiness in her giving touched his mind with a glowing warmth; but more than that, she received his own gifts with the same unfettered joy as she gave, and this above all stirred the deepest wells of his being.

He marvelled, as he had marvelled before, that this rare and unknowable girl could so easily lay aside the almost tangible composure which armoured her.

She lay, an hour later, with her head on the crook of his shoulder, a hand resting on his chest. Thin blades of sunlight through the shutters of the bedroom window glinted upon her long legs.

'Tarrant,' he said, and began to laugh softly. 'Jesus, he'd blow his top. This is a hell of a way to start an operation.'

'We're not in the ring yet. Just waiting.' Lightly she hammered on his chest with her fist. 'Do you know a better way to wait?'

'They'll never invent it. What are we waiting *for*?'

'Willie Garvin.'

He sat up, looking down at her. 'Coming here?'

'He's been here. We caught an early plane and arrived a couple of hours before you expected us. Willie let us in with a strip of celluloid. His bags are in the small bedroom. Mine are in the corner there.'

Hagan rubbed his brow. 'I guess I had some questions about all that earlier, but something came up.'

'Yes.' She stretched, thoroughly and at length, extending every muscle. For a few seconds she lay relaxed, then got up and went to one of the two big cases which stood in the corner. Hagan watched with artist's eyes the intricate play of sinew and muscle in her body as she lifted one of the cases on to a chair and opened it. He got up and pulled on his shirt and trousers, slipping his feet into open brown sandals.

Modesty was buttoning a three-quarter length house-coat in pale blue waffle nylon, her feet in white mules. Her hair was loose and she looked very young. He went to her and put his hands on her shoulders, looking at her, not speaking.

'Have you got coffee in the house?' she asked.

'Sure. Like some now?'

'I'd love it. Give me five minutes.' She went up on her toes to kiss him, then picked up a small leather toilet-case and went through to the bathroom.

In the kitchen, Hagan put the kettle on and ground coffee-beans in the little aluminium hand-grinder. He set out two large cups and the perforated metal containers for making café filtre. When the coffee was made he carried it through the smaller bedroom and out on to a narrow balcony with a table and two chairs. Beyond the roof-tops which fell away down the slope lay a line of yachts and launches moored in the harbour, with the placid blue expanse of the Mediterranean beyond.

Modesty came through from the passage, and his heart lifted at the sight of her. The loose black hair was clipped back at the nape of her neck now, and her face was free of make-up. She smelt fresh and warm, like new-baked bread. Standing on the balcony, blinking a little in the bright sunlight, she might have been no more than twenty. Hagan remembered the reason that brought her here, and sudden fear twisted his stomach.

'Black and sweet,' he said, holding a chair for her. 'That's how I remember you liking your coffee. Unless I'm thinking of some other girl.'

'That wouldn't surprise me.' Her swift smile warmed him. 'But I like it her way, so this is fine, darling.'

He sat down, absorbed in the study of her profile as she looked out over the sea. 'In Paris,' he said after a few moments of silence, 'this girl who liked her coffee your way, and who made love the way you do, and whose picture I painted—she called herself Lucienne Bouchier.'

'That was because I thought the name Modesty Blaise might have rung a bell with you.'

'It would have. A carillon of bells. Is Modesty Blaise the real name?'

'Real enough.' She watched a seagull glide down in a wide curve towards the sea. 'When you don't have a name you have to choose one.'

His eyes moved to the line of her shoulder and neck, printing the curve on his memory. It wasn't quite right in the painting, he would have to make it right sometime. He said: 'I'm not with you. The Modesty Blaise I'd heard of wasn't a no-name. She was big-time, and she ran The Network. Why did she go out of business, by the way?'

'Voluntary liquidation.' She spoke absently, with no deep interest in the subject. 'When I was seventeen I set my sights on half a million sterling. I made it, and I quit.'

'That's one ambition you didn't pick up at Miss Mabel's School for Young Ladies.'

'I began to pick it up at my kindergarten. That was a prison camp in Greece, soon after the war started. But we were on the run in the Balkans for a couple of years before that, I think.'

'Who's we?'

She shrugged. 'I don't know. It's always been hazy, like a dream you can't quite remember. But I was alone from as early as I can really remember clearly.'

'And without a name?'

'There wasn't anybody to call me by my name, so I don't know what it was.'

'No friends?'

'Not till a lot later. Then I had one friend—an old man I found in a refugee camp in Iraq.'

'That's a long way from Greece.'

'Yes. I'd made my way across Turkey by then.'

'Across Turkey,' Hagan said. 'Just like that.' He looked at the small foot which hung relaxed as she sat with one leg crossed over the other knee. 'Quite a little walk. But then you found this old man and he looked after you?'

'No. I looked after him. In and out of half a dozen refugee

and D.P. camps for about five years.' Her eyes were distant, remembering with a shadow of sadness. 'He was Jewish and spoke five languages. He'd been a professor of philosophy at Budapest. Six hours a day he used to teach me.'

'Teach you what?'

'Everything.' She drank some coffee. 'I hated it at first, but I pretended to listen because I didn't want to hurt him. And that was strange, because I was as hard as nails with anyone else. Then after a while I became interested in the things he was trying to teach me.' She gave a little shake of her head. 'That old man knew everything, and he knew how to teach. But he'd let the food be stolen out of his hand. He'd have starved without me.'

'You played hatchet-man?'

'I could have used a hatchet sometimes. But I had sharp teeth, long nails and a little knife. And I knew the targets.'

'How old were you then?'

'Around twelve, I suppose.'

'And you'd tackle a man?'

She smiled. 'It wasn't so hard. For one thing I wasn't scared. I'd had all that burnt out of me long before. For another thing I had the right attitude, the right frame of mind.'

'Meaning?'

'Most people scare easily. They're afraid of getting hurt, even by something small, if it's fierce. So they have to work themselves up to a certain pitch before they'll risk fighting. Watch two men at it; there's usually a lot of words and jostling first. All preliminaries.'

'True. But not with you?'

'There's a point where you're committed, and from then on it's dangerous to pussyfoot around. You have to throw the switch. Go in like a ball of fire and finish it as quick as you can.' She looked at him. 'I'm not telling you anything. If you work for Tarrant you must know it.'

'I know it. But I hadn't thought about it before. It sounds as if you must have been a little hell-cat.'

'I was.' She smiled briefly, then lapsed into silence, watching a yacht come into the harbour.

'Go on,' he said. 'What happened between then and Modesty Blaise running The Network?'

'It's too long a story, and too long past.' She looked at her wristwatch. 'How much did Tarrant tell you about this job, Paul?'

'Everything, I guess—but that's little enough.' Hagan gave her a carefully judged smile. 'Oh, he said I take orders from you.'

'Yes.' She finished her coffee. 'I wanted him to make that clear.'

Hagan stiffened. In the last seconds there had been a subtle change in her, an imperceptible hardening. It was alien to the femininity of the small foot in the dangling mule, the smooth bare leg, and the warm body beneath that pale blue housecoat. Hagan didn't like the change.

'I haven't taken orders from a woman since Miss Peake,' he said, holding the smile. She looked a question at him and he added: 'Miss Peake taught school when I was six. I worked pretty well under her. But I may be a little rusty in that situation now.'

'Don't be, Paul.' She spoke without heat. 'We can't afford it.'

He jerked his head towards the house and said: 'You didn't give the orders a little while back.'

'That was a little while back. And that was fine. But we're on our feet now.' She looked out over the town and the long coastline stretching eastward into the heat-haze. 'We're playing in my back yard with my ball. If you don't play my way, Paul, you have to quit.' There was no challenge in her tone, no provocation.

Hagan sat very still, waiting for the surge of resentment to die down within him. He wanted to take her in his hands and shake her, dominate her, use his strength to hurt her. He knew it was an atavistic urge that sprang from the wounding of his male ego, and the civilised part of his mind held contempt for the emotion.

'Don't make it hard for me, darling,' she said quietly.

'I'll try not to. What's the first order?'

'There isn't one. I'd just like to hear any ideas you've got on where to start.'

'Any ideas...' he repeated, and shrugged ruefully. 'That spikes me. I haven't been able to pick up a smell of Gabriel so far. Where do *you* figure we should start?'

'We've started,' she said. 'You haven't met Willie Garvin, have you?'

'I know of him. The word is that he's good. I guess if he rode ramrod for your outfit he'd have to be.' Hagan found that a breath of mockery had crept into the last words, and he cursed himself. Modesty seemed not to have noticed.

'Yes,' she said. 'Willie's good. I've sent him off to locate Pacco.'

'Pacco?' Hagan rubbed his chin. 'Sorry, I'm not so well up on the criminal side.' He hesitated, realising that his own words supported her argument; she must have seen it too, but again she gave no sign. 'Wasn't Pacco the man in charge of this area for you in the old days?' he ended.

'Yes. He managed operations from Perpignan to Menton, but only as far north as Avignon. I made the area over to him when I split up The Network. The point is that if Gabriel or anyone else has been setting up a job from here, Pacco will know about it.'

'Will he tell?'

'We'll know when we find him.' She stood up and moved to the balcony rail. 'Pacco likes to walk in the shadows. But there's a girl Willie knows ... he's gone to look her up.'

'And she's close to Pacco?'

'Nicole is as close to him as a girl can get. It's not because of her voice that she sings in one of his night-spots—though it's not a bad voice at that.'

'If she's Pacco's girl, will she talk?'

'I got her out of trouble with the police once, and she was grateful. But I think she'll talk to Willie anyway. Pacco is her meal-ticket, but she's a little bit crazy about Willie.'

'Enough for him to get her talking?'

'More than enough.' Modesty's teeth showed white in a quick smile. 'But if I know Willie he'll take time out to persuade her anyway. He's quite a gentleman.'

Hagan spread his hands. 'It must be that sort of day. Everybody's doing it.'

'We'll have other things to keep us busy soon,' she said thoughtfully, and took a packet of Gauloises from the pocket of her house-coat. 'A cigarette, and then I'll get dressed. Have you got a light?'

Hagan slapped his pockets and got up. 'Left my lighter in the kitchen,' he said. 'Don't go away.' At the open French windows he stopped and looked back at her. Now he could see her full-length in profile, and the artist in him was at work again, absorbing the blend of colour and composition. A wisp of black hair blew across her face in the warm breeze, and she absently lifted a hand to push it back. He wanted to cry out to her to hold that position, just there, like that, while he rushed for a sketch-pad.

She turned her head to look at him curiously: 'What is it, Paul?'

'Nothing. I'll get that light for you.' He lifted a hand with the little finger extended. 'Another few degrees and I could light you with this.'

He went through the small bedroom, across the studio and into the kitchen. As he came out with the lighter, the door-buzzer sounded.

Mister Garvin, thought Hagan. Do I take orders from him, too?

He opened the door and looked into the muzzle of an automatic. Holding it was a dark, chunky man in a black suit with a pale grey shirt and red tie. He wore a black mohair hat with a band of brocaded silk satin, and pointed shoes with plaited leather toe-caps. His face was square, with a spreading nose and very small eyes. The gun was a nine millimetre Beretta Brigadier.

Hagan registered every detail in one instant mental snapshot before he felt any emotion at all. Then sickness hit him hard in the stomach, a sickness of rage against himself. For the last hour he had been thinking with his body, not his mind. So had Modesty, but she had stopped from that moment when she had stretched long and lazily like a cat, and got up from the bed. Now, because his mind had remained warm with the memory of firm flesh and strong limbs and her body united with his, he was looking down the barrel of a gun.

With a job begun, with one of Tarrant's men dead and another missing, he had opened the door wide without the precautions any novice would have taken.

A bloody fine start, he thought savagely, then closed his mind to all else but the man and the gun. A finger flicked, motioning him back into the room. He obeyed, keeping his hands low. The man moved in and shut the door, holding the gun steady on Hagan.

Hagan's face was slack with pretended shock; his mind was racing. A shout would warn Modesty. It would also tell this man that she was here—and he might not know that yet. Modesty had no weapon; at least, not on her. But if he could start talking and make it loud enough to reach her ears, then maybe she could——

The gunman lifted his free hand and twirled a finger in a clear command to Hagan to turn round, at the same time shifting his grip on the gun slightly, ready for a blow.

'Just like that,' Hagan thought grimly. He turned, and kept turning fast, his right hand scything in a backward chop to sweep the gun-hand aside and grab the wrist. But the man was waiting for it. Hagan glimpsed the fleshy lips parted in a grin as his chop was blocked by a forearm, and then the gun-butt smashed against the side of his head. He felt his legs folding under him, and the rough scrape of matting against his face as he hit the floor.

With an enormous effort he tried to draw breath for a shout, but the links between mind and muscle were dead. The world spun sickeningly away from him, and with the last shreds of awareness he felt a harsh stricture on his wrists.

Modesty stood looking out over the harbour below, the cigarette in her fingers. She was uneasy about Paul. Behind the sensitive artistry which made him so splendidly satisfying as a lover, there was a steely core of male pride. She wondered how it might affect the job ahead. You couldn't make this business work by committee; Paul would probably hold the same view. But in spite of Tarrant's orders he would want to

do things his own way. The last hour hadn't helped. Because **she** had lent him her body, she had created in him an element **of** protectiveness towards her.

She had known it might not be wise to let it happen. Correction. To make it happen. But it had been wonderful, and she had no regrets. Turning, she walked through the small bedroom where Willie's cases lay and into the short passage leading off the studio. The unlit cigarette was in her hand.

'Paul, don't you approve of women smoking?'

She saw him lying on the floor on the far side of the studio. There was a red abrasion on the side of his head and his wrists were tied behind him with a piece of sisal cut from a wrapped canvas. She knew the man who knelt on one knee beside him, small eyes watching her as she entered.

'Ca va, Didi?' she said, and kept moving towards him without change of pace or expression. With a man less alert, it might just have brought her within kicking distance; but not with Didi. On her second pace he brought up the gun. His other hand, holding the flick-knife he had used to cut the sisal, lowered the blade to rest on Paul Hagan's carotid artery.

'One step more,' he said in French, and she stopped. Hagan's eyes flickered open, staring blindly at first, then slowly focusing. She saw the muscles of his arms twitch as he strained against the bonds. The blade pressed down very slightly, and Hagan relaxed.

'Put both hands on your head,' Didi said to Modesty. 'And move two steps forward. Just two. Very slow.'

She obeyed, and said quietly: 'Pacco won't like this.'

'No?' Didi grinned. 'I will tell you what Pacco will not like. He will not like you and Garvin and this Hagan all together here. Pacco is boss now, not Modesty Blaise.' There was sudden venom in the last two words.

Hagan's head was turned towards Modesty, but he could feel the hair-trigger tension in the man who knelt over him, and it left him shaken. Modesty was six paces away, unarmed, and at the psychological disadvantage of wearing nothing but the thin nylon house-coat. Yet this man was watching her as a hunter might watch a trapped tigress.

'*Alors* ... you remember me?' Didi used the familiar '*tu*' with insulting inflexion.

'I saw you in '61 when I came over for a conference with Pacco,' she said.

'And do you remember '62? The time you sent Willee Garvin to see me, after I ran a small packet of heroin?'

'We never touched drugs.' She spoke with a blend of contempt and boredom. 'Everybody who worked for me knew that.'

'I know that after Garvin came my arm was in plaster for five weeks,' said Didi viciously, and Hagan felt hatred surge through the man.

'I'll speak to him about it,' Modesty said. 'For drugs, it should have been your neck.'

'No, *I* will speak to Garvin. Where is he?'

'He went to see a friend.'

'I want him here. Pacco tells me to watch Hagan. I watch, and I find Modesty Blaise. Where she is, Garvin will not be far away. And that one I fix before I tell Pacco.'

He stuck the knife in the floor and instantly pressed the barrel of the Beretta to Hagan's throat, never taking his eyes from Modesty.

'You move, I kill him,' he said simply, and with his free hand threw a twelve-inch length of sisal towards her. 'Pick it up ... but very slow. Good. Now turn round, with hands behind you, and make the thumb-tie.'

Slowly she turned, knowing that the first hint of a false move would send a bullet through Paul's throat. Behind her back, her fingers gave a twist to the sisal, making a small double-bow in the middle of it. She slipped a thumb through each loop of the double-bow, and waited. Didi wasn't going to make a mistake. She could get him, perhaps, but for the loss of Paul. And in a moment Paul would have the bare chance of a move, but then the bullet would be for her.

'Lie on the couch, face down,' Didi said. She moved to the studio-couch which stood against one wall, lay down on it, and turned on her face. Didi rose, very light on his feet, and moved quickly across the studio, keeping the gun trained on her. Now the flick-knife was again in his other hand.

Head turned to watch, Modesty saw Paul stir and start to bring his legs round. The gun jabbed into her neck, and Paul froze. Didi stuck his knife in the wall, took the loose ends of the sisal and jerked hard. The bow-knot tightened brutally on her thumbs. He twitched a half-hitch with each loose end and secured the knot.

Now the gun was trained on Paul again.

'The legs,' Didi said flatly. She knew what he meant. With this tie-up you could secure a man with six inches of string and hold him more helpless than if you used handcuffs.

She considered going unconscious. This was a trick she could perform at will, a self-induced faint. It had its uses, but it would serve no purpose at the moment. She bent her knees, lifting her feet and resting one ankle in the crotch formed by the bent knee of her other leg. Didi gripped the raised foot and forced it down hard, trapping the other foot between the back of the calf and the thigh.

With his gun-hand he reached quickly for her bound thumbs, lifted her hands, and hooked them over the instep of the raised foot. When he released the pressure on that foot it sprang up against the thumb-tie, so that her arms and legs were painfully and helplessly locked. The last move had taken only two seconds but Hagan was up on his knees, face bone-white with fury.

'Gently, Paul,' Modesty said quietly. Didi walked across the studio, gun in hand, and kicked him in the stomach so that he fell on his side, gasping for breath.

'Now,' Didi said, and moved back to the couch. Taking the knife from the wall he sat down sideways on the edge of the couch and looked at Modesty. 'When will Garvin come?'

He waited three seconds, and when there was no answer he slid the blade under the collar of her house-coat and slit it carefully all down the back.

'Late tonight,' Modesty answered, watching Paul. 'Or it could be tomorrow.'

Didi rubbed his chin, eyes narrowed. 'You will know how to reach him.' It was not a question.

'Antibes 26-3157,' she said.

'*Verrons, alors.*' Didi got up and lifted the telephone from the small side-table. At the extreme length of its flex it could stand on the floor just below Modesty's head.

'You will tell Garvin to come,' he said, dialling the number. 'And speak with great care, *ma belle*.' He straightened up, the phone in one hand, and ran the point of the knife skilfully down her bare back, not breaking the skin but leaving a thin red hair-line. 'With great care,' he repeated.

EIGHT

'COME on now, love, speak English.' Willie Garvin settled his head back more comfortably on the pillow. 'It's good practice for you.'

'I know. But I can't do it when we are making the love, Willie. It takes my mind away from what I am doing, and I don't like that.'

'I should 'ope not. But we're not making the love now, Nicole.'

'And I am speaking English now.'

'Well all right, then.'

She lay half on top of him, folded arms resting on his chest, looking down at him. Nicole was twenty-three, a small girl with dark red hair and a body well-fleshed without being plump. She knew that she was feather-brained, but the knowledge did not disturb her. Nicole's attitude to life was very simple. She did whatever she had to do to get along comfortably, and the rest of the time she did whatever she enjoyed doing. She was happy and generous, and rarely thought about tomorrow; but she was thinking about it now.

Of the men she had known, she was now quite sure that she liked Willie Garvin by far the best. When he had appeared beside her, in the bustling market in the old part of Antibes an hour ago, her heart had jumped in the strangest way.

Willie had helped her with the shopping, and then sat on the pillion of her scooter with the two big baskets while she drove home to her small flat off Avenue de Verdun.

Nicole sighed and kissed him gently on the nose. 'It's so good to see you again, Willie. Really, you are more pretty than ever.'

''Andsome,' he said absently. 'You're pretty, I'm 'andsome.'

''Andsome. Thank you. How long will you stay in Antibes?'

'Can't say yet, chick. It just depends.'

'Oh.' She was disappointed. 'But last year you stay three weeks on holiday. I could say to Pacco that I must visit my grandmother in Grenoble, like before, and then we can go away——'

'Sorry, love. I'm 'ere on business.'

'Business? Ah, with Modesty?' Her eyes sparkled. For her, part of Willie Garvin's cachet lay in his unique relationship with Modesty Blaise, whom Nicole adored without a trace of envy. 'With Modesty?' she repeated. 'Like the times before?'

'Not quite like the times before,' Willie said, kneading her shoulder gently. 'Where do I find Pacco?'

'At *Le Gant Rouge*, in Juan les Pins. He has made a very nice apartment at the back now.' She studied him anxiously. 'But please don't go to Pacco, Willie darling.'

'Why not? He's a funny bloke, but we never 'ad any trouble with 'im.'

'It is different now.' She lay down and put her head on his shoulder. 'Since Pacco becomes boss, he is not nice. He has fear for somebody to take over from him, so he does bad things to make people afraid. He will think Modesty has come back with you so he will not be boss any more.'

She cupped a hand to Willie's cheek and spoke earnestly. 'Believe me, Willie, he will do bad things against you. And he has more than fifty men now, between Cannes and Nice alone.'

'Overstaffed,' Willie said with faint scorn. 'Modesty would never 've run up the over-'eads like that. Still, it's Pacco's business now. All I want from 'im is a bit of information.'

'Listen, Willie, I will find what you want to know.' Nicole rose on one elbow and looked down at him with a rueful grimace. 'I am sorry to say this thing, but tonight before I sing I must be with Pacco for a little while. You know, it is part of the job.'

'He'll be on a dusty wicket tonight,' Willie said, and grinned.

'How is that?'

'Never mind. What were you saying?'

'Well maybe it's good that I must be with Pacco tonight, because I will get him to tell me what you want to know.'

Willie frowned. 'Pacco's fly,' he said.

'Fly? *Une mouche?*'

'No. Fly—dead crafty. *Il est malin.*'

'Ah, ça. But I am a fly too, Willie. When Pacco makes to—to have good time with me he tells many things. He knows I don't listen, I don't care. So he tells. He likes for me to say yes and no, and how is that, and oh, you are clever.'

'Sure you won't be taking a chance?'

'Truly. It is easy.'

'All right. But you better not go to 'im looking all big-eyed like you are now. Pacco might wonder what you've been doing this afternoon.'

'Pooh!' She was contemptuous. 'Pacco does not notice me like that.'

The telephone beside the bed rang, and she wriggled across Willie to reach out for it, lying on his stomach. Thoughtfully he began to walk two fingers up her spine.

'Yes,' she said into the phone. 'Ah! Modesty?' A puzzled note. 'But this——' She interrupted, and listened with a little frown. 'Yes, but ... yes, he is with me. You want to speak to him?' A pause. 'All right. I will tell him at once.' She took the phone from her ear, stared at it, then put it back on the rest and turned her head to look at Willie.

'It was Modesty,' she said. 'But so strange. She didn't let me speak, really. She said I must say to you to go back right away. It is urgent. But Willie, she didn't say my right name ... all the time she called me "Jacqueline".'

Willie's hand stopped moving on her spine. 'Jacqueline,' he echoed quietly, and there was no query in his voice. ' 'Op off love.' He delivered a light smack to her buttocks. 'I got to get moving.'

She climbed off the bed and picked up a dressing-gown. Willie began to put on his shirt and trousers. 'About Pacco,' he said. 'I want anything he knows on a man called Gabriel, and anything he knows about a big shipment of diamonds. Right?'

'Yes, Willie. Gabriel and diamonds. I will remember.' Frowning in concentration, she moved to the window and adjusted the plastic venetian blinds to allow more light.

'Don't push it too 'ard, though,' Willie said, pulling on his shoes. 'I don't want Pacco to guess——'

'Willie, come here!' She was parting the slats of the blind to peer out, and her voice was urgent. Willie moved to her side and bent to look through the narrow gap. The flat was part of a corner house, and an alley ran along the side and rear. In the alley stood a red Vespa.

'I think you are followed here, Willie!' Her voice trembled a little. 'That scooter. It belongs to one of Pacco's men.'

'Which one?'

'Chaldier. He is from Algeria, and joined Pacco after Modesty's time.'

'You reckon 'e followed me? Or would 'e be watching you?'

'Ah, no. Pacco does not care about me like that. I am afraid for *you*, Willie. I know Pacco will do bad things.'

'Don't you worry, love.' He put his arm about her shoulders and squeezed comfortingly. 'Go and look out front, see if you can spot the bloke.'

She hurried away, barefoot. Willie picked up his jacket. It was a lightweight wind-cheater with a long zip up the front. Inside the left breast was stitched a twin sheath of thin but stiff leather, holding his two knives. Carrying the jacket, he went into the bathroom and washed his face and hands. It was as he ran a comb through his hair that he saw a bottle on the shelf behind the lavatory, and began to grin. The bottle held spirits of salt.

Nicole appeared at the bathroom door. 'He's there, Willie,' she breathed, round-eyed. 'Outside the café across the road.'

Willie picked up the bottle carefully and slipped it into the pocket of his jacket. He took Nicole's arm and went through to the living-room. Standing well back, he could see the pavement on the far side of the road, with a few tables outside a café. At one of the tables was a small man with a thin dark face. He wore narrow cream trousers and a dark green linen jacket. His thick hair was long and carefully styled.

'I'll put 'im out of the way for a bit,' Willie said. 'You still ready to get Pacco talking tonight, chick?'

'Sure, Willie.' She hesitated. 'But after, I think I will go away. It's not very nice with Pacco sometimes. I will go to Paris. Maybe London.' She touched his arm. 'You think I could get work in London, Willie?'

'Reckon I could keep you busy.' The innuendo was automatic and she saw that his mind was busy with other matters.

'When shall I meet you to tell you what I find from Pacco?' she asked.

'You name it, love.'

'I finish late at *Le Gant Rouge*. Be in the old market here at two o'clock. It is empty then.'

'Right. Can I borrow your scooter now?'

'Anything you like, Willie. I can get a taxi tonight from Juan les Pins.'

'You're a living doll.' He took her by the arms and kissed her. 'See you tonight, then.'

'All right. I would like to see Modesty, too, if she can come. It's funny she was so strange on the telephone, calling me Jacqueline.'

'It meant she was in trouble. I'll take care of Chaldier, then sort it out. So long, love.'

'So long, Willie. And please——'

He halted by the door and looked back.

'Please be a fly,' she said anxiously.

Willie went down the stairs and out into the tiny back yard. He passed through a gate into the alley where the red Vespa stood. It was a new machine, beautifully kept. The saddle had a cover of tartan cloth with foam rubber beneath it. Willie strolled to the scooter, took the small bottle of spirits of salt from his pocket, and emptied it on to the saddle. The liquid soaked in immediately.

He dropped the empty bottle in a dustbin and went back through the house and out of the front door. Nicole's Lambretta stood by the kerb. Taking plenty of time, he switched on the petrol and primed the carburettor. From the corner of his eye he saw the figure of Chaldier move quickly across the road and into the alley.

Willie kicked the scooter to life and straddled it. As he drove slowly off, there came the sound of angry revving from the alley and the Vespa appeared. He could see Chaldier in the mirror. The man was scowling, and Willie saw him ease himself up on the foot-rests and reach behind with one hand to pluck at the seat of his trousers.

Opening up a little, Willie turned left along the Rue Vauban towards Place General de Gaulle. Behind him, Chaldier was driving erratically. They made the circuit of the *place*, and Willie glanced back on the corner. Chaldier was half standing now in a grotesque crouch, one hand reaching down between his legs to tug at the damp crotch of his trousers.

'Seen blokes nicked for less than that,' Willie thought contentedly. A rich enjoyment began to spread within him, then was snuffed out as he remembered Modesty's phone-call from Hagan's flat. How the hell could trouble have started already? And what kind of trouble was there that Modesty couldn't cope with, anyway? Uneasiness gnawed at him. Somebody must have the drop on her, or she would have spoken freely on the phone. And she must have rung him under orders, to bring him back to Hagan's flat. There was a grain of comfort in that. It meant that whoever had the drop wanted Willie Garvin in the net before making the next move.

He put speculation out of his mind and concentrated on driving, watching Chaldier in the mirror, growing a little impatient. The bastard's wedding-tackle must be case-hardened; surely he'd have to stop soon and make a dive for a gent's—or at least get out of sight somewhere so that he could get those trousers off. And so that he could be dealt with.

They were almost at the bottom of the Rue Albert now, and still Chaldier followed. Willie turned to look back, and saw the agonised bewilderment on the man's face as he lurched dangerously across the road and swung back to the shriek of a horn.

Willie turned right, along the road by the sea, where a low wall bordered the scrubby grey strip of beach. Suddenly Chaldier seemed to go mad. He tried to get off his scooter without stopping. It hit the kerb and he rolled sprawling across the pavement. Willie braked to a halt and turned to watch.

Chaldier was struggling to tear his trousers off, and at the same time jumping down the low wall to the beach. It was not

101

a good combination of actions. He landed in a sprawling heap, panting wildly and kicking to get free of the trousers.

'Strewth!' Willie muttered, awed at his own success. Fascinated, he watched Chaldier hurl the trousers away. Underneath he wore vivid shorts of white and mauve stripes. A mixed crowd was gathering rapidly, and there were cries of indignation.

'*Est-il fou?*'

'*Ah, c'est dégoûtant!*'

'*Devant les enfants, voyons!*'

A gendarme moved across the road, pushing through the crowd. Chaldier was stumbling into the sea, the striped shorts round one ankle. He sat down waist-deep, one hand clutched to his head, the other under the water. The striped shorts floated away. Grimly the gendarme strode to the water's edge. He blew a shrill blast on his whistle to attract Chaldier's attention, and beckoned with a menacing finger.

Willie felt it would have to do for now. He let in the clutch and opened the throttle, heading for the road which cut across Cap d'Antibes. He was thankful that he had borrowed the Lambretta instead of picking up the hired car he had left near the market. With the weight of traffic, the scooter would get him to Cannes a lot faster than the car.

Twenty minutes brought him to the Boulevard de la Croisette and the port. As he drove up the narrow, winding streets of the old quarter he saw a man walking ahead at a casual pace, carrying a walking-stick. The man was tall and grey-haired. He wore dark trousers with a light beige linen jacket and brown brogues. Willie drew into the kerb ahead of the man and got off the scooter.

''Allo, Sir G. Didn't reckon on seeing you 'ere.'

Tarrant leaned on his stick. He detected a hint of tautness in Willie Garvin, and wondered if Hagan was being difficult.

'It's not exactly official,' he said. 'I'm overdue for a holiday, and His Highness made a strong request that I should come out here with him. Since I was told to give my personal attention to this business, I thought it a good idea to come.'

'The Sheik's 'ere too, then?'

'Complete with retinue.' Tarrant rubbed his brow wearily.

'We're all established at the Gray d'Albion, a happy band of brothers. I'm beginning to feel like Lawrence—except that he apparently *enjoyed* bizarre company.'

'Cheer up, my old darling.' Willie's manner was light, but there was still the underlying tension. *''Eaviness may endure for a night, but joy cometh in the morning.'*

Tarrant stared. 'I beg your pardon?'

'Psalm 30. Verse 5.'

'You—ah—you have another calling, then?'

''Ardly a calling. But I once spent a year in the coop at Calcutta with only a psalter to read, so I got the psalms by 'eart.'

'I see.' Tarrant paused. 'What's troubling you, Willie?'

'I'm not sure yet. Could you do a little thing for me?

'What is it?'

'Give me two minutes, then walk on to Hagan's place. That's first left, number sixteen. Go up the stairs an' press the buzzer.'

'And then?'

Willie shrugged. 'See what 'appens.'

Modesty sealed off the throbbing agony of her hands, excluding it from her consciousness.

Just half-an-hour since the phone-call to Nicole, so Willie should be here any minute now. Her ears were strained for the slightest sound of movement—not on the stairs outside but within the apartment. This concentration helped to eliminate the pain. It also helped to eliminate any awareness of Didi's hand moving upon her.

Across the room, Paul Hagan lay staring fixedly towards them, pure hatred burning in his eyes, face shining with the sweat of it.

Didi looked at his watch and stood up. 'When Garvin comes,' he said, moving the gun from Hagan to Modesty and back, 'if one cries out, I shoot the other first. *Entendu?*'

He froze suddenly, listening. There came the faint sound of feet mounting the stairs, growing louder. Somebody stopped outside the door. The buzzer sounded. Hagan's eyes were on Modesty, urgently willing her to shout. She moved her head slightly in negation, and turned her eyes to watch the passage which led off to the bedrooms and bathroom.

Didi, gun in hand, walked softly to the door. He gripped the handle and suddenly flung it open. As he did so, Willie Garvin stepped out from the passage behind him on the far side of the studio.

There was a knife in Willie's hand, held by the point; then there was no knife, only a glittering blur in the air. The blade drove into the back of Didi's gun arm, biting into the bone. He whinnied in shock, still staring at the tall grey man who stood before him in the open doorway. The gun toppled from nerveless fingers, and the tall man caught it calmly, pushing Didi back into the room and closing the door behind him.

Whimpering, Didi turned, knowing he would see Garvin. The second knife was poised in a big, powerful hand, and two arctic-cold eyes promised death.

'Want 'im finished, Princess?' Willie asked quietly.

'No, Willie. Get me loose, please.'

The secondary wave of shock hit Didi and he collapsed on a chair, half-sprawled over the table, the knife jutting from the back of his arm. Tarrant weighed the gun in his hand and said nothing. Willie Garvin was bending over Modesty now. He freed the locked foot hooked under the bound thumbs, then delicately nicked through the sisal with his knife.

As she moved stiffly to sit up, the slit house-coat fell away to the waist, and for a moment Tarrant saw her splendid body. Willie drew the house-coat up and about her shoulders again, then ripped the collar slightly so that he could knot it at the back of her neck. Her thumbs were blue-black and horribly swollen. Willie took them in his palms and began gently to massage. His whole attention was on her, and the others in the room might have been forgotten.

'I'll get a couple of basins of 'ot and cold water,' he said. 'Keep dipping your thumbs in alternate. It'll soon get 'em right. But you're in for a bad ten minutes, Princess.'

'I earned it, by God. All of it.' Her voice was hard with self-contempt. Then it softened. 'Thanks, Willie love. The thumbs can wait. Get the medical kit and fix up Didi before he bleeds too much. I'll see to Paul.'

Clumsily she picked up Didi's flick-knife and got to her feet. Willie crossed the studio, giving Hagan an amiable nod of greeting.

''Allo, Paul. Glad to meet you. 'Ow's your luck, matey?'

'Better than I deserve, goddam it.' There was bitter savagery in Hagan's voice, and the sweat was running on his face. Modesty knelt beside him, the knife in her hand.

Willie stood in front of Tarrant, and Tarrant saw two frosty blue eyes challenging him, daring him to comment on anything at all that he had seen or surmised. Tarrant looked at Modesty and Hagan, tight-lipped, then back at Willie. After a moment's hesitation he gave a slight nod of acquiesence.

Willie relaxed, looking down at Didi, who still lay sprawled across the table, half-fainting. He took the man by the hair and lifted his head.

'Didi,' he said cheerfully. 'I remember 'im now. Always 'aving trouble with 'is arms, Princess.' He went out into the bedroom and returned a minute later with a small attache-case. Hagan was in the kitchen, heating water. Modesty stood by the kitchen door, massaging her thumbs, her mouth a thin hard line. Nobody was speaking.

'I'm not ecstatic about being used as a decoy,' Tarrant said as Willie put down the case and opened it. 'He might have shot me.'

'Somebody 'ad to take a chance,' Willie said reasonably. 'And I'm chicken meself.' He neatly cut away the sleeve of Didi's jacket, then the shirt-sleeve, exposing the bare arm with the black-hilted knife jutting from it. Putting a hand on Didi's shoulder, he gripped the hilt and looked at Tarrant. 'Right. Will you get ready to whop on one of those field-dressings, Sir G.?'

Ten minutes had gone by. Modesty was dressed in skirt and blouse, and wearing a pair of cotton gloves with pads of lint soaked in witch-hazel in the thumbs. Hagan stood by the window, hands in pockets. The hands were balled into fists. Didi, his face a dirty grey, sat on the couch. His shoulder was thickly bandaged, the arm in a sling.

'And how does *he* fit in?' Tarrant asked.

'He doesn't.' Awkwardly Modesty took a cigarette Willie had lit for her. 'He's a random factor. Apparently Pacco was suspicious of Paul and had him watched. When I came on the scene Didi thought it over and decided he ought to nail us. But he wanted a little personal revenge before he reported to Pacco.'

'Pacco's got a lot of eyes,' Willie said, coming through from the kitchen with a tray of coffees. 'There was a tail on me, too, but I don't reckon he got a chance to report either.'

'What did you do with him?' Modesty asked.

'I just fixed 'im temp'ry, Princess. Either the police have got 'im for indecent exposure, or 'e might be in 'ospital.' Willie frowned. 'I'm not quite sure what spirits of salt does to the old family jewels.'

'In clear, Willie love.'

He told the story briefly, and she turned to Tarrant. 'Can you liaise with the Deuxième on that? We want the man kept out of the way for a few days. The same with Didi here.'

Tarrant picked up the telephone. 'Léon Vaubois gave me direct access to Inspector Durand for any co-operation needed,' he said. 'The advantage the French police have is that the laws here are actually designed to *help* them do their job.'

Fifteen minutes later a grocer's van called at the house and two businesslike men took Didi down the stairs with a raincoat draped round his shoulders.

'Thank you for the coffee.' Tarrant got to his feet and picked up his walking-stick. He looked at Modesty. 'I'm sorry this random factor caught you unprepared,' he said politely. 'And please don't think I want to breathe down your neck, but I'd be glad to have a progress report whenever you can manage it.'

'You're at the Gray d'Albion with Abu-Tahir?'

'Yes.'

'We'll see you there when we've heard from Nicole. It won't be till very late.'

'I shall be up. And so will His Highness, I expect. Goodbye for now, my dear.'

When Tarrant had gone there was a long silence in the

studio, broken only by the faint sound of Willie Garvin whistling in the small bedroom as he unpacked.

Hagan said: 'How are your hands?'

'They'll be as good as new in a few hours.'

'They must hurt badly.'

'They might, if I let them.'

He looked at her, grim-faced. 'I'm sorry. Christ, I'm sorry. When I think of that bastard sitting there, handling you, mauling you——'

'Don't be a fool.' She dismissed the subject impatiently. 'I've known a lot worse than that, and it's not important. What's important is that you slipped badly and I slipped badly.'

'You?'

'Of course.' Her voice was taut, almost harsh. 'If I hadn't been...' she gestured, 'relaxed, from being in bed with you, I'd have known something was wrong. Will you get Willie in here, please?'

Hagan stared. He went to the passage and called. Willie came through, holding a knife in one hand, the knife he had pulled out of Didi's humerus; in his other hand was a small stick of carborundum. He wore a reminiscent grin.

'You should've seen this bloke on the scooter,' he said. 'It was dead funny, Princess——'

'Just a minute, Willie. I've got to ask you something.' She looked at him soberly. 'Do you want to quit?'

He understood, and made no pretence otherwise.

'Go easy on yourself, Princess,' he said gently. 'I don't think you've weighed it up yet. This is about the best thing could 've 'appened.'

Hagan said bleakly: 'Don't pat *me* on the head, Willie boy.'

'I'm not.' Willie was unruffled. He began to hone the blade carefully, with small circular movements of the carborundum. 'You fell flat on your face, matey. So did the Princess. And so did I, not so long ago, before this started. So now we've all 'ad a decoke and got it out of our systems. It might 'urt a bit, but if you get sharpened up in the first round you're less likely to take a belting later on.'

Hagan breathed hard and started to speak, but Modesty

silenced him with a gesture. 'Be quiet. He means it. And he could be right.'

She moved to the window and stood looking out, her eyes distant. Watching her, Hagan saw the tension in her body gradually slacken, and the hard lines of her face grow softer. She gave a little sigh, and when she turned from the window there was something of a smile about her lips.

'He's right,' she said simply. 'Nobody's going to walk flat-footed from now on. Listen, we'll have to move out of here, Paul. If Pacco's taken an interest in you this is no good as a base. Can you find us a villa out of town somewhere? Back from the coast, at Biot maybe, or Valauris.'

'Sure. Give me a few hours.' Hagan felt a sudden sense of relief. The bitter black cloud was lifted from his mind, though he could not have told how or why.

Willie had stopped honing his knife. He stood in front of Modesty's picture, lips pursed, studying it with absorbed interest.

'You ought to finish this sometime, Paul,' he said seriously. 'You've done it lovely. Very nice indeed.' He bent forward, a finger almost touching a painted leg, high up towards the back of the right thigh. 'See this, Princess?' he said admiringly. 'He's even got the little scar where I dug that bullet out of you.'

NINE

NICOLE sat looking at herself in the ornate, cream and gold mirror of the dressing-table. She wrinkled her nose in a tiny grimace at her own reflection.

On the other side of the big rumpled bed, Pacco was putting on his shoulder-holster, a George Lawrence design with the gun held in a spring clip and only the butt showing.

It was a large bedroom, with expensive and sickly décor. Nicole's nightdress was pink and blue, semi-transparent, with infinite bows and frills. She hated it. She also wore stockings, because Pacco liked her to; she hated this as well. Pacco slipped on his tuxedo. He was a big man, carrying a lot of flesh, and with a heavy-jowled face. He moved round the bed to Nicole, put his hands on her shoulders, and bent to kiss her neck. She looked at him in the mirror and smiled.

'Nicole, little pigeon ... something troubles you.' There was distress in his eyes. 'You have not been quite yourself this evening.' He shook his head with profound anxiety.

Nicole thought of her own small bedroom and Willie Garvin. She shut the thought hastily out of her mind, and sighed. 'I am sorry, Pacco. It's nothing. Only I am a little worried about my grandmother in Grenoble. She has not been very well.'

'You are a good girl, Nicole.' Pacco squeezed her shoulders. His eyes were moist. He was a cruel man of almost limitless sentimentality. 'Always we should think of the old people. I remember my own dear grandmother, when I was small...' He swallowed, and looked at his watch. 'Ah, I must attend to some business, little pigeon. Rest for a while, and I will come back to watch you dress for the first cabaret.'

He slid his hands down her body to her thighs. Nicole braced herself inwardly, knowing what was to come. His fingers suddenly pinched hard, nipping the flesh, and he chuckled fatly. She gave the expected small squeal of surprise, and patted his cheek, thinking how she would like to rake it with her nails.

Still chuckling, Pacco went to the door. He put his fingers to his lips and blew her an arch kiss. When the door closed after him she let the smile drop from her face. Gently she rubbed her sore thighs and glared sulkily at herself in the mirror.

She shrugged, and whispered softly: 'I'm sorry, Willie. He didn't talk, the big pig.' A sparkle touched her eyes, and she winked. 'But he didn't get much fun, either.'

Pacco walked down the wide, thickly carpeted passage. There were two pictures on the walls, and a recess holding a small-scale replica of Rodin's *The Kiss*. One of the pictures showed a small girl in a long nightdress at her nurse's knee, saying her prayers. The other showed a bloodstained French cavalryman of the First War, kneeling and holding the head of his dying horse amid a scene of carnage. Underneath was the printed caption: *Adieu, mon vieux*.

His face thoughtful, Pacco walked along the passage to a square lobby with several doors leading off and another passage running at right-angles to the first. Here a man sat by a French side-table of gilded wood, reading a newspaper. In the lobby were several small pictures and statuettes. Beneath a wrought-iron vase-holder containing artificial flowers stood a small urn. Pacco touched the urn and sighed.

'The ashes of poor Joseph,' he said. 'It's good to remember old friends, Maurice.'

The man glanced up from his newspaper and gave a meaningless shrug.

Pacco shook his head. 'I wish he had not made it necessary for me to kill him,' he said unhappily. He went through one of the doors into his study. It was a long room with a short turn at the end, like an elongated L. Pacco crossed the white carpet, sat down at a large, ornate desk, and unlocked a drawer. He took out a message-pad and a small red book.

For ten minutes he was busy encoding a message. When it was done he went through a door into a narrow room where a man sat in front of a transmitter, headphones hanging round his neck, reading a paperback book with a garish cover.

'When is the next call, Pepe?' Pacco asked.

The operator glanced at the watch in the fascia of the transmitter. 'In five minutes. They will be listening out at twenty-three hundred.'

A pink message-slip in his hand, McWhirter paced reverently along the stone corridor behind a file of monks. At the end of the corridor they turned off towards the cells where they would stay under guard throughout the night. McWhirter lengthened his stride and moved on towards the sanctum.

Gabriel was sitting at the desk, pen in hand, reading papers clipped in a dull red file.

'Fleet Hermes comes on winged foot,' announced McWhirter, waving the message. 'A most interesting communication from our friend Pacco——'

'Wait.' Gabriel went on reading. McWhirter pursed his lips and began to pace a slow, intricate measure on the patterned carpet. Two minutes passed. Gabriel closed the file and looked up. 'In a nutshell,' he said briefly.

McWhirter put the message down in front of him. 'From Pacco. It seems a young girl o' close acquaintance wi' the said Pacco has been carrying out a wee probing operation on him—or trying to. She's mentioned Gabriel and she's spoken o' diamonds. Pacco says somebody must ha' put her up to it, and shall he try to find out who?'

Gabriel sat back, his colourless eyes looking through McWhirter. 'Pacco might give away more than he finds out,' he said. 'We'll just discourage whoever it is. Tell Pacco to kill the girl tonight.'

'Aye.' McWhirter picked up the message, turned it over, and jotted on the back. He looked at his watch. 'Time of origin, twenty-three thirty.'

Gabriel said: 'Is that all? Nothing from any of the other stations?'

'Only routine. Kalonides ran the first rehearsal tonight. They have to trim five minutes on time, but he's no' worried. It was their first run.'

'All right. Get that message off to Pacco.'

111

'D'ye no' think there's a chance he might jib? I gather this is his sleeping girl.'

Gabriel opened another file and looked at McWhirter. 'Pacco knows me too well. He won't jib. He might even enjoy it. It'll give him something to cry about.'

Twenty minutes later, in his study, Pacco decoded the reply. Slowly he set a match to the message and watched it burn out in the ashtray. He sat back, thinking of Nicole, of the soft warm body beneath the splendid frou-frous of the night-dress, and of those wonderfully agile legs, sheathed in long taut nylons, gartered at the thighs.

A tear brimmed from his eye and rolled down his fat cheek.

'I don't get Sibelius meself,' Willie Garvin said quietly. 'All noise and no tune. Now you take old Mozart. There was a kiddy who really knew how to write music with a bit of melody.'

'I'm not saying he didn't,' Modesty answered, keeping her voice low. 'If I had to do without one or the other, I'd keep Mozart. I'm just saying that if you really try with Sibelius it's well worth the effort.'

It was a little before two in the morning. The old market was empty, and the dark huddled houses around it were sleep-ing. Overhead, a wide patch of high cloud was passing slowly over the moon. They had arrived fifteen minutes ago, Modesty on the pillion of Nicole's scooter, which they had left five minutes' walk away to save attracting attention here.

Modesty wore a grey sweater and a full black skirt, with black stretch tights. Her shoes were flat walking shoes. She carried a handbag with a shoulder-strap. The clasp of the handbag was large, consisting of a thick rod of polished black wood with small hemispheres at the ends. The rod meshed into a clip on the other side of the handbag. Willie Garvin had made the clasp for her. When the black rod with the mush-room-shaped ends was jerked hard it came loose—and she had a kongo in her hand.

Willie was smoking a cigarette, the glowing end cupped in his hand. He wore dark narrow trousers and a matt black wind-cheater, belted at the waist, the zip locked halfway up.

They sat in darkness on a low wall some distance from the *musée*.

'All right,' Willie said reluctantly. 'I'll give Sibelius another try. But I don't think he'll get through, Princess. So it's not likely he'll be able to go around bragging that *I'm* one of 'is fans. I get browned off with a bloke who makes me listen too 'ard.'

'Courage, Willie love. I know what you mean, but you can always go back to old Mozart and the more tuneful kiddies.' Modesty stretched her legs. It was good to be here in the darkness, waiting for something important, and talking to Willie. There had been many such times in the past.

Sometimes, she knew, people had wondered what Modesty Blaise and Willie Garvin could find to say to each other outside shop-talk and the business of The Network. That was ironic when you thought of the average suburban coffee-table talk. Willie had seen more and done more and lived more than an average twenty people put together. She was always finding something new in him; she thought the same thing probably applied in reverse. And Willie had views. They were sometimes surprising, but they were his own and always worth listening to.

'What do you think about Paul Hagan?' she asked.

'Sharp. Plenty of brains. All right in a caper—get 'im in a rumble and he'll throw the switch, nothing barred. I could see that in 'im this afternoon.' Willie carefully stubbed out his cigarette in a crevice, and considered. 'Works on 'is nerves a bit, though. Do better if 'e cooled down.'

'I think he was mad at himself today, Willie.'

'That could be it. I s'pose he can use 'imself all right in a rumble, Princess? I mean, I like the way 'e moves, but what about muscle-tone. Does 'e strip well?' There was no prurience wrapped in the question. She knew Willie accepted her affairs without curiosity, as she accepted his.

'Yes. He's in trim, Willie. I haven't seen him go, but I'd say he knows the rough stuff. I'm more worried about how he's going to take orders from me.'

'He's got to,' Willie said gently. 'If he wants to stay in. I mean ... it's your game. You knew more about staying alive

113

when you were twelve than Hagan's going to know when he's fifty.'

'Yes. But I'm still a woman.'

'He'll 'ave to forget that. Really forget it.'

'You don't forget it, Willie. You're always fussing over me.'

'Not once a caper's got 'ot, Princess,' he said soberly. 'If I'd ever done that we'd 've been tucked up in wooden overcoats a long while back. Go into a caper thinking you've got to do a bit of the other man's job, and you're cooked. You taught me that yourself.'

'No. You knew it long before, Willie. At Dien Bien Phu and a dozen points west. Maybe you didn't verbalise it as a principle before, but you knew it.'

She heard him chuckle. 'I didn't verbalise anything as a principle before. Just used to react like one of Pavlov's ruddy dogs. But the thing is, Paul Hagan's got to play it your way, Princess, or——' He broke off.

From somewhere in the darkness, perhaps a hundred yards away, there came the faint click of high heels on the cobbles. Modesty touched Willie's arm and they rose. He picked up the newspaper he had put for her to sit on, and together they peered into the darkness. The tall houses which hemmed the market and the approach road from the west showed no light in any window. The whole area was a well of blackness, with only a single pool of light from a distant lamp.

The brisk footsteps halted suddenly. There was a long pause, then they broke into a run, coming closer. Modesty and Willie moved forward. Again the footsteps halted, and there was silence.

Willie rubbed an ear uneasily. 'Something's up,' he murmured. 'Sounds like she's spotted someone after 'er.'

'I think she's in that dark patch beyond the lamp,' Modesty whispered. 'You make straight for her, Willie. I'll move down on this side and——' She stopped, her hand tightening on his arm. A figure flitted through the pool of light, running hard but making no sound—the figure of a girl.

'Takes 'er shoes off so she won't be 'eard,' Willie said grimly, 'then she runs through the light.'

'Let's get to her. And fast.'

They started forward, rubber-soled shoes making no sound, and in the same moment other shapes darted across the pool of light. Two men. One, a big man, was outflanking Nicole. She swerved, heading for a flight of broad stone steps which led up and over a narrow pathway below. Modesty and Willie were only fifty paces away when the second man vanished up the steps in pursuit. At the same moment the big man saw them and stopped dead.

'That one,' Modesty said, pointing, and Willie veered away from her. The big man hesitated, then turned and ran. Modesty swung round the big stone post at the bottom of the steps and went up them fast. The kongo was in her hand now.

Something lay on the flags at the top—a girl, on her side, with legs sprawled. Shoes and a handbag lay scattered nearby. She was curled up, forearms clasped across her stomach, air rasping in her throat as she panted noisily, horribly.

Modesty's eyes swept the darkness beyond. There was no movement. She went to Nicole, dropping her handbag and going down on her knees. The girl jerked in terror as Modesty's hand touched her shoulder, then recognition came into her eyes.

'Modesty...' The voice was a painful whisper, and Modesty saw blood pumping between the clutching forearms across the stomach. For a moment pity and searing anger swept her, then she gripped her mind and drew a steel barrier down upon all emotion.

'Let me see, little one.' She spoke gently, taking one of Nicole's arms and trying to ease it away from whatever it hid.

'No ... please——'

The eyes widened in terror again, staring beyond Modesty, and the white-lipped mouth opened cavernously in an inaudible cry of warning. Modesty threw herself sideways, rolling on her back, feet drawn up. The smaller man was there, knife glittering as it slashed down in a blow already launched at her back.

Her long legs flashed up, ankles crossed in a vee, skirt falling back to her hips. There came a jarring shock as the man's wrist was solidly blocked in the crotch of her ankles. She

115

turned her toes in, locking the wrist, and in one smooth movement she arched up on to the crown of her head and twisted the full length of her body with all the power she could muster.

The man gave a gasping scream, and whirled in a cartwheel on the axis of his viciously twisted arm. He hit the stone flags on his back with a bone-jarring thump, the knife clattering to the ground.

Modesty knelt up, took his trapped wrist in both hands, and came to her feet. The kongo was gripped against his wristbone, pressing on a nerve. It was a secondary use for the little weapon; an arrest-grip which could produce pain so intolerable as to kill all resistance in the strongest man.

She stood poised, one foot jammed against the man's neck, holding the arm rigid, crushing the kongo against the nerve.

'*Qui t'a envoyé?*' Who sent you? Her voice was a cold, deadly whisper. The man arched in pain but said nothing.

'*Qui?*' She tightened her grip, and he began to whimper, his whole body twitching.

'Pacco! Pacco!' The croaking words came as if torn from his throat.

'Pacco will join you soon,' she said. She put a foot in the man's stomach, lifted herself, and swung across his body, turning so that she fell on her back, and always keeping his captured arm rigid, to act as a lever. He rose in the air, hoisted on her slim straight leg, and went soaring on in an arc which carried him just clear of the stone balustrade. The beginning of a scream was cut short as he smashed head-first upon the cobbles twenty feet below.

Modesty came to her feet with the completion of the roll, and moved to kneel again by Nicole. The girl's eyes were closed now, and in the darkness her face was shiny white. She was barely breathing, and the blood no longer flowed freely.

'Pacco,' she said in a tiny whisper. 'He didn't tell me anything ... I tried, but ...'

'Don't talk, darling.'

The girl was dying quickly, and dying was a lonely thing. Modesty lay down, easing an arm under Nicole's head, trying not to move her. Nicole relaxed a little, her head nestled into

Modesty's shoulder. She sighed, and there was relief in it. Modesty knew that the pain had left her now.

A few seconds passed. Suddenly Nicole spoke quite clearly. 'Please say to Willie I am sorry——' Her voice stopped in mid-sentence. Modesty felt a sudden fierce tremor pass through the body and then it went limp.

She rested Nicole's head gently on the ground and got up. There was blood on her skirt. She went to the balustrade and looked down. Below, the man lay quite still. He seemed to be headless in the darkness, and she saw that his neck was un-naturally bent so that the head was almost obscured by the shoulder and arm.

She picked up her handbag, and slipped the kongo inside it. Leaving the killer's knife where it lay, she went down the steps and turned along the dark street. Every ten seconds or so she paused and gave a soft, two-note whistle in a minor key. Fifty yards past the street-lamp was a narrow alley leading off to a communal open washplace with stone troughs. As she reached the opening her whistle was answered, and she turned along the alley.

Ahead, a lamp set on a wall-bracket threw the giant and grotesque figures of two men on to the wall beyond the stone troughs; the shadows moved, blending and separating in an eerie saraband, with the occasional harsh scrape of metal on metal as the only music.

Where the alley opened out, she stopped. Willie, knife in hand, had the big man backed into a corner. The man held a knife also, a knife twice the size of Willie's, and he held it in the way of a knife-fighter, thumb on the blade, point angled up for the rising thrust. But he was panting, and there was desperation in his face. Slowly he edged forward, feinted, and darted in.

Willie Garvin moved with flowing ease, parrying with knife against knife, the most skilled of all manoeuvres in the art. He swept the bigger weapon casually out of line, and Modesty waited for the riposte to the exposed throat. But instead the small blade swerved and nicked an ear. The man sprang back, breath hissing through teeth bared in a rictus of fear. Willie took two shuffling steps back, and waited.

Modesty moved forward and spoke, her voice low and hard. 'What the hell are you fooling about for, Willie?'

'Thought you might want a talk with 'im, Princess,' he said reasonably, not turning his head. 'Nicole all right?'

'No.' She stood at his shoulder now, looking at the big man. 'Nicole's dead. Pacco sent the two of them to kill her.'

'Ah.' The syllable held no expression.

'I've put the other one down,' she said. 'And I don't want to talk to this one.'

Willie nodded bleakly. His knife hand came up to breast-height, the knife pointing towards his opponent. The big man crouched, eyes narrowing; this time he waited for the attack, bracing himself for a last desperate effort in what was to come.

Willie Garvin did not move his feet. In one eye-baffling movement he spun the knife, caught it by the point, and threw. It thunked home solidly, the black hilt quivering in the centre of the chest. The big man looked down, dull-eyed, and his poised knife-arm fell limply. Leaning back against the wall, he slithered down with legs folding under him and toppled to one side.

Willie moved forward, jerked the knife free, and wiped it clean on the dead man's jacket. He straightened up and went back to Modesty. She had taken off her skirt and was swilling it in the cold water which lay in one of the stone troughs. There was a small rent in one leg of her black tights, just above the knee.

'Pacco had 'er killed?' Willie said.

'Yes.' She wrung out the skirt and handed it to him for a more powerful wringing. 'Nicole must have overplayed it. Pacco knew she was trying to pump him, and he had her killed to scare off whoever was using her.'

'He can't 've known it was us, then.' Willie's hands crushed the fabric. 'Poor little kid,' he said softly. 'She was so sure she could 'andle it.'

TEN

IT was half past two when Modesty and Willie climbed the service stairs of the Gray d'Albion. The hotel was silent, and they saw no staff.

Willie Garvin broke a long silence. 'What 'appens to Pacco, Princess?'

'You want to see him off.' It was hardly a question.

'Yes. As long as it don't mess the job up. If it was you or me that got done, fair enough. But that poor little bint . . .'

'It won't mess the job up. And it might give us a breakthrough. We know Pacco's against us now, anyway. We know he wouldn't have killed Nicole for choice, so he must have done it under orders. And I still say it's Gabriel. Sign Pacco off, and his whole organisation along the Riviera will be in chaos for a while. We might find somebody who knows something—and can be persuaded to talk.'

She glanced sideways at Willie as they walked along a wide corridor. 'It needs to be soon, though. And we can't just charge in at *Le Gant Rouge*. We need a play.'

'I got a play,' he said slowly. 'It leaves you out and brings in Paul Hagan. But we could work it right away. Would that be okay, Princess?'

'Yes.' She put a hand on his arm. 'She was your girl, Willie —one of them, anyway. I'm sorry.'

'I feel like I'd done it meself,' he said bleakly. 'She wasn't all that smart. I should 've known she'd never fool Pacco.' He shrugged a little wearily. 'Still, it always comes out the way it's written.'

Abu-Tahir and Tarrant sat on cushions playing backgammon, with half a dozen Arabs watching. Hagan was sprawled with one leg over the arm of a deep chair, sketching on a pad. Everybody started to rise as Modesty and Willie came into the big suite.

'Please.' She gestured for them to remain seated. Sinking down on a cushion between Abu-Tahir and Tarrant, she

119

opened her handbag and took out cigarettes. Hagan sat up on the arm of his chair, watching her. Willie prowled the room, hands in pockets.

Tarrant put down his dice-box and took out a cigarette-lighter. 'What did Willie's young lady have to tell you?' he asked.

'Nothing.' Modesty took the light he held for her.

Abu-Tahir said: 'Your skirt is wet, Modestee, and your leg grazed. Has there been troubles?'

'Yes, Abu-Tahir. The girl is dead. A man called Pacco sent two of his men to kill her. They succeeded. And they are also dead now.'

There was silence for several seconds.

'It means we're prodding the right nerves,' said Tarrant, 'if we weren't sure of that already. Where do you fit Pacco in, Modesty?'

'I'd say the job was planned here, probably at Gabriel's villa. Pacco was hired for security in this area. That's how Gabriel would work. He's big. He spends big money retaining big people to cover him.'

Hagan got up. 'What happens now?' he said.

She looked at him without expression. 'Willie would like you to go along with him now to *Le Gant Rouge* and kill Pacco.'

Hagan stared for a long moment, then turned to Tarrant. 'May I go along with Willie and kill Pacco?' he asked politely.

Tarrant fingered his chin. 'It's best when I don't know about these things,' he said slowly, and looked at Modesty. 'Pacco does sound the kind of man who would be improved by death. But isn't this a digression?'

'No. If we're going to get anywhere we have to take Pacco out before he takes us out. And we might win a point or two in the confusion afterwards.'

'Sir Tarrant, let it be done,' said Abu-Tahir.

Tarrant picked up his dice-box. 'My ears are closed. But if you want a few hours off, Hagan, I've no official work for you tonight.'

'You won't find Pacco asleep,' Modesty said. 'He's a night-bird. And he'll have men with him.'

'I also have men, Modestee,' Abu-Tahir said hopefully. 'Twenty good men. And myself is like another ten.'

'I'm sorry, Your Highness.' She put her hand on his sympathetically. 'This is not good ground for you to fight on.' Then, to Hagan: 'Did you fix the villa, Paul?'

'Just east of Biot,' he answered. 'We'll be well out of the way there, but in easy reach of any place along the coast. We move in tomorrow morning—sorry, this morning. I cleared all your baggage out of the flat and brought it here.'

'I'll be wanting something from one of the cases,' said Willie. 'Come on, matey.'

They went out and into an empty room across the corridor. Hagan said: 'Do me a favour, Willie.'

'Sure.' Willie opened a case.

'Don't call me matey.'

'Okay. What you carrying where?'

Hagan's hand moved, and there was a gun in it. He opened his jacket. Underneath he wore a modification of the Bucheimer Semi-Shoulder holster; it lay snugly in a cross-draw position between waist and armpit. The gun was a Colt Cobra, a .38 Special. Hagan slipped it back into the holster.

Willie nodded approvingly. 'Very nice.' He rummaged in the case and put something in his pocket; rummaged again and produced an automatic, a Smith & Wesson Model 39. He grimaced at it, said: 'I wish I liked these bloody things,' and tossed it to Hagan.

'What's this for?'

'Put it in your pocket, please Mister Hagan. Right 'and jacket pocket. We'll run through the script on our way to Pacco's place.'

In the big drawing-room of the suite Tarrant was saying: 'I'm one of those unprogressive people who actually approve the principle of retribution. I also agree with your thought that removing Pacco might provide us with some kind of opportunity.' He paused, calculating his words. There was a brooding look in Modesty's eyes. He guessed that she was feeling now whatever she had not allowed herself to feel an hour ago, when she had knelt over a dying girl. It seemed good to him that he should try to break her mood.

121

'But I must confess to some anxiety,' he went on, 'that you've sent Hagan off with that barman of yours on such a risky affair.'

Her eyes snapped to life. 'Instead of feeling anxious,' she said with cold anger, 'it would be more to the point if you rehearsed a few tactful words to say to your friend Inspector Durand. There are three bodies at Antibes, and there'll be more at *Le Gant Rouge* before dawn.'

'Yes,' said Tarrant. 'But I thought I ought to wait for the tally before getting in touch. One likes to be precise.'

'How do you think he'll take it?'

'With relief, in my opinion. Over the past few years the crime situation along this coast has developed into something like Chicago in the twenties.'

'I know it.'

'Quite. And the police situation is critical. I think Durand will be particularly pleased about Pacco—assuming it works out as we hope.' He picked up a small black object which had rolled from her open handbag. 'And what is this pretty thing?'

'A kongo. Or yawara stick.' Her tone was suddenly lighter, and he knew she had realised the purpose of his provocative words. 'It's a very old oriental weapon, and very simple. You can strike up, down, from any angle.'

Tarrant gripped it in his hand. 'Hardly weighty enough, I would have thought.'

'You use it against vital points. Nerve-centres. Then it's as effective as a lead fist.'

'I see.' He raised his eyebrows at her. 'And from whom does one learn the subtle art of usage?'

She smiled and opened her eyes wide. 'Why, from that barman of mine, of course.'

Hagan moved along a broad carpeted corridor to a square lobby where a man sat reading a newspaper. Willie Garvin, walking to one side and just behind Hagan, said: '*Ca va, Maurice?*'

The man looked up, stared without pleasure, then got to his feet. 'Willee,' he said in uncertain greeting.

'This one is called Hagan,' said Willie. His French was

122

fluent, with little accent, and far better enunciated than his English. He turned Hagan slightly, so that Maurice could see the knife held against Hagan's back. 'He has been asking me many difficult questions concerning Pacco, so for the sake of old friendship I have brought him here. It seems better to me that Pacco should answer for himself. *D'accord?*'

Maurice licked his lips and forced a smile. 'No doubt,' he said, and moved to the door of Pacco's study. He went in, closing the door after him. Ten seconds later it opened and he beckoned.

'*Bien*, Willee.'

Hagan walked in, feeling the point of Willie's knife-blade against his back. Behind an intricately carved desk sat a heavy man with a fleshy face. He wore a light grey suit. Around the right arm was a black mourning-band, two inches deep. There were four other men in the room. They were of a type Hagan knew well. Hoods. They looked the same in any country. The tension in the room was a palpable thing.

'Pacco, mon vieux.' Willie spoke cheerfully as Maurice went out and closed the door. 'I present to you a M'sieu Hagan, who is much interested in you.'

'It's good to see you again, Willee.' Pacco did not get up, and his eyes were watchful.

'He carries a gun,' said Willie, and one of the men moved quickly forward. 'The pocket.' Willie nodded towards the jacket pocket. The man's hand slid inside and brought out the automatic.

'Right. There's the man you wish to see, M'sieu Hagan.' A push in the back from Willie sent Hagan stumbling towards a chair which stood across the desk from Pacco. He recovered and sat down, staring around him with angry eyes. Willie's knife had disappeared.

'So you are interested in me?' Pacco said.

'Why not?' Hagan's voice was belligerent. 'You're interested in *me*. The type who called on me with a gun made that clear enough.'

'Didi?' Pacco sat up a little straighter. 'So that is why he has not reported. I wish to know what happened to him, M'sieu Hagan. Also about another of my men, Chaldier.'

'Before you get going Pacco...' Willie walked forward, hands in trouser pockets. He settled himself on the corner of the desk and smiled. 'I have a small favour to ask. You may spend some time with this fellow, and I don't wish to hang around.'

Pacco rubbed a smooth cheek. 'A favour? You are not here on business, Willee?'

Willie laughed and said something coarse. 'No. Not on business. Just a little holiday, Pacco. The weather at home is not good. Apart from bringing our friend here, I was coming to see you in any case, to ask where I can find Nicole.'

'Nicole?' Pacco stared. Slowly his face crumpled and a tear rolled down his cheek. He took out a lavender-scented handkerchief and mopped his eyes. 'My God, Willee, I have a bad thing to tell you. I remember now that you liked Nicole very much.' He smiled pathetically. 'Sometimes I was jealous. But now ... it is all over.' He choked on the last words.

'All over?' Willie looked round at the silent men. Two stood behind Hagan, the other two against the wall behind Pacco. Willie looked back at Pacco. 'What is it with Nicole?'

'She is ... dead, Willee.' The tear-damp jowls quivered, and Pacco touched the black mourning-band on his arm. 'Our poor little Nicole. Oh, my God, I am sad. For me, life will not be the same without her.'

'Dead?' Willie stood up, staring. 'But how? What happened?'

'It was only tonight.' Pacco rubbed a hand across his brow and gestured vaguely towards the telephone. 'I don't know all about it yet. I am still waiting to hear.' His voice failed, and he sniffed noisily.

Willie shook his head slowly, fingering the tie he wore. It was of red suede, with a large imitation diamond in the centre of the flap. 'You know something?' he said sombrely. 'I put this tie on tonight to please her. It was a present she gave me, one time when I came over here from Tangier for a week or two.'

Pacco looked up, blinking moist eyes. 'The tie was from Nicole?' he said.

Willie nodded. He lifted his shirt collar, unclipped the tie at the back of his neck, and took it off. He looked at it sadly. 'I can't wear it again,' he said. 'She was a lovely girl, and I really liked her. It only hurts to keep being reminded . . .' He drew a deep breath and forced a smile. 'Well, you have your own sadness, Pacco—and work to do, also.' He glanced at Hagan. 'I must let you continue with it. Perhaps it will help to take your mind from thoughts of Nicole.'

'Ah, I am not like you, Willee. I like to think of her and remember her.' Pacco got up. 'That tie. If you don't want to keep it I would like very much to have it. As a souvenir of . . . of my little pigeon.'

Willie considered doubtfully. 'I suppose I should keep it,' he said. 'But for you, Pacco, as a parting gift, here . . .' He held out the tie. 'Try it for size, and we can adjust the clip at the back.'

Pacco swallowed hard in wordless gratitude. He took the tie and moved to the end of the room, where it turned at an angle. On the wall at the end of the turn was an ormolu mirror. Willie stood behind Pacco, watching him take off his own tie and put on the red suede. Pacco studied his reflection and nodded with melancholy pleasure.

'I will always wear it on her birthday,' he declared shakily.

'There's something I forgot,' said Willie. 'You can unscrew that stone. Nicole had her name engraved on the mounting underneath.'

'So?' Intrigued, Pacco lifted the flap of the tie and unscrewed the imitation diamond. Willie moved casually away and round Pacco's desk. He stood with his back to the two men by the wall, facing Hagan across the desk, but not looking directly at him.

'I'll take the high road and you take the low road,' he said absently, in English.

'What do you say, Willee?' Over by the mirror, half-screened by the angle of the wall, Pacco stopped peering at the base of the mounting and looked up with sudden suspicion.

Willie grinned coldly, without a trace of humour. 'I say you shouldn't have killed her, you snivelling bastard.'

The explosion was sharp and vicious, not very loud. It came from behind Hagan and away to one side. With it came the shattering of glass as the mirror smashed into fragments. In his mind's eye, Hagan saw the two-legged thing with the ruined head remain upright for a long second before toppling to the floor. He saw the frozen horror on the faces of the two men behind Willie, and knew that it must be duplicated on the two who stood behind his chair. The thoughts were instantaneous with the swift reaction of Hagan's muscles, and only microseconds after the explosion itself. Yet Willie Garvin had already moved, was diving straight at him, hands going down flat on the centre of the desk. Hagan ducked, barely in time. He saw Willie swing round, pivoting on his arms with the poised perfection of a gymnast on a vaulting horse, seemingly unhurried yet making all other movement appear to be in slow-motion. Then Willie's feet shot out to smash viciously against the heads of the men behind Hagan's chair.

Hagan only heard the impact. He was taking the low road, down under the open well of the desk. As Willie's weight came off, Hagan heaved up, lifting the whole desk-top on his shoulders, and lunged forward. He felt it smash splinteringly against the two other hoods, crushing them against the wall. Hagan let the desk-top drop, and the men went down with it. Blood poured from the nose of one; the other, dazed, had a gun half out of a shoulder-holster. Hagan's right hand flicked the Colt Cobra from the Bucheimer under his jacket. With neat precision he clubbed the second man, then Bloodynose. Straightening, he swept the room at a glance.

The thing that had been Pacco lay sprawled in the turn of the L. Willie's two victims were huddled in a limp tangle on the floor, and Willie was halfway to the door at the far end of the room, a knife in his hand.

The door swung open. Maurice stood there, white-faced, gun levelled. Willie swerved smoothly and hit the floor, rolling, just as the gun spoke. Hagan fired, and Willie held his throw at the last moment. He came to his feet and moved to look down at Maurice. There was a neat hole in the middle of the forehead, and a far from neat hole in the back of the skull.

'You're a fair old shot, Mister Hagan,' Willie said with quiet approval. 'Modesty couldn't beat that.'

Hagan inclined his head, amused, wondering why he felt no rancour at the comparison. 'Praise indeed, Mister Garvin.'

'It's that all right,' Willie agreed, and nodded at the wrecked desk. 'See if you can find anything worth taking. I'll see what's in 'ere.' Warily he threw open the door which led off the middle of the long room. Beyond it, the small radio-room was empty. Willie ran his eye over the transmitter, noted the frequency setting, then began to search.

Sixty seconds later he came out with a thin bundle of papers. 'Anything good, Mister Hagan?'

'A code-book of some kind.' Hagan held it up, then slipped it into his pocket. He waved his gun towards the window. 'Shall we go?'

Five minutes later they were in the small Renault, driving at a leisurely pace along the road through Golfe-Juan to Cannes.

Hagan relaxed and fumbled for his cigarettes. He felt good. The growing tension of the last half-hour, erupting into swift and dangerous action, had acted as a catharsis, cleansing him of the nagging resentment which had simmered within him through all the long hours since the fiasco in his apartment that morning. He lit two cigarettes and passed one to Willie.

'Do me a favour, Willie.'

'Sure.'

'Call me matey.'

'Okay.' Willie glanced at him with an amiable grin. 'How's the old head?'

Hagan touched the bruise made by Didi's gun-butt. 'It's in a hell of a good shape compared with Pacco's head.'

He sat back, smoking quietly, thinking about Willie Garvin. Christ, but Garvin was good all right. Hagan had never seen a man move so fast, yet with such an appearance of unhurried precision. And Willie wasn't only good at the strong-arm stuff. The way he had played Pacco, used the big slob's maudlin sentiment, suckered him with that tie ... it was something for the record.

They were turning left on to the main road.

'Tell me, Willie,' Hagan said. 'How is it with you and Modesty. I don't quite have it figured.'

'There's nothing to figure. I work for her. She knocks 'em down, I jump on 'em.'

'Sure. I know that bit.'

'That's all.'

'You've been working pretty close for a long time, Willie.'

'She's been knocking 'em down for a long time.'

Hagan drew on his cigarette, frowning. 'Look,' he said slowly, 'you have to feel something about each other.'

Willie rubbed the back of his neck and looked baffled. 'Well, 'course you 'ave,' he said. 'But, I mean—well, 'ow d'you feel about someone who's got all that Modesty's got, and who picks you out of the gutter and makes you so different you walk like a bloody king?'

'I guess you'd feel at least halfway crazy about someone like that.'

'All the way. But not your way, matey. That's something else. It'd be a liberty.'

'That's what I don't get. Why not my way?'

Willie moved uneasily. His thumb kept flicking the butt of his cigarette in a fidgety manner. Suddenly Hagan saw that he was deeply embarrassed, as a devout believer might be embarrassed by a friend's unwitting sacrilege.

'Sorry,' Hagan said. Then, after a moment's silence: 'That's a mighty tall pedestal you've got her on, Willie boy.'

'She's never fell off. And it's been a long time.' Willie relaxed gratefully. 'Only twenty she was, when she first picked me up, but she was big-time already. I was in the coop in Saigon, and she bought me out some'ow. She was over on a trip from North Africa, and she'd seen me fight in a Thai-style match the week before. That's when she'd marked me down.'

'Thai-style.' Hagan tossed his cigarette end out of the window. 'That's elbows, knees, feet, head-butt—everything, isn't it?'

'Yes. Combination moves. The Thai boys have had a few karate experts down from Japan and eaten 'em. It's the speed that gives 'em the edge. Not that I go a bundle on any one system, mind——' He broke off with an apologetic shrug, as if veering away from a subject on which he knew himself to be a possible bore. 'Anyway, Modesty took me out of gaol and

128

along to this 'otel. I looked a right mess ... and she looked like a princess.'

Willie slowed for yellow winking traffic lights at a crossroads.

' *"Willie Garvin,"* she says, *"they tell me you're a dangerous rat. I've got no use for rats, but I've got a hunch there's some sort of man inside you trying to get out. Come and work for me, and at least he'll get a chance."*' Willie shook his head wonderingly. 'How's that for a turn-up?' he asked.

'It worked, Willie. You must have earned your luck.'

'I couldn't earn that kind of luck in a lifetime, matey.'

'I wouldn't think it was all one way.'

'Maybe not. I'd been around, done a lot of things. There was stuff I could teach 'er, sure. But she'd lived twenty years that would 've killed most people a dozen times over. And she'd done that without Willie Garvin.' He shrugged. 'I'd never bloody lived at all till she came along and changed everything.'

'Yet she's all woman,' Hagan said, and felt his loins throb with sudden memory of her. 'You'd wonder how the hell she could have managed to stay that way.'

'She's out on 'er own,' Willie said simply. 'You can't go comparing.'

There was silence. They were turning into the grounds of the Gray d'Albion when Hagan spoke again.

'I'm scared,' he said softly. 'My God, it's all so crazy, Willie. She quit. And she's got everything. So why does she have to come back and mix in this stinking job? It's not even a living.'

Willie stopped the car and switched off the engine.

'It's one way of knowing you're alive,' he said.

ELEVEN

THE villa stood at the end of a short dirt road above the village of Biot, perched on the hills south of the Préalpes de Grasse. It was screened on two sides by pines, and on the other two by a tall hedge and an ancient dry-stone wall. There were four bedrooms and two large living-rooms, a kitchen, and a small spare room on the ground floor. The early-morning sun slid over the bougainvillaea-topped wall and fell upon the green confusion of the uncared-for garden at the back.

Modesty backed the Renault along the sideway and lined it up with the Peugeot. She got out and went into the kitchen. Willie Garvin was tinkering confidently with a gas-boiler in the corner.

'Thought I'd get this going right away, Princess. You'll be wanting a bath.'

'Thanks, Willie. Look, one of us had better sleep downstairs in that small room, just in case anybody comes around at night.'

'That's what I thought. I've put my gear in there and brought a folding bed down.'

She nodded. The bath and the precaution. It was never any surprise to her that Willie anticipated her wishes, but it always gave her pleasure. 'Where's Paul?' she asked.

'Humping the other stuff upstairs.'

'How did he go at Pacco's place?'

'Good.' Willie lit the pilot jet and blew out the match. 'Very good. He's got the flow.'

'Reacts?'

'Only a fifth slow. He's a natural.'

'No trigger-nerves?'

'None. He throws the switch.'

'And appreciates?'

'High speed and wide angle.'

They were talking in shorthand on a subject both had

studied in theory and practice with sober intensity for many years. Willie opened the main jets of the boiler and straightened up. ''Ave a look at that Bucheimer semi he uses for the Cobra,' he said. 'You might gain about a tenth on it, Princess.'

'What about the bosom?'

'I don't think that 'd get in the way. It's worth trying sometime.'

'All right. You might bring the groceries in from the car when you've finished with that contraption, Willie love.' She went along the passage and up the stairs. Paul was in the large bedroom looking out over the garden. He had brought his own cases in as well as hers.

'I'll take the room next door, Paul,' she said.

He stared. 'What's wrong with this one?'

'Nothing. But we're not sleeping together, darling.' She smiled and touched his arm as she moved to the window. 'It'll be all the better afterwards.'

Hagan sat down on the bed and lit a cigarette. 'I know we have a lot to do,' he said carefully. 'We have to go out and work like beavers, trying to dig up something while the mob here's still in a state of shock. But we also have to sleep sometime. Why not together?'

'It makes a difference,' she said. 'Only a small difference, but we can't afford it.'

Hagan felt his muscles twitch. The quiet patience of her answer sent a spurt of resentment through him. He crushed out the cigarette, went across the room and took her by the shoulders, jerking her round to face him.

'What the hell are you talking about?' he said. 'We're on a job. Okay. It's not a search for the Holy Grail. Fasting and a bed of nails won't help. Look, I can put you across that bed and take you now, and still go out and move as fast as the next man.'

'Not quite.'

'The lady tells me,' he said. He was suddenly furious to find that half his mind was studying the line of her cheek-bone and contours of her lips. 'I'd like to know how you manage to be so goddam sure of yourself,' he said.

'You want me to hit you in the face with it, Paul?'

131

'Go ahead. Hit me in the face with it.'

'All right. You're an amateur. I'm a professional. You're smart, fast, good with a gun, good with your hands. It's not enough. You rely on your gifts, and it's not enough.' There was no cruelty in her eyes, but neither was there any mercy.

'Go on,' Hagan said.

'I wasn't good with a gun, like you. I spent two hours a day for two years, making myself good. It might not seem worth it. How often do you really need to use a gun—I mean, to shoot with it? Once in three, four, five years? All right, I spent fifteen hundred hours making myself ready for that one time. Because I'm a professional, Paul. I've spent thousands of hours making myself ready in all kinds of different ways for those few times when being ready means living instead of dying. Thousands of hours. Because I'm a professional. I'm not proud of being a professional, or ashamed of it. But that's what I am.'

She stopped abruptly, and smiled. 'I'm sorry. Here endeth the lecture.'

Hagan lifted a hand and turned her head gently towards the sunlight which poured through the window. He ran his finger-tips down from one small flat ear, following the line of her neck and shoulder.

'That curve,' he said. 'I've got to get it on canvas.'

'You're not going to change that picture?'

'I must. When will you sit for me again?'

'Afterwards. Sit, stand, lie—anything you want. But afterwards, Paul.'

He nodded and let her go. Picking up his two cases he went out and across the passage to the other bedroom.

On the third day, soon after dusk, Willie Garvin picked up Tarrant at La Brague and brought him to the villa.

Hagan had roused from sleep only half an hour earlier, after being out until just before dawn. He came down freshly bathed and shaved.

Modesty was in the kitchen, preparing a meal. She wore a blue and white check pinafore over a shirt-necked sweater and slim skirt.

Tarrant kissed her hand. 'I had a cryptic conversation on the phone with Fraser an hour ago,' he said. 'He's had no reports through that give us any help. Gabriel's yacht is still at Haifa. Gabriel himself might be anywhere. Have your own researches produced anything?'

'No.' Modesty turned the four escalopes of veal under the grill and shook the pan of sauté potatoes. 'Between us we've checked nearly every contact we've got from Toulon to Menton.'

'Thank God for the new auto-route,' Hagan said, and started to collect cutlery from a drawer. 'I'll help Willie with the table. It's his turn, but I'm like that.' He went through into the small dining-room.

'No break-through then?' Tarrant said.

'We still have a few more checks to make,' she answered. 'But I don't hold out much hope.'

'*The Tyboria* sails from Cape Town in a day or two, with the diamonds. Something could happen any time from now on.'

'I know. But that's your end of it. My brief was to work from the other end. The Gabriel end.'

'If it's Gabriel.'

'It's Gabriel. Did you get Léon Vaubois' backroom boys to go through Pacco's code-book and the other stuff Willie and Paul brought back?'

'Yes. Unproductive. No messages had been kept, so the code-book didn't help. We just know that Pacco was in radio contact with somebody on a particular frequency.'

'With Gabriel. And Pacco wouldn't be the only out-station on the group. Have they listened out?'

'Without result. I imagine the frequency was changed as soon as Pacco failed to come up on the next routine call.'

Tarrant watched her slip the escalopes into a hot dish. She placed capers and slivers of anchovy on each one. Four eggs were frying in a large pan. Using a slice, she placed an egg on top of each escalope.

'Where do you go from here, Modesty?' he asked quietly.

'I'll tell you in two days, when we've checked the last contacts,' she said, and took off her pinafore. 'Ready now. And we have a rule, Sir Gerald—no shop while we eat.'

'Most civilised. It also makes for efficiency. Are we secure here?'

'Willie's rigged a series of alarms. If anybody did come along, we'd know. Will you bring that bowl of salad along, please?'

It was a simple but handsome meal, and the talk was good without being too clever. Tarrant registered that the three of them were at ease with each other, and that they all had the knack of contributing by the positive way in which they listened when another was talking.

Modesty herself was in a new mood, one he had not seen in her before. He found it hard to define. She was almost gay, almost tense, almost excited, but none of these words could be accurately applied to her. When he congratulated her on the meal she gave her sudden sparkling smile in acknowledgment of the compliment, and shook her head. 'I'm rather limited, really. You should be here when Paul presides in the kitchen. He's quite a master.'

'Don't come when Willie presides,' Hagan said.

'Bangers and mash.' Modesty wrinkled her nose. 'And usually burnt.'

'Ingrates,' Willie said without resentment. Tarrant was now used to hearing Willie use words rarely found in an East End vocabulary. 'And burnt is sort of relative. I'd say crisp, meself.'

'A question of semantics,' Tarrant agreed. 'But I still hold that this is an excellent meal, Modesty. Is there anything you don't excel at?'

'Many things. Let's see now ... I can't sew and I haven't green fingers; whatever I plant is doomed. I daren't sing, even in the bath, because my range is about half an octave. I can't play any instrument. I've no palate for wine—I prefer a rough red Algerian to a vintage claret. I can't do crossword puzzles. I don't understand modern sculpture——'

'You don't *what*?' Hagan said, astonished, and put down his fork. 'Look, all anyone needs is one eye and a few grey cells.'

'They're off,' said Willie.

The conversation flowed. It was fresh and stimulating, and

to Tarrant's surprise Willie Garvin carried his share with ease. More surprising, his views were not taken second-hand from Modesty and sometimes differed from hers. He was strong on anything technical and well-read on current news. On the arts his knowledge was limited, but detailed within those limits.

'He astonishes me,' Tarrant said quietly to Modesty at a moment when Willie and Hagan were engrossed in argument.

She nodded agreement. 'He's a voracious reader, and he's got a good mind. With a different start, he could have gone anywhere.'

'What does he read?'

'Biography, military history, technical books, science-fiction —almost anything but general fiction and travel. And he has total recall.'

'I envy him,' said Tarrant. 'When I think of the documents I have to plough through . . .' He hesitated. 'It's a pity he can't lose that accent.'

'He can. I think he hangs on to it because it fits the niche he's found for himself. He likes that niche. But he can lose the accent when he wants to.' She lifted her voice a little. 'Willie, love. We'd like a comment on the claret. Wine Society style.'

Hagan broke off the argument and grinned at Tarrant. 'This slays me,' he said.

Willie picked up his glass and held it to his nose. He sniffed appraisingly. Taking a little wine into his mouth he rolled it around and swallowed. Tarrant noted that the mime and the expression were exact, without exaggeration.

'A good little one,' Willie said. His voice was low and rich, the voice of a well-bred gourmet. 'Splendid quality of tonal sonority in the shape . . . but rather thick legs, perhaps.'

Tarrant laughed and shook his head a little ruefully. He was wondering if there were times when he had been a target for Willie's mimicry.

Hagan said: 'You should get the two of them to do an American couple sight-seeing in Venice. It's for real.'

'Is this for amusement only?' Tarrant asked Modesty.

'No. For practice. We've had to act a lot of parts, over the years.'

'It amuses *me*,' said Hagan. 'Do the Venice bit.'

'Another time. I interrupted you and Willie. What were you arguing about?'

'Weapons. I think I'm winning.'

'A gun's noisy and a knife's quiet,' Willie said patiently. 'A gun can jam and a knife can't.'

'A gun's faster. And you can use a silencer.' Hagan made the point reasonably. There was no patronage in his manner, Tarrant noted.

'I wouldn't say it's faster, matey.'

'Ah, look, maybe not against you, Willie. But how many people could use a knife as fast as they can use a gun?'

'We're not talking about people. We're comparin' weapons. You got to compare 'em at maximum efficiency of usage.'

'I don't think so, Willie,' Modesty said thoughtfully. 'If you're going to say one weapon's better than the other you have to gauge it on average efficiency of usage.'

'M'mm. But then you've not got much average on knives. So it comes down to what's the best for a particular person, Princess. And then you got nothing to argue about.'

'You can hold half a dozen men at the end of a gun,' Hagan said.

'You can 'old 'em at the end of a knife, matey. Maybe you got to drop a man, to show you're in business; but that's why I carry two knives.' He drank some claret. 'You don't honestly go for a silencer, do you?'

'They're clumsy,' Hagan admitted. 'But they're okay for the right occasion.'

'I don't reckon 'em. Much better to get the noise down by rigging the cartridges. You might lose a bit on feet-per-second, but there's nothing in it if you're accurate. You got to be accurate with a hand-gun anyway.'

'Whatever you do, you've still got noise,' Hagan conceded, 'but I reckon you can fire a shot in an hotel room and you'll be unlucky if anybody comes running. They always think it must have been something else.'

'I'll give you that,' Willie said. 'You know, they've just come up with a caseless point two-two at the Daisy plant over in the States. Gives seven-fifty f.p.s. from a standard air-gun, and 'ardly makes any noise at all. I'd like to get a good look at one sometime.'

He glanced at his watch and got up. 'Will you excuse me, Princess? I'm seeing Varron tonight with a bit of luck, and I want to change that plug in the Peugeot before I go. I can drop Sir G. off on the way.'

'All right, Willie. Pass Sir Gerald those cigars, will you? And don't turn your back on Varron.'

'I'll watch 'im.'

'May I see one of your knives, please?' Tarrant asked.

'Sure. In the jacket there.' Willie nodded to the dark windcheater hanging on the back of a chair, and put down a box of cigars on the table. 'I'll be ready in about twenty minutes, Princess.' He went out.

Tarrant got up and lifted the breast of the jacket. The twin knives lay in their sheaths against a thin backing of leather stitched to the lining. Gently he gripped the hilt of one of them. There was the slightest resistance, and then the knife slid smoothly out. He went back to his chair, studying the weapon.

Modesty said: 'He sometimes carries them in a harness-sheath under his shirt, but he prefers the jacket.'

Tarrant nodded, turning the knife over in his hands. The blade was five and a half inches long, of fine steel honed to a perfect edge along the full length of one side. The curve to the point was very slightly asymmetrical, and he realised that this was to balance the other edge, which was honed for only three inches from the point and then flattened out slightly up to the hilt. On this flattened edge, only a sixteenth of an inch thick, a slim fillet of brass had been bonded.

There was no cross-guard, only the elliptical base of the hilt, which extended a quarter of an inch all round the blade. Tarrant had expected that the hilt would be of sharkskin, but it was of black, sharply-dimpled bone, rough to the touch—to guard against slipping in a moist hand, he guessed.

Tarrant looked at the top of the hilt and saw the small dot of metal which showed that the tang of the blade ran the full length of the hilt.

'Why the fillet of brass?' he asked.

'The Bowie principle,' Modesty said. 'If you guard against a thrust with steel on steel, the other blade skids off too easily. The brass is soft metal, so the other blade nicks in and catches.'

'I would have thought the hilt a little short for a secure grip,' Tarrant said, absorbed.

'It gives three fingers and a thumb; that's enough for Willie.' She refilled Tarrant's glass. 'It's basically for throwing, and it has to be carried comfortably, so there's a limit on the overall length.'

'I've always felt that throwing a knife was more of a circus trick,' Tarrant said. 'Until that business with Didi the other day.'

'It's about the hardest trick in the book—except that it's not in the book. With a normal throw, held by the point, that knife makes a full revolution in twelve and a half feet; so it's travelling point-first between six and seven feet, and again between eighteen and nineteen. Any different range, beyond or between, you have to give more spin or more drag to change the rate of revolution.' She smiled. 'That's something else I don't excel at. I'm no good at it at all.'

'But Willie excels?'

Hagan answered. 'I saw him working-out yesterday. Draw and throw. He's machine-accurate. I might just beat him with a gun, but I wouldn't lay odds on it.'

'He was only working-out then,' Modesty said. 'Let's go into the other room and look at the map. Bring your drinks with you.'

They rose, and followed her through, Tarrant pausing to put Willie's knife back into its sheath.

The map spread on the table was small-scale, showing Africa and the whole of the Mediterranean. Modesty lit a cigarette. 'We haven't made any progress getting a lead on Gabriel through his sub-contractors,' she said. 'So let's think about Gabriel himself.'

She drew a finger along the map from south to north. Tarrant noticed that her nails were not coloured now.

'The ship leaves Cape Town,' she said. 'It sails up the east coast of Africa, through the Red Sea to Suez, then on to

Beirut. Three weeks. How do you go about taking two crates of diamonds worth ten million pounds from the ship's strong-room?'

'How crazy can we think?' Hagan asked.

'As crazy as you like.'

'Fine. Well, maybe Gabriel has hired a destroyer, for a little piracy. Or maybe he's going to shadow *The Tyboria*, and somewhere along here he's going to crash-land a glider on the boat-deck, a glider full of armed men. You know, I could have earned myself some wages there. I flew gliders for two years in the States.'

Tarrant was frowning at him, and Hagan shrugged. 'We're supposed to be thinking crazy,' he said.

'That's right.' Modesty waved a hand to clear the cigarette and cigar smoke. 'It might strike a spark.'

'If I had to plan it,' said Tarrant, 'I would have tried to introduce men into the passengers or crew.' He sighed. 'But every soul on board has been vetted, and the guard arrangements are more than adequate. So by this time I would have had to cancel the plan and go home.'

'With Gabriel,' said Modesty, 'it's bound to be something that's not in the book. He has a bizarre imagination, with the practical genius to make his ideas work. Let's say the ship is going to be attacked from outside in some way. Forget how, Sir Gerald. Think about where.'

Hagan leaned over the map. 'I'd say somewhere here, in the Indian Ocean rather than the Med. It's a whole lot bigger and there's more scope for a getaway. I guess the only place you can be pretty sure it won't happen is there.' He put his finger on the Suez and Port Said area. 'Right in the middle of everything.'

Modesty looked at Tarrant. 'They might get away overland if they got the diamonds short of Suez, somewhere in the Red Sea. But I still don't see how they get them. I just hope you've got your end sewn up tight.'

'I hope so too.' His voice was a little grim. 'I'd be happier if we were making any progress at all at your end, though.'

There was silence for a moment. Modesty drew on her cigarette, looking at the map, her face impassive.

'What the hell do you expect her to do, for Christ's sake?' Hagan said in a dangerously quiet voice.

Tarrant looked at the ash on his cigar. 'If I could answer that, Hagan, I wouldn't have needed to ask Modesty's help in the first place.'

'Be'old,' Willie's voice intoned from the doorway. 'Be'old 'ow good and 'ow pleasant it is for brethren to dwell together in unity. Psalm hundred and thirty-three. Verse one.' He came in, zipping up his jacket. 'You ready, Sir G.?'

The moment of tension passed. Hagan laughed and relaxed. Tarrant lifted apologetic eyebrows and took Modesty's hand. 'I'm sorry if I was terse,' he said, 'but I'm increasingly worried. Living with Sheik Abu-Tahir is an additional burden. Tell me, if your last contacts fail is there anything at all that you'll be able to do?'

'Yes.' She spoke absently, still looking at the map. Her face was calm, almost dreamy. It was only now, by contrast, that Tarrant realised how much tension had lain beneath the surface during these past two hours. He wondered what had brought the sudden release, and waited for her to go on. When she remained silent he lifted her hand and touched her fingers to his lips.

'Then I'll see you again in two days,' he said. 'Thank you for a very stimulating evening, my dear.'

TWELVE

HAGAN reached the villa at noon, after driving from Ste. Maxime. Willie Garvin was tuning the engine of the Renault, and spoke without looking up.

'Any luck, matey?'

'No. How did Modesty make out with that fence in Nice?'

'He talked. He'd 'eard about a load of diamonds going from somewhere to somewhere else, but didn't believe it. Then he told her the police 'ad put Pacco down but rigged it to look like a gang-fight.'

'My guy told me it was a Kabyle bunch taking over from Pacco. He didn't know anything about diamonds or Gabriel. And brother, he didn't *want* to know.'

Hagan went on into the house. Modesty was nowhere downstairs. He went into the bathroom, washed his face and hands, then tapped on the door of her room. There was no answer. Puzzled, he opened the door.

She was sitting on the floor, on a small rug, facing the window. Her back was towards him. She wore only a pair of opaque black pants, like swim-trunks, and a plain black bra. Her hair was loose and tied back at the neck. Her feet were bare. Full sunlight through the unshuttered window fell about her in an aura of gold.

'Modesty . . . ?' Hagan found he had spoken in a whisper. Uncomprehending, he moved forward so that he could see her face. She sat with her feet drawn up, ankles crossed, her knees spread wide and close to the floor. Each hand lay palm upwards, resting on a thigh, the fingers slightly curled. Her back was perfectly straight. She sat so tall, yet so relaxed, that it was almost as if she were fractionally suspended above the floor.

For long moments Hagan could detect no sign of breathing. Then he saw that the breasts were rising slowly, almost imperceptibly, and that the stomach was sinking gradually in beneath the rib-cage. The indrawn breath lasted for well over fifteen seconds, the exhalation no less. And between there was a five second period of no movement at all. Hagan thought of an animal hibernating, the life-process slowed almost to a standstill, and he felt the tiny cold feet of horror crawling up his spine.

He looked at her face. It was moulded in soft lines of complete serenity. The eyes looked through him as if he were invisible. They were empty, unaware. But no, not empty; only filled with a tranquillity so deep that it gave the impression of emptiness.

The sense of her total alienation from him brought a surge of anger.

'Modesty!' His voice was sharp now, but there was no reaction. A footstep sounded in the doorway. Willie Garvin walked in and put a hand on Hagan's arm, saying quietly: 'Not now.'

For a moment Hagan resisted. Then he turned, shook Willie's hand off, and walked out of the room. As he went down the stairs he heard Willie close the bedroom door before following him. In the living-room Hagan went to the sideboard and poured himself a drink. He turned to look at Willie.

'Yoga,' he said. 'Yoga, yet!'

'Why not?' Willie sat in a chair and put one leg over the arm of it.

'Why?'

'It 'elps, that's why.' For the first time Hagan saw Willie Garvin look hostile. 'For God's sake, Paul, you know as well as anyone that if you don't get your mind right before you get stuck into a rough caper you're 'alfway beaten.'

'I've never had to sniff up *prana* or whatever it is, to get my mind right. Have you?'

'No.' Willie relaxed a little. 'We're different. Listen, when we went into Pacco's that night, did you think about a lot of things that could 'appen? Not getting killed—that's nothing. I mean getting maimed, maybe coming out with 'alf your face carved off or the old joystick shot up.'

'What the hell are you talking about?'

'Women 'ave got different imagination from us.' Willie got

up to pour himself a drink. 'They've got a bleeding sight more sense, I suppose. We know what could 'appen, but we don't really believe it. A woman can see it 'appening to her. So Modesty does some yoga stuff to kill the imagination. She knows if she goes into a rough caper scared, she'll buy it. She'll 'esitate, maybe just blink at the wrong time, flinch a bit, get stab-fright or trigger-freeze. Not scared, she knows she's got a fifty per cent better chance.'

Hagan stared wonderingly. His unreasoning anger had gone now. Something else was nagging in his mind, but he could not pin it down for the moment.

'She's studied yoga—for that?' he said.

'She's studied it a bit. Just the practical side. But she found 'er own way long before that. It sort of came natural. She's always been able to block things out of 'er mind, but the yoga 'elps.' Willie emptied his glass and put it down. 'Did you know she's been raped twice?'

'*What?*'

'First time, she was about twelve. Some peasant around Baalbeck. When she couldn't fight any longer, she made 'erself unconscious. Self-induced faint, I suppose you'd call it. Second time she was twenty-two. That was when we ran into a bit of bad trouble in Beirut.'

'It ... didn't affect her.' Hagan made it a statement rather than a question.

'She went unconscious. Never knew anything about it. But that's the sort of thing I mean, matey. It's something else that's different for a woman. Something that can't 'appen to us.' He walked to the window and looked out. 'Unless you count ol' Lawrence of Arabia,' he added, with a touch of surprise at the random thought.

'What happened to the man—the second one?'

'I went after 'im later and signed 'im off.' Willie shook his head ruefully. 'Modesty gave me a right rollicking for that. Said she didn't like me takin' unnecessary chances just for personal revenge. She doesn't reckon revenge much, an' neither do I. But I couldn't let this bastard go around boasting he'd had her.'

Hagan stared down into his drink, trying to get his bearings.

Suddenly he stiffened. The hidden thing nagging at the back of his mind had emerged.

'A rough caper,' he said, and moved across to Willie. 'Twice you've said that. But we're at a dead end on this job, so why is she getting geared up for trouble?'

'You'll 'ave to ask Modesty that,' Willie said politely. 'She's be'ind the wheel on this job.'

'*Is she?*' Hagan heard the ugliness in his own voice. He put down his glass and went out through the kitchen into the garden. Sitting on a bench in the sunshine, waiting till his anger had faded, he tried to look into his own mind.

He felt the warm sun upon him, and he thought of his paints and his canvases and of Modesty Blaise. In the retentive eye of his artist's mind he remembered the long, firm curves of her body, the texture of her skin and the warmth of her flesh as she strove and yielded in his arms. He remembered a hundred small things of the past few days; the poise of her head when she was thinking; the sudden rare smile; her way of pushing back a wisp of hair with the inside of her wrist; the small vases which stood in every room, filled with wild flowers she had cut.

It was suddenly incredible to Hagan that all these could be facets of the same woman Willie had been speaking of; the woman who had run The Network, who only days ago had killed a man with her hands in the old market of Antibes; the same woman who had sent him with Willie to kill Pacco, and who had driven all three of them relentlessly over the past days in search of a lead to Gabriel; who was so hard and competent and sure of herself that she would never play second fiddle to any man.

It not only seemed incredible to Hagan now. It had suddenly become unreal. Reality lay in other things; in the warmth of her mind and the wonder of her body. This only was important—herself. And was this to be put at hazard for the sake of two boxes of pebbles? Or for Tarrant? Or for Sheik Abu-Tahir? Or for what?

The lunacy of it hit Hagan with the impact of an ice-cold shower falling upon a man asleep. He knew now what Willie Garvin had been talking about when he spoke of imagination and the things that could happen when the guns spoke and the knives were out—the things that could happen to Modesty Blaise.

Sweat broke on Hagan's brow, and he was suddenly a frightened man.

A clear moon was rising over the trees. Hagan closed the shutters, switched on the bedside lamp, and took off his dressing-gown.

Tarrant would come next day. He thought about that as he pulled on his pyjama trousers and sat on the edge of the bed, picking up a half-smoked cigarette from the ashtray.

It had been a curious day. Modesty had appeared towards four o'clock. She looked strangely different to Hagan's eye. She was cleansed of the slight tension that had been showing around her eyes, and there was a quality of newness about her. She made Hagan think of a knife-blade, freshly tempered, fine-honed, and polished bright.

She had gone out in one of the cars and returned after two hours. In answer to Hagan's casual question she had said: 'Oh, just seeing to one or two personal things, Paul.'

The rest of the day had been quiet. Nothing important had been asked or answered or done. Willie Garvin had been busy in his own room for most of the time.

Hagan ground out his cigarette. His jaw muscles were aching with tautness. He had asked no more questions of Modesty because his mind was made up now. As he picked up his pyjama jacket there came a tap on the door. It opened, and Modesty was there. She wore mules, and a house-coat of crisp cotton in thin stripes of pale green and white.

'I've brought us a night-cap,' she said, and moved across the room to put down a small tray with two glasses. 'Gin and french for you. The old rough red for me.'

Hagan saw that she had pushed the door shut behind her as she came in. He threw the pyjama jacket on the bed and looked at her. 'Just a night-cap?'

'Unless there's anything else you want while I'm here.' Her eyes were wide and solemn, but there was a hint of mischief in their depths; of mischief and of something else, very

145

strong, that leapt out and kindled a flame in the pit of his stomach.

'Anything?' he echoed.

'Yes.'

Slowly he took her by the shoulders. 'You told me that was for amateurs, not professionals. What's changed your mind?'

She gave a little shrug, and for a moment there was weariness in her eyes. He wondered if she was acting. 'I'm not sure,' she said. 'Failure, maybe. I don't relish having nothing to say to Tarrant tomorrow.'

'Willie Garvin spoke of a rough caper.'

'He was just hoping. Willie thinks I'm infallible. He's in for a disappointment, too.'

Hagan began to unbutton the house-coat, starting at the top. There were six buttons. After the third, he knew that she wore nothing underneath. He slipped it off her shoulders and let it fall, then held her at arm's length, looking at her. She did not move.

'I've something to tell Tarrant,' he said. 'And you. We're quitting, Modesty.' His hands tightened almost brutally. 'I've suddenly gone sane.' His eyes swept down her body and back to her face. 'I'd have to be a raving madman to risk all this for a box of stones, even if they were mine.'

'Is that how you feel about me, Paul?'

He slid his hands down to her waist and drew her towards him, feeling the warm points of her body against his chest.

'All of that,' he said. 'You're all that matters. Now I know it, and I have to take over the show. Only there isn't going to be any show. Just you and me. I'm taking you away, Modesty.' His eyes were narrowed and diamond-hard, watching her like a hawk ready to swoop. 'Tarrant won't stop me. Neither will Willie. Neither will you.'

Her head was drawn back to look at him. Suddenly she moved so that her face was against his shoulder. He felt her teeth bite gently into the muscle, and her hands held him urgently.

'Stop talking,' she said, her voice husky and muffled. 'Stop talking and do something.'

He picked her up and turned to the bed.

It was different from the time before, but no less wonderful. Now it seemed that the core of her desire was for complete dominance by him, and that her source of mounting joy was to sense his needs and give unstintingly to fill them.

He lay spent at last, and after a while she disengaged from him and rose to her knees. 'There,' she said softly. 'Now you can talk if you want to.' She went to the dressing-table, took two cigarettes from the packet there, lit them, and came back to him. 'Here, darling.'

He sat up lazily, luxuriously, and took the cigarette from her. Though his body was quiet now, he felt strong and sure of himself. 'What's left to talk about?' he said, and ran his finger-tips down the line of her cheek. 'We've just said it all.'

'Yes.' There was a shadow of sad acceptance in the single word. She looked small and young, and Hagan felt protective-ness growing within him as he looked at her.

'Don't get cold.' He lifted a blanket and drew it round her shoulders.

'I'm fine.' With the blanket about her she got up again and brought the small tray with the two glasses. 'Here's to us, then.' She sat down on the bed, and Hagan took the glass of gin and french.

'Don't worry about Tarrant,' he said. 'I'll tell him the score.'

Willie Garvin was lying on his bed fully dressed. The cases had been checked and packed with great care. He heard the faint creak of the stairs, and a moment later Modesty came into the room.

'All right, Willie. If you'll bring my dress-cases down now.' She wore a skirt and sweater, with flat shoes and a head-scarf, a light coat over her arm.

'You slipped 'im the mickey?' Willie asked quietly.

'Yes. He won't wake up till dawn at the earliest.'

'Going to raise Cain when 'e finds us gone, Princess.'

'It was the only way to shake him off, Willie. And we had to shake him if we're going to play the live-bait caper. He was getting scared for me.'

'I know. Comes out more dangerous than being scared for yourself, that does. What d'you reckon Tarrant will do?'

'I don't know and it doesn't matter. We'll get nowhere with people breathing down our necks all the time; Tarrant, Abu-Tahir . . . and Paul.' She gave a little shrug. 'They complicate everything. We have to do it our way, Willie. On our own.'

'I reckoned it would come to that,' he said, and she smiled at the touch of relief in his voice. 'I'll get your things down, Princess.' At the door he paused and looked back. 'Where've you booked us for?'

'Paul put his finger on it,' she said. 'Suez. But we're going a long way round, Willie. We've got to set ourselves up for Gabriel.'

THIRTEEN

FRASER sat at Tarrant's desk and read through the full report again.

It was a bloody rum do, he reflected.

Boyd, the new man, standing across the desk from Fraser, said: 'See the last paragraph. It looks like the old man's missed them again.'

Fraser had discovered that if he tautened his chest and stomach muscles, and restricted his breathing, he could make his face go slowly red and cause the veins to stand out on his forehead. It produced a terrifying simulation of anger. He tried it now, allowing several seconds for the build-up as he stared glassily at Boyd.

'Are you referring to Sir Gerald?' he said at last.

'I—I beg your pardon, sir.' Boyd flushed, and to Fraser's delight actually shuffled his feet. 'You—er—you wanted to be reminded that Sir Gerald's call from Tel Aviv should be through in five minutes.'

'Thank you, Boyd.' Fraser allowed his choler to fade, and beamed archly at the baffled man. 'You seem to have a splendid grasp of your duties.'

When Boyd had gone out, Fraser lit a cigarette and returned to the report.

A bloody rum do. It was eleven days ago that the Blaise girl and Garvin had vanished from Biot. They had appeared two days later in Rome; and, according to the Department's man there, had made contact with Sacchi, who was suspected of being a high Mafia man. They had left Rome six hours before Tarrant and Hagan arrived. The next report was from Athens, where they had been seen dining at the Hilton with Ypsilanti. Ypsilanti was the wealthiest fence in the Balkans. From Athens they had moved on to Beirut and then to Haifa.

The old man, Fraser reflected, was falling behind. Modesty Blaise and Garvin had left Haifa thirty-six hours ago. With relish Fraser looked forward to the phone-call Tarrant was making from the Embassy in Tel Aviv; they could not use scrambler, so the conversation would have to be partly in established code and partly in free cryptic.

The phone at his elbow rang. He picked it up and heard Tarrant's voice: 'That you, Jack?'

Fraser pitched his voice a little high and said: 'Yes, Dad. Having a good trip?'

There was a pause before Tarrant answered heartily: 'Not too bad thanks, son. A little tiring. I'm worried about Auntie Pru and young Willie. How are they getting along?'

'Well, they haven't been in touch, Dad. But there was a letter from Uncle Bert this morning, and he said they'd arrived safely in Blackpool.' His eyes flickered to the code-card. Yes, Blackpool was Cairo.

'Blackpool,' said Tarrant. 'I see. Oh, by the way, I went to have a look at that boat for you, Jack, but it had gone.'

'Old Gabby's boat?'

'Yes.'

Fraser giggled. 'Maybe Auntie Pru's a bit sweet on him and she's got an assignation with him in Blackpool, eh?'

'I hardly think he's her type.'

'You can never tell. And he's got good prospects. Any idea how much longer this business trip will take you, Dad?'

'God knows. Is everything all right at home? No problems?'

'Gosh, no. We're managing fine.'

'Good. Well, I'll be in touch with you again soon. Send any urgent messages to our Blackpool office to be dealt with.'

'Okay. 'Bye, Dad.'

Fraser put the phone down. He sat back and thought for a while, then swore softly. He didn't like the way things were shaping. Didn't like it at all. Their man in Cairo, Albert Alexandrou ('Uncle Bert'), was a very good man. Fraser felt glad of that. Tarrant looked like needing all the help he could get.

The window of the big Pontiac convertible was wound down. Modesty Blaise took the binoculars from her eyes and passed them to Willie. He looked out across the harbour of Port Said, where a dozen or more ships lay at anchor. Among them was a white yacht, an elegant conversion of an ex-German deep-sea patrol craft, one hundred and twenty feet long, powered by two 950 h.p. diesels.

Through the powerful binoculars Willie could see the name *Mandrake* on the bows. He traversed to the deck, studying the half-dozen people there. Two were in deckchairs, another leaning on the rail. Two more were exercising with a medicine ball, one throwing the heavy ball to strike the other's stomach. He saw that the figure on the receiving end was a woman in a T-shirt and slacks, with bright hair. On the forepeak a figure stood alone, hands behind back, looking shoreward.

Willie lowered the glasses. 'Well, there 'e is, Princess. Right on the spot where the job can't be done.'

'That's how Gabriel figures,' she said. 'I wonder where *Mandrake* picked him and the others up after she sailed from Haifa.'

Willie shrugged and took another look through the Zeiss binoculars. 'The blondie doing the muscle-stuff ... she'll be that Mrs. Fothergill we 'eard about, I suppose. Joined 'im a couple of years back, didn't she?'

'About that.'

'You reckon Gabriel's got word about us making a come-back, Princess?'

'He should have, Willie. We laid it on hard enough. But it probably doesn't worry him yet. Let's slip down to Cairo and change all that.'

Willie started the engine, and the Pontiac moved smoothly away. Outside the town he accelerated, turning on to the overland route across the desert.

Two hours later they drove through the Copt quarter of Cairo and into the open courtyard of a large house built in elaborate arabesque style. A fountain played in the centre of the courtyard. The windows, shaded with *mushrebiya*, held the rich tones of stained glass.

A servant, a young man in white jacket and trousers, conducted them to a large room paved with marble and furnished

151

with a magnificent collection of European and Oriental antiques.

'Old Hakim still does 'imself very well,' Willie said, studying an intricately chased falling-ball clock which hung suspended from a gold chain in one corner of the room. A door opened and Hakim entered. He was a slim, elegant Egyptian in a dark, lightweight lounge suit with a white shirt and maroon bow tie. He was at least seventy, Modesty knew, but he could have passed for fifty-five.

'Miss Blaise,' he said in soft, liquid voice, 'what a pleasure to receive your message.' His English was barely accented. He came forward, smiling, and shook hands with her. 'And Mr. Garvin also. We have had many pleasant business chats together, have we not?'

He pulled a chair forward for Modesty, gestured courteously for Willie to be seated, and sank gracefully on to a narrow divan against the wall.

'We're on business again, Hakim,' Modesty said. 'It's bigger than anything you've handled for us before. Diamonds. Ten million poundsworth.'

Hakim's smile became a little fixed, but otherwise his air of pleasant interest did not alter.

'How much?' he asked.

'For you, half a million.'

Hakim stared, and gestured deprecatingly with long fingers. 'Oh come, Miss Blaise. To dispose of such an enormous quantity of stones is a long and expensive matter. This you know well. Now for twenty per cent one could see a reasonable profit, taking a long-term view.'

'I'm not giving twenty per cent on a parcel this size, Hakim. I have my own expenses.'

'Fifteen, perhaps? I do not think any of my competitors in Europe will take so little. Certainly not anywhere in the Middle East.'

'They want diamonds behind the Iron Curtain,' Modesty said. 'I've got a firm offer from a Government-backed agent on the other side to buy the whole parcel for nine million sterling.' She gave him a friendly smile. 'Ten per cent. If you can't do better than that, I'm afraid we're wasting your time.'

'May I ask where these diamonds are now, Miss Blaise? And if they are not in your possession, how you propose to secure them?'

'Please don't be stupid, Hakim.'

'I apologise.' Hakim spread his hands regretfully. 'Also for being unable to do business with you in this matter, Miss Blaise. Unfortunately my expenses do not allow me to compete with political gentlemen.'

Modesty studied him. 'If I went to seven-fifty thousand?'

'I am sorry, but no. Can I offer you some refreshment?'

'Thank you, but we have many things to arrange. It's a pity we can't make a deal, but I'm sure I can rely on you not to speak of this, Hakim.'

He rose, smiling. 'How foolish that would be for me. Now that you are again engaged in business I hope there will be other matters in which we can be of help to each other, Miss Blaise.'

'I'm sure there will be. Goodbye, Hakim.'

When the Pontiac had driven out of the courtyard, Hakim called his servant. 'I have an important matter to consider, Nasir,' he said slowly, 'and I must first relax. Tell Fiama I shall want her this afternoon.'

It was nine o'clock in the evening when Modesty sat with Willie in a small café-bar in the Muski district. Her hair was down, bound in a short club at the nape of her neck. She wore little make-up and her nails were unvarnished. A light nylon mack did much to hide the roll-neck sweater and black denim slacks she wore beneath it.

Willie was in his dark wind-cheater. They both wore boots which laced-up to four inches above the ankle. The boots were of strong leather, with a waterproof rubber covering bonded over the thick soles and heels, sealing all round the welt.

They were drinking beer and speaking very quietly in German. The waiter thought they were from one of the German technical contingents in the area.

'Do you think Gabriel will move tonight?' Modesty asked.

'Perhaps. But tomorrow is more likely. It depends how long Hakim takes to make up his mind.'

'You handled most of the deals with Hakim, you know him better than I do. Are you sure he will tell Gabriel?'

'I'm sure. But Hakim never hurries. This afternoon or this evening he will have a girl, and then he will eat and drink and listen to music. In the end he will decide to tell Gabriel.'

'Why?'

'It's safer for him. Gabriel kills people who annoy him. You don't. Hakim will come to that conclusion in the end.'

'Good.'

Willie drank some beer and looked about him. 'We have a week to wait before that ship is due through the canal,' he said. 'We may have to stake ourselves out for some days before Gabriel jumps.'

'Yes.'

'Let's hope he doesn't jump too hard.'

'He won't, Willie. The story I told Hakim will stop that. Gabriel won't get rid of us as long as he thinks he can use us.' She pushed her half-empty glass aside. 'Let's move on. We want to give them a chance.'

Willie paid the bill and they went out into the narrow street. The Pontiac stood by the kerb, its top up. A beggar whined softly, squatting against a wall. Willie tossed a coin to him and gave another to the small boy guarding the car. He got in behind the wheel and Modesty settled beside him.

When the car had moved fifty yards a figure rose from the floor at the back and a gun was pressed to Willie's neck. A voice said in accented English: 'Head for the Place Atabeh. I'll direct you from there.'

Modesty felt a warm glow of relief tingle through her body. She said quietly: 'Suppose we don't want to go?'

'The gun is silenced,' said the voice from the darkness behind. 'I think first I would shoot through your leg.'

Modesty nodded. 'All right, Willie,' she said.

From Place Atabeh they turned south and through the Abdine Square. Five minutes beyond, in an alley which ran behind small houses, the voice halted the car.

'The gun is on Garvin while you get out, Miss Blaise,' it said. 'Please think of him. And then you will stand with your

154

back to me, very close, and the gun will be on you while he gets out.'

It was efficiently performed. She caught a glimpse of the man as she opened the door. He was small and wiry, brown-skinned, with a blue pin-stripe suit and a dark hat. He shepherded them up a short path and through a door at the back of the house. Beyond the kitchen lay a passage, with two doors off on the right.

'The second door,' said the man with the gun. Willie opened it for Modesty and followed her in. The man came in close behind him and closed the door.

'Christ,' said Willie Garvin in disgust.

Tarrant was getting up from a worn leather armchair. He looked placidly unruffled, but there was a hint of strain about the eyes. Hagan stood by the curtained window, his back to it, hands driven deep into trouser pockets, shoulders a little hunched. The muscles of his jaws twitched slightly, and his eyes were cold.

'Thanks for the mickey finn,' he said in a metallic voice, looking at Modesty.

'Please, Hagan.' Tarrant lifted a hand. 'Modesty, will you sit down?'

She stood still and said: 'Who's this?' A movement of her head indicated the man behind Willie.

'Albert Alexandrou. Our man in Cairo,' Tarrant answered. 'He's been close to you ever since you arrived.'

'I see,' she said shortly. 'Do you know you may have destroyed the only chance we have?'

'Chance of what?' Tarrant's voice was equally terse. 'I'm reliably informed that Modesty Blaise has made a comeback, that she's setting up The Network again. She's known to have been picking up old contacts in Rome, Athens, Beirut and elsewhere. I'm also informed that today she visited the biggest fence in the Middle East. I ask myself—why?'

Modesty turned away. She took a packet of cigarettes from the pocket of her neat black denims and sat on the arm of a chair.

'You tell him, Willie,' she said.

'Glad to.' Willie turned without apparent haste, the edge of his hand catching Albert Alexandrou's forearm and carrying the gun outwards, then instantly sliding to the wrist and forcing the arm back against the door. With a jutting knuckle, Willie rapped sharply on the dorsum of the gun-hand, and caught the gun as it fell from momentarily powerless fingers. The whole movement occupied no more than a second.

Willie put the gun down on a small dining-table and hitched himself on the corner. 'You know what the Princess is doing to clean up this lousy job for you?' he said mildly. 'She's playing the live-bait caper.'

Tarrant glanced at Hagan, who had not moved, then back at Willie. 'Will you translate that for us?' he said.

'All right, Sir G. Nice and simple. The only way to find out 'ow Gabriel's going to snatch them crates of ice is by getting right next to 'im. So we've set things up to make Gabriel come and get us. That's why we are staked out tonight. That's why the Lone Ranger didn't get 'is arm broken off when he popped up with the gun. We reckoned 'e was one of Gabriel's boys.'

There was a long silence. Tarrant and Hagan turned their heads to stare at Modesty. Hagan moved his shoulders uneasily. 'You've flipped,' he said at last. 'You're headed straight for the Napoleon factory.'

Modesty looked at him and exhaled smoke. 'We've done it before,' she said simply.

'What do you think will happen if Gabriel takes you?' Tarrant asked. 'Are you hoping he'll tell you all about it?'

'He might.' It was Willie who answered. 'And if not, we'll be there when they bring the job off, 'owever they do it.'

Hagan gave a grunt of contempt. 'You'll be at the bottom of Port Said harbour with concrete boots on, you goddam fool,' he said bitterly.

'No.' Modesty shook her head. 'We've got a stopper on that. He'll keep us undamaged.'

'For how long?' Tarrant asked quietly. 'And what happens if and when you've found out what you want to know? How will you get out with it?'

'For long enough,' she answered. 'As for getting out, that's the hard bit—just the kind of thing you brought us in for. We'll play it by ear.'

'I don't think I can allow it,' Tarrant said slowly, and looked at Hagan. 'Do you think it could work?'

'It's kamikazi stuff,' Hagan said flatly.

Tarrant nodded. 'I think so, too. I'm sorry, Modesty.'

'You can't veto anything,' she said, looking him in the eyes. 'Willie and I are going to finish this, and you'd do well to accept that. We're in Egypt now. Not a country where you can pull many strings, Sir Gerald. But I can. There are friends I made in the past who are in very high places now.'

Tarrant fingered his chin. 'We're not quite so badly placed. His Highness Sheik Abu-Tahir is here in Cairo—and a very welcome guest. Nasser is wooing him for the United Arab Republic. It's not likely that Abu-Tahir will bite, but he's happy to enjoy a lavish wooing. I think that at the moment Nasser would act very promptly to oblige him in any way.'

Willie Garvin laughed. Modesty said: 'If you go to Abu-Tahir and say you want to stop me, you'll be in trouble.'

'Are you sure? I know he regards his diamonds highly, but——'

'He regards *me* highly. He'd consider that you were insulting me.'

The silence grew. At last Tarrant said: 'Will you talk to her, Hagan—alone?'

Hagan went to the door and opened it. He waited for Modesty to pass through, and followed her. As the door closed Tarrant relaxed a little and rubbed his eyes with finger and thumb. 'I suppose she might listen to him,' he said.

Willie took out a cigarette and offered one amiably to Albert Alexandrou. '*Like the deaf adder that stoppeth her ear,*' he said, '*which will not 'earken to the voice of charmers, charming never so wisely*. Psalm fifty-eight, verse four.'

In a small bedroom Modesty said: 'I had to walk out on you, Paul. Sorry about the mickey, but it was the best way. You'd only have fussed.'

'I'm not fussing now,' he said curtly. 'I'm not even trying to stop you, as Tarrant imagines. I just want to know why.'

She smiled. 'Look, try not to hate me too much.'

'I don't hate you.' He loosened up a little and rubbed a hand over his face. 'But I can't be like Willie. I can't walk around at your heels like a tame dog. And with you, there's no other place for a man.'

'I thought you'd found other places to be. And liked it.'

'For that you could hire a gigolo.'

Her smile vanished, and he felt disgust at his own satisfaction in hurting her. It was made worse when she did not hit back, but said quietly: 'I've never wanted you to walk around at my heels, Paul.'

'That's true. On this job you left me a few hundred miles behind.'

After a long silence she said: 'I'm not going to apologise for being the way I am. You've had all of me that I can give, Paul. If it's not enough, there's nothing I can do about it.'

He came close to her but did not attempt to touch her. 'I know,' he said. 'I know there's nothing you can do about it. It's hard to take, but I've taken it now. What I still don't know is *why* you have to do what you're doing.'

'Perhaps I don't know myself. And the reasons don't matter anyway. I'm doing it because I must. But if you want to, Paul, we'll have a wonderful time afterwards.'

'I can't think about afterwards. It's too far away. What do you want me to say to Tarrant now?'

'That the job's on. And as he can't stop it, the next best thing is to help. We could use a communications-link. I've been uneasy about that.'

'Communications?'

'A tracer. We've got what's necessary, but that's only one end of it.'

'All right. I don't see how you're going to work this, but let's go and tell Tarrant the score.'

In the other room Willie was smoking in silence. She was familiar with every nuance of his expression, and knew that something was wrong.

'What is it, Willie?'

'That bloody nit of a Minister. Sir G.'s just told me, Princess.'

'Told you what?'

'I had a message,' said Tarrant, 'when we were in Athens. Thornton decided that it would confuse the "supposed opposi-

158

tion" as he called it, if *The Tyboria* left with the diamonds before the due date.'

'My God,' she said quietly. 'Surely he'd realise they have a man in Cape Town who'd see the ship sail?'

'I wouldn't care to analyse his thought-processes,' Tarrant said carefully. 'The fact is that *The Tyboria* sailed six days early. No attempt on the diamonds has been made so far.'

'Where is she now?'

'Due to pass through Suez and reach Port Said in thirty-six hours.'

'Dawn, the day after tomorrow?'

'Yes. This makes things difficult, no doubt. I'm taking it for granted that Hagan has failed to dissuade you.'

'We reckoned on another week,' said Willie. 'There's not much time, Princess. We'll have to chuck ourselves in their laps some'ow.'

She stood with head a little on one side, thinking. 'Yes,' she said at last. 'Yes . . . it might even be better this way.'

'Dear God.' Tarrant closed his eyes prayerfully. 'Don't tell me Pompous Percy has done the right thing *again*.'

FOURTEEN

McWHIRTER came up the gangway from the motorboat and mopped his brow. He looked round the harbour and gave a grunt of satisfaction as he saw a grey-painted 7,000 ton cargo boat under the Liberian flag, lying a quarter of a mile west of *Mandrake*.

He went along the deck. Mrs. Fothergill was leaning on the rail. She wore grubby white shorts and a deep bra. Her body looked like polished hickory.

'Dear lady,' said McWhirter, laying his hand over hers. 'I would ha' brought ye violets. I scoured the bazaars——'

'I get sick of you, McWhirter,' she said, knocking his hand away. 'I keep hoping you'll shoot off your big funny mouth at Gabriel once too often, and he'll tell me to work you over a bit. I'd like that.'

'Och, I'm no' worthy of ye, Mrs. Fothergill,' he said cheerfully, snapping his fingers. 'Is there anything new to tell now?'

She hesitated, then shook her head. 'What about ashore?' she asked. 'Did Rashid have anything on the Blaise girl and Garvin?'

'A few bits and pieces. They're making a comeback right enough.'

'What d'you think Gabriel will do about her?'

'Nothing. Unless she gets in our way. Och, there's a fascinating thought, Mrs. Fothergill. How d'ye fancy a match wi' Modesty Blaise? She's a bonny talent by all accounts.'

The woman grinned. 'Stick to your accounts, McWhirter. You're a fool on the real stuff. That skinny bitch wouldn't last me ten seconds.' Her heavy, bovine face grew thoughtful. 'But Garvin now . . . he might be interesting.'

Borg came along the deck and stopped. 'Have you told him?' he said to Mrs. Fothergill.

She shrugged. McWhirter looked hard at her and said: 'Told me what?'

'Basilio's broken his leg.' Borg was scowling. 'Fell down a companionway.'

'God Almighty,' breathed McWhirter.

'I was hoping you'd go blundering in with one of your bloody stupid jokes,' Mrs. Fothergill said regretfully. 'That would have got Gabriel going all right.'

McWhirter gave her a venomous look. He jerked his head at Borg. Together the two men went along the deck and into the handsomely furnished stateroom. Gabriel stood with his hands behind his back, staring out of the window.

'Borg's just told me,' McWhirter said. 'How bad was it?'

'Bad enough.' Gabriel's voice was cold and flat. 'A double fracture of the femur. He was taken ashore an hour ago.'

McWhirter sat down on the long couch fixed to the bulkhead. 'An' the reserve technician went down in Haifa wi' appendix,' he said emptily. 'Could anyone in the crew handle Basilio's job, Gabriel? I wouldn't think it was that specialised. One o' the engineers, perhaps?'

'There's nobody I'd rely on.'

'Or in Kalonides' crew?'

'I've just checked. No.'

McWhirter plucked nervously at the skin of his neck. 'Ye have three quarters of a million sunk in this. We'll have to bring a man in.'

Gabriel turned from the window. His colourless eyes were flecked with red.

'*Who?*' he said viciously. 'We've got eighteen hours. The job needs skill. It needs nerve. It needs stamina. It needs a man who's idiot enough to come in from outside, pick up ten million poundsworth of loot for us, and think we'll let him live to talk about it afterwards. *Who?*'

McWhirter sat very still, avoiding Gabriel's eyes. The door opened and Mrs. Fothergill came in with a young Egyptian in a white suit.

'He's from Hakim,' she said, 'with a message. For your hands only.'

The young Egyptian took a photograph from his pocket, looked at it, then looked at Gabriel carefully. He nodded, put the photograph away, and brought out a sealed envelope from his inside pocket.

Gabriel took the envelope, ripped it open, and unfolded the single sheet of paper within. After a long time he looked up with blank eyes and said: 'All right.'

Mrs. Fothergill opened the door and saw the Egyptian out. Gabriel moved to the long window of the stateroom. He read the message again.

McWhirter cleared his throat. 'About finding a technician wi' the necessary skill and nerve——' he began, then broke off at a warning glance from Borg.

When Gabriel looked up his face was without expression, but for once there was a tinge of colour in the putty-like cheeks.

'We've found one,' he said. 'Modesty Blaise is getting under our feet. *And she owns just the man.*'

Willie Garvin stood by the curtained, second-floor window of the hotel bedroom. Through an inch-wide gap he could look out upon the west side of Ezbekeya Gardens, busy with evening traffic. The black Chevrolet was still there.

A few feet away from him Modesty Blaise lay on the bed, looking through a French fashion magazine. She wore a white wrap over black stretch tights and bra. The communicating door to Willie's room stood wide open.

'They've been there two hours now,' Willie said, and looked at his watch. 'Must be sweating a bit. D'you reckon there's any chance they might come in an' try to take us?'

'Us?' Modesty said seriously, and turned a page. 'No, not from a hotel full of people. They'll have to pull some stroke to get us out, Willie love. And we'll have to wait for them to pull it. The thing's got to look right. How many in the car?'

'Four. One of them's Borg. I don't know about the others.'

The telephone beside the bed rang, and she picked it up.

'Yes?' A long pause. 'Oh . . . ? But I thought the commission was too low for you, Hakim. No, I haven't made final arrangements yet.' Another pause. 'Tonight? Yes, I think so. We'll be leaving in twenty minutes.'

She put down the phone and sat up. 'Hakim thinks he'd like to handle that deal for us after all. He wants us to meet him in Ismailia.'

'Very nice little stroke,' said Willie. He picked up a large suitcase, put it on the bed and opened it. ''Ere we go, then. Sunday best for the party.' He began to take off his shirt.

Modesty stood up on the other side of the bed, took off the white wrap and unhooked the back of her bra. The thought touched her mind that if Tarrant could see them now he would be shocked. It amused her.

She knew that if Willie looked at her it would be because he happened to look at her. The caper had begun, and to Willie she was no longer a woman. If he looked at her body deliberately it would be a sharp, professional look, an instinctive checking of movement and muscle-play, as a man might run a knowledgeable eye over a race-horse. It was always so while a caper lasted; and sometimes afterwards, when there were hurts to be nursed. In the years past she had sick-nursed Willie—from very close to death on one occasion. And twice he had nursed her, with gentle and objective skill.

There were no mysteries between them. Paul had spoken of Willie as a tame dog walking at her heels. Perhaps it was so. If Willie had heard the tag he would probably have grinned agreement. But she knew, with great humility and without believing it herself, that Willie would still consider walking at her heels as setting him head and shoulders above any other man; even above any who had possessed her. At one time this attitude of his had troubled her, but no longer. A man couldn't be more than happy, and Willie Garvin was a happy man.

She dropped the bra on the bed and leaned over to take the other bra that Willie handed her from the suitcase.

Twenty minutes later they went down the stairs. They were dressed as they had been dressed the night before, when Albert Alexandrou had put a gun to Willie's neck. The open Pontiac stood in the hotel courtyard with half a dozen other cars. Willie took the wheel, and she sat beside him. She liked to drive, but Willie was better, and they would need the best tonight.

'Sorry it's been a long wait, Paul,' she said quietly.

Hagan lay curled on the back seat, almost hidden by a dark rug. 'Be my guest,' he murmured. 'Are we off now?'

'Yes. The Ismailia road. Has anybody been snooping around the car?'

'No. Is there a good place on the Ismailia road?'

'This side of Bulbeis,' said Willie, and eased the car out into the square. The big black Chev fell in fifty yards behind them as they circled Ezbekeya Gardens.

'How did Tarrant make out with the Egyptian top brass?' Modesty asked.

'Abu-Tahir handled it,' said Hagan's voice from the back seat. 'He got all we asked for, and earnest promises for any further co-operation he might need.'

'Where will you and Tarrant be?'

'In a room looking out over the harbour at Port Said.'

'And the D.F. stations?'

'Fixed. One listening out at Air Force H.Q. here, one at the Cyprus base, and the Lebanese have got their station in the hills behind Beirut on the job.'

'It should be enough coverage.'

As they left the last straggling outskirts of Cairo behind, Willie eased his foot down. The lights of the following car stayed two hundred yards behind. There was no other traffic on the road.

''Bout twenty minutes,' Willie said, and switched on the beam.

They spoke no more. After ten minutes, when Cairo was only a glow in the sky behind them, the Chev suddenly swept closer. Willie waited until it had closed to fifty yards, then accelerated hard. The Pontiac leapt forward.

Hagan had thrown off the rug but still kept low on the back seat. 'Can you hold them off long enough?' he asked.

Modesty looked back at him and smiled briefly, the smile not touching her eyes. 'Yes.'

The Chev crept up again.

'They're not shooting,' Hagan said. 'Looks like your stopper's going to work. They want you whole.'

The Chev had moved out to overtake. Willie eased out,

crowding the other car steadily. It fell back. Modesty looked at her wristwatch. 'Not long now.'

Ahead, at the farthest range of the long headlight beam, the straight road narrowed and wound briefly through a low, rocky outcrop. Willie braked smoothly, holding the middle of the road, and the Chev tore down upon them, tyres screaming as the wheels locked intermittently under the stab of the driver's braking-foot. Willie whipped down a gear and accelerated with full power. The Chev, almost halted at the end of a long skid, fell back far behind them.

Willie slid into top. There came the sound and bluster of air beating back from the walls of the outcrop as they moved into the first of the twisting curves. Leaving the gear in top, Willie let the speed drop to fifty, forty, thirty...

He said: ''Old tight.'

Hagan braced himself and Modesty turned, gripping the back seat. The Pontiac touched the wall with a grinding scrape of metal on rock, and swung away. It moved in a controlled skid across the road, side-swiped a jutting corner, and kept going. The wall on one side fell away to no more than a lumpy ridge bordering the road. Willie eased the nearside wheels up the ridge so that the car tilted dangerously. It was barely moving now.

'Out,' he said, bringing it to a halt. Modesty swung over the top of the door and Hagan dropped to the ground beside her. The car hung teetering. Willie slid out on the nearside, keeping his weight on it. Hagan moved round beside him and together they heaved. The Pontiac crashed over on its side.

Willie walked quickly to where Modesty stood in the middle of the road and took her arm. 'Right, Princess,' he said. 'See you later, then.' His other hand came up. He hit her with the point of his elbow, just below the ear; a short blow, travelling only four inches. Her head lolled and she crumpled. He let her fall, not lowering her, and as she rolled over her face scraped along the ground.

Hagan felt his stomach contract. Suddenly he knew what she meant about being a professional. He didn't like it, but he understood it now.

Headlights flickered across the sky as the Chev topped the

low rise which lay two hundred yards back, round the long S-bend. The snarl of the engine grew louder. The driver had dropped a gear for better control on the bends.

Willie stepped three paces away from Modesty and said: 'Right, matey.' He was close to Hagan, facing him, head turned and tilted a little to expose the jaw.

Hagan swung hard with his right. It connected perfectly. Willie's body went limp, and collapsed in a sprawl on the road. Hagan turned and ran for the car. He passed it and went on beyond into the seamed slope of rock. As he dropped flat, the lights of the Chev swung round the bend.

Tyres squealed for long seconds and the car halted with a jerk. A man and a woman got out of the back seat. The man held a gun. He covered the woman as she moved forward warily, first to the overturned car and then to the two figures lying in the road. Bending over Modesty she lifted an eyelid with her thumb. Abruptly she swung an open hand in a vicious slap across the unconscious face, and waited for any reaction.

Hagan wanted to kill her.

'She's out,' the woman called, and moved to Willie. She lifted his head by the hair and thumbed back an eyelid. 'This one, too.'

The woman stood up and grinned. Hagan saw a heavy face with a bright fuzz of dyed hair.

'Gift-wrapped,' she said. 'Here, Gasparro.' Another man slid out from the seat beside the driver. 'Help Borg lift him in,' the woman said, jerking a thumb at Willie. She moved to Modesty, slipped an arm under her shoulders and another under her knees. Without effort she straightened up and carried the limp form to the car.

Hagan watched as the two unconscious captives were crammed into the back with Borg. The woman squeezed in front with the driver and Gasparro. Doors slammed and the car moved away, quickly gathering speed.

Resting his damp forehead on his hands, Hagan lay cursing monotonously. After a while he got up and began to walk towards the railway line running east to Bulbeis.

FIFTEEN

THERE were six people in the cabin. It was of fair size, but any greater number would have made it crowded.

Gabriel sat behind a plain oak table, his back to a white-painted bulk-head. Borg and Mrs. Fothergill sat on a long locker beneath a port. Borg held a gun on his knee. Mrs. Fothergill was smoking a cheroot.

McWhirter stood by the door, flexing his knees and humming a dirge. He was watching Modesty Blaise and Willie Garvin with great interest. They stood before the table, their hands in front of them, La Trobe handcuffs on their wrists. Both were dusty and dishevelled. There was a slight gravel graze on the woman's cheek from being thrown out of the car.

They'd been lucky to be thrown clear, McWhirter thought, and then amended the opinion. No, unlucky ... for them, at least.

On the table in front of Gabriel lay a pile of objects. Two slim throwing knives, and a Colt .32 in a holster on a narrow leather belt; a packet of cigarettes, a box of matches and a lighter; a lipstick and a pocket-comb in a leather case; money and some keys; a small handkerchief and a large white one.

Gabriel went through the pile methodically, examining every object. He looked carefully at the cigarettes, broke one open, then tossed the packet to Willie Garvin.

'Thanks.' Willie caught it with handcuffed hands. 'Any chance of a light?'

Gabriel examined the lighter thoroughly and threw it across the table. 'You can smoke later,' he said coldly. 'Not here.' He picked up the lipstick, uncapped it, slid the button up the curving groove, then drew it back again and put the cap on. He threw it to Modesty; then the comb and the handkerchiefs.

Sitting back in his chair, he studied the two captives. The pupils of his eyes were very small, one of the rare signs of excitement in Gabriel.

'Check them again,' he said. Borg passed his gun to Mrs. Fothergill and got up, moving to Willie Garvin. He ran his hands down Willie's chest, probing hard. He checked the empty twin-sheath, then ran his hands over Willie's back and down the arms. Kneeling, he felt carefully down each leg. He picked up first one foot then the other, looking at the soles of the boots. They were enclosed in the same rubber covering that was bonded over the line of the welt.

Straightening up, Borg went through the same methodical process with Modesty. She stood looking past him as his hands probed her body.

'Both clean,' Borg said at last, and went back to his seat.

Gabriel looked at them in silence for several moments. 'Mrs. Fothergill would very much like to kill you,' he said.

Modesty gave a slight shrug. 'I understand she likes to kill anybody. Why us?'

'Because you're here. And because I want you to talk. If you don't, she gets her kick. Right away.'

Modesty lifted her hands and rubbed the back of one wrist against the graze on her cheek. 'You know about me from before, Gabriel,' she said. 'You know I'm not in business to get hurt. There's no profit in it. What do you want me to talk about?'

'Diamonds. A parcel worth ten million pounds. You've been offering them.' Gabriel leaned forward. 'Where are they?'

'On a ship coming through Suez in the morning, for Beirut.'

'Check.' Gabriel nodded. 'And what were you planning to do?'

'Lift them from the strongroom of the Anglo-Levant Bank in Beirut sometime in the next week.'

McWhirter choked back a sudden cackle of laughter. Gabriel's lips thinned till they almost disappeared, and he shook his head slowly. 'Don't get smart, Blaise. I had a detailed study made for that operation. It's a loser.'

'For you, maybe. But there's a factor you don't know about. I'm an old and trusted friend of Sheik Abu-Tahir. I've got access to the strongroom, on his authority, for valuing and conversion as and when.'

Gabriel considered. 'That makes it work,' he said after a

moment. 'But you'd have been disappointed. I'm taking the diamonds before they reach Beirut.'

She stared, and exchanged a look with Willie Garvin. Gabriel saw that she was shaken.

'Piracy?' she asked, unbelieving. 'It's simpler just to cut your throat. That ship's been fitted with a 5.2 gun and four pompoms.'

'I know. There's a factor *you* don't know about—yet. We'll come back to it. How were you going to handle distribution?'

'I've got a buyer for the lot. He's from the other side of the curtain.'

'How much?'

'Nine million. In various proportions of gold, hard currencies and soft currencies.'

'Check. You haven't got yourself hurt so far. Keep it that way.'

'I suppose Hakim talked?'

Gabriel ignored her and looked across at McWhirter. 'That's half our distribution costs, right?'

'Aye. We could make an extra million doing it her way.'

Gabriel looked at Modesty and said: 'How do you make contact with your buyer?'

'I don't. He's going to make contact with me in Istanbul. And in his own way. All I have to do is be there, ten days from now.'

'With the diamonds?'

She made a gesture of impatience. 'Not at that stage. Look, it's a complex set-up. I couldn't handle the sale with Interpol on my tail, so the diamonds in the Anglo-Levant were to be replaced by imitations. That would have given me time to——'

'Never mind what your plan was. How solid is this buying arrangement?'

'I could tell you a hundred per cent. But nothing's that certain. I'll make it not less than ninety-five per cent. They want those diamonds badly.'

'All right. You'll be in Istanbul ten days from now—under supervision.' Gabriel leaned back in his chair. 'It's a good set-up. A nice deal. Consider yourself bought out.'

She moved her shoulders. 'I've been expecting that. For how much?'

'For your neck. And Garvin's. We'll find somebody else for Mrs. Fothergill.'

After a long silence she said in a flat voice: 'Okay. I only came back because this thing was the biggest I'd ever seen. I should have stayed home.'

Willie Garvin gave a little sigh of mingled acceptance and relief. He looked round at the unresponsive faces and grinned. 'Well, that's the way it goes. All settled, eh? So 'ow about getting these cuffs off—and a little drink?'

Gabriel got up and walked round the desk. He stood in front of Willie and suddenly hit him back-handed across the face.

'It's not settled yet,' he said. 'You work for me now, Garvin, until this is over. And you talk soft, not clever. How well can you handle a torch?'

'You want a safe opened?'

'A big one. Can you work fast and under tough conditions?'

'I'm not just a pretty face, y'know.'

'I told you,' Gabriel said. 'Not clever.' He turned and hit Modesty hard across the face. 'Now ... ?'

Willie drew a deep breath. 'I can use a torch,' he said quietly, 'and I can work fast under tough conditions.' He was hoping that he hadn't folded too easily. The vicious blow across Modesty's face had moved him no more than the blow across his own. It had been necessary to show a measure of jaunty independence before capitulating. He thought it was just about right.

'That's better.' Gabriel turned to Borg. 'Brief him. Let him try out the gear. Make sure he knows the route, the distances, the timing and the floor plan. Everything. How long?'

'If he's bright, two hours.' Borg stood up.

'You've enough time, then. Get busy.' Gabriel looked at McWhirter. 'Benzedrine half an hour before the job starts.'

'Aye. He'll have had a hard night. And what about Madame?' He nodded towards Modesty.

'Number four cabin. Leave the cuffs on and put a man on the door.'

Three hours after she had put herself to sleep, Modesty opened her eyes. There was no moment of uncertainty about her surroundings. She saw that the other bunk in the small cabin was still empty. Willie's wind-cheater lay on it, his boots stood beside it.

So Willie had not slept. He was still being briefed. She got up and washed her face in the corner-basin, the handcuffs clinking on her wrists. Looking in the spotted mirror, she pushed a few wisps of hair into place and felt the chignon at the nape of her neck to make sure it was securely bound. Cigarettes and lighter were in the pocket of Willie's wind-cheater. She lit a cigarette and sat down on the bunk.

The ship moved gently to the harbour swell. It was still at anchor. The port-hole cover was locked. She knew that Tarrant and Paul would be somewhere overlooking the harbour, in one of the port offices, perhaps. They would be watching Gabriel's yacht, *Mandrake*. But Gabriel was here, on a small cargo ship lying a quarter of a mile away. She had glimpsed the name as she and Willie were brought aboard in the darkness ... *Andronicus*.

She wondered about Willie's briefing, but only for a moment. Speculation was pointless. She felt no sense of anxiety, for this was weakening and she had laid it aside many hours ago, when the call from Hakim had started the first move of the live-bait caper. Her mind was a carefully controlled instrument, rejecting all considerations except those which were or could be vital—and to these it was infinitely sensitive.

The door opened and Mrs. Fothergill came in. The unintelligent eyes surveyed Modesty with a touch of greediness, like a mastiff scenting a bone. 'Gabriel wants you to see how it works,' she said, and chuckled. 'He's a bit proud of it, and I can't say I blame him.'

'May I have these cuffs off—just for two minutes?'

'Eh?' Mrs. Fothergill's suspicious stare slowly faded and comprehension dawned. 'Want the loo, eh? All right, ducky, but the cuffs stay till Gabriel says otherwise. You look limber enough to manage. This way.'

Ten minutes later Modesty stood with Mrs. Fothergill on a narrow catwalk, looking down into a hold some forty feet square. The catwalk ran round three sides of the hold, and the only floor was the ship's bilge itself, the plates clean and dry. There were a dozen men here, some on the catwalk and some below.

A grotesque object rested on wooden chocks on the hull-plates of the ship. One part of it she recognised—a big flattened doughnut of forged steel with a streamlining shell of green Fibreglass round the rim, pierced by two huge Plexiglass ports. From fins on either side at the stern, two short right-angled tubes projected—jet nozzles which pumped out water for propulsion and steering.

The grotesqueness lay in the great inverted bell which surmounted the diving saucer and appeared to be secured to its upper surface by a four-inch deep steel collar. Around the rim of the bell was a thick rubber flange. From the catwalk she could look down into the bell and see the open circular hatch in its flattened base.

From a gantry above, three braided nylon cables spread from a central point, their ends secured to small steel hoops set into the metal hull of the diving saucer. Six men were busy making a final check on the power assemblies which lay between the inner shell of steel and the outer shell of Fibreglass. Willie Garvin stood watching. He wore lightweight coveralls, borrowed plimsoles, and was no longer handcuffed. A small dark man in similar coveralls was climbing a rope-ladder to reach the rim of the bell. He scrambled over, lowered himself to the base, and disappeared down through the double-hatch leading through to the interior of the diving saucer.

Willie Garvin looked up and saw her on the catwalk. She lifted her 'cuffed hands in acknowledgment. He smiled, made a small gesture towards the saucer, and wagged his head with reluctant admiration.

Gabriel, Borg and McWhirter stood on another stretch of the catwalk, near a control panel and telephone bolted to the wall. McWhirter saw Modesty and Mrs. Fothergill and came bouncing along to join them, rubbing his hands.

'D'ye like it, young lady?' he grinned.

'I don't know yet,' she answered slowly. 'It's the Cousteau diving saucer, isn't it?'

'No. The Giolitti. Very similar.'

'How did Gabriel get it?'

'Och, he's a man wi' many enterprises. Among them he owns a sizeable documentary film company.'

'And they're shooting some underwater sequences?'

McWhirter nudged her with a bony elbow, and winked. 'You're a deductive young woman. Aye, there's a unit making the right sort o' documentary around the Greek Islands. They hired the saucer at great expense and in due form.'

'You've added that superstructure,' she said, nodding towards the inverted bell.

'An' we'll subtract it when it's served its turn, ma'am.'

'Not without leaving any trace.'

'True. But on the last day o' filming, the saucer will suffer a wee accident, damaging the top o' the hull.'

'For which it's insured, of course.'

'Why don't you two shut up,' said Mrs. Fothergill without heat. She was leaning on the rail of the catwalk and watching the scene below with vacuous interest. 'Talk, talk, bloody talk. If ever I do you, McWhirter, it'll be your larynx that gets the first chop.'

McWhirter laughed gaily and said, 'Dear lady.'

Modesty saw Willie climb up into the bell and vanish through the double hatch. His hands drew the outer hatch, in the base of the bell, down into place. She saw it tighten securely. Gabriel was speaking on the telephone, watching the saucer, and for some time there appeared to be a test procedure going on.

'Is Gabriel in contact with them?' Modesty asked.

McWhirter shook his head. 'Not direct. Through the radio-room. That's where we have a long-wave link wi' the saucer. We'll be going up there later.'

Gabriel put down the phone and spoke to Borg, who shouted: 'Stand by.' The men on the floor moved back, well clear of the area on which the saucer stood. On the catwalk two men moved round closing watertight doors. They signalled to Gabriel and there was a sudden taut silence in the hold. Nobody moved.

'Launch her,' said Gabriel.

An engine whined, and the nylon cables lifted the saucer a few inches from its chocks. Men darted forward and drew the chocks clear. Gabriel signalled to somebody below, out of Modesty's sight. After a moment there came a soft rumbling sound and the steel plates of the hull slid slowly back in two sections, a long strip of caulking breaking away as the sections parted.

The dark, oily sea of the harbour lapped quietly in the bottom of the hold, but the water barely rose, for the airtight hold itself was functioning like a massive diving-bell. Another signal, and the saucer with its cumbersome superstructure was lowered slowly into the water. As it floated, half-submerged, men moved to the edge of the open hull and detached the nylon cables.

Gabriel picked up the telephone and spoke. Five seconds passed. Modesty saw water begin to rise within the bell.

'They're pumpin' it in,' said McWhirter. 'It'd come in over the top wi' a rush otherwise, an' might topple her.'

As the water in the bell rose, the saucer sank lower. Soon only a few inches of the bell's rim were left above the surface. Then there was nothing more to be seen. The plates rumbled back into place, and men moved forward through a few inches of water to caulk the overlapping joint.

'We'll take it from the radio-room, McWhirter,' Gabriel called. 'Bring Blaise along.'

There was a plan pinned on the wall of the radio-room, a long strip of paper with a scale drawing of a ship and of the saucer, with times and distances measured out along a scale at the foot of the plan.

Through an open port on the far side of the cabin Modesty could see a white-painted ship lying just outside the approach to the canal. She knew it must be *The Tyboria*. Tarrant and Paul would be watching through glasses from their vantage point overlooking the harbour. They would be watching *Mandrake* too, believing that she and Willie were prisoners aboard her. They would not be watching the cargo ship, *Andronicus*, as it made ready to sail.

The Tyboria and *Andronicus* would sail. Gabriel's yacht

would remain. She wondered how long it would be before Tarrant and Paul discovered what had happened. There was no way of making an estimated answer, and she put the matter out of her mind.

Gabriel said: 'I've told Garvin what happens to you if he fumbles this job or tries to get smart. Told him in detail.'

'He'll remember,' she answered, and lifted her wrists. 'You've bought me out for my neck, and you want me to sell the diamonds my way for you. Do you still have to keep these things on me?'

'The 'cuffs?' Gabriel grinned without showing his teeth. It was a curiously repellent expression, artificial and without emotion. 'They're for your own protection—in case Mrs. Fothergill gets a sudden compulsion. With the 'cuffs on you're safe. Like if you wore glasses.'

Mrs. Fothergill sniggered. Gabriel turned and looked out of the port.

'May I ask questions?' Modesty said.

'You won't have to. McWhirter doesn't often have a captive audience. You're a gift for him.'

'Come over here, young woman,' McWhirter said contentedly, and led her to the plan on the wall. 'Now, the saucer has to travel approximately half a mile to reach *The Tyboria*. It can only do one and a half knots wi'out the superstructure, less than a knot wi' it.'

'Why doesn't the extra weight of the bell overturn her?'

'Heh?' McWhirter glared, then his face relaxed. 'The mercury ballast compensates,' he said. She knew that he was guessing. But somebody had not guessed. This was a Gabriel project, and every aspect of it would have been tested.

'You have to be sure the saucer will reach *The Tyboria* in time,' she said, studying the scale. 'It needs half an hour just to reach her.'

'Aye. But we launched twenty minutes ago, as the ship was comin' through the last stretch from Raz-el-Esh.'

'I still think the timing's a hazard. Do you know how long *The Tyboria* will be hove-to there?'

McWhirter glanced out of the port at the white-painted ship. 'No. If there's no passengers or mail, there's still the

175

formalities an' the cutter for the pilot. Minimum thirty minutes. An' the job's been well-rehearsed, d'ye see.' He paused, rubbing his chin, and added slowly: 'Not wi' Garvin, though.'

'What has he got to do?'

'Nothing till contact's made—an' that's the pilot's job.'

'A precision job. How does the saucer home-in and locate itself?'

'Ah...' McWhirter beamed and rubbed dry hands together. 'By instruments. She'll come up right below the strongroom. There's other things in yon strongroom besides the diamonds, an' among them a crate o' valuable porcelains four feet square and a foot deep.'

She nodded. 'Shipped by one of Gabriel's companies—and with something inside to put out a homing beam?'

'Aye. As soon as Garvin transmits from the saucer on the frequency that triggers the homer.'

'There's still a margin for error. How do you know the crate with the homer is lying just where you want it in the strongroom?'

Gabriel answered, not turning from his position by the port. 'We know every item in the strongroom,' he said. 'The exact position. It cost money to get that floor plan, but we expect to show a profit.' He looked up at the clock on the wall over the radio-operator's table. 'We should be hearing from them soon.'

Mrs. Fothergill lit the stub of a cheroot. She looked around her vaguely, then bent and picked up a chair by one leg. Gripping it at the foot, she held the chair at arm's length, the sinews standing out on her arm, and began to watch the big second-hand of the clock.

'What happens when the saucer makes contact?' Modesty asked.

'She comes up here.' McWhirter put a long finger on the drawing of the ship, and chuckled. 'I'll confess I always thought a ship's bottom was sharp, but no. It's flat here, d'ye see. The saucer comes up.' He used his hands to demonstrate. 'The bell makes contact wi' the ship's bottom. Magnetic contact, just enough to hold. Two-fifty pounds o' iron ballast is dropped, an' ye have upward pressure. The water's pumped

176

out o' the bell, an' ye have the added adhesion o' water pressure outside.'

'What about barnacles?'

'The rubber flange keeps the bell water-tight. It's been tested.'

'So you've got the bell, with the saucer below it, lightly stuck to the bottom of *The Tyboria*.'

'Aye. It should be happening about now. And it'll hold as long as the ship doesn't move.'

'That could be in the next twenty minutes. So now Willie gets busy?'

'He'd better, lassie.' McWhirter looked at her and she saw the cruelty that lay deep in the twinkling blue eyes. 'Aye, he'd better.'

SIXTEEN

WILLIE GARVIN crouched in the inverted bell, his back braced against one curving side, his legs straddling the double hatch. A thick disc of rubber covered the opening between his feet. From below, tubes passed through the disc to the oxy-acetylene torch he held. Another tube led to an aqua-lung mouthpiece gripped in his teeth, and there was a clip on his nose. He wore dark goggles, and a small powerful lamp was strapped to his forehead.

With a scraper, he had cleaned the lightly-barnacled plates close to the rim of the bell, and the metal rim was now pressed hard against the ship's bottom. The flange of rubber bonded to the exterior made a water-tight seal.

Willie set the torch going, adjusted the flame, and took a stick of weld from the long pocket in his coveralls. Carefully he began to melt the weld into the thin, V-shaped gap between the hull-plates of the ship and the bevelled edge of the bell's rim.

In seconds the interior of the bell was thick with fumes. Breathing evenly, sucking in air through the tube, Willie carefully tack-welded along an eight-inch length of the curving perimeter. When it was done, he edged awkwardly round in the confined space and began to apply another fillet of weld on the opposite side.

Six minutes had passed when he finished. Sweat ran from his pores. The heat in the bell was ferocious, despite the cooling effect of the surrounding water.

Patiently he settled in a new position to apply more weld at a third point of the circumference. The muscles of his legs and arms protested fiercely against the unrelenting strain. He closed his mind to the pain and worked on. As he began the fourth and final weld a tremor passed through the bell and settled to a steady vibration. The ship had begun to move.

Willie looked at the flame of the torch. The inner cone was

irregular and poorly defined. He reduced the flow of acetylene until the flame was right, and carried on. Even with the bright light on his brow it was hard to see now through the dense fumes. The fourth weld took longer than the rest, and when it was done he doused the torch and leaned back limply, dragging in gulps of air from the aqua-lung cylinder in the saucer below.

Bending down, he banged three times on the edge of the hatch. Moments later there came a faint hissing sound, and the foul air began to thin. It was being pumped out and replaced by fresh air. Now that the ship was moving, the bubbles rising to the surface would be lost in the bow-waves which creamed back along the ship's sides.

Willie kicked the rubber disc down through the hatch and handed the torch to the pilot below. Taking out the aqua-lung mouthpiece he slid down into a squatting position and allowed all his muscles to go slack.

The pilot's head appeared between his feet. 'Continue!' the man said urgently, and gestured for haste.

'Get knotted.' Willie pushed back his goggles and gave his mind to deliberate relaxation, head resting back against the side so that he could watch the fillets of weld in the light of the inspection lamp on his brow. They were holding. The moment of greatest stress had come when the ship began to move and the welds had borne the strain of the bell's inertia. Now that moment was past they would continue to hold.

After five minutes Willie signalled to the pilot and a long limp tube of cellophane was passed up to him. It contained a mixture of hemp and plastic metal. Willie opened the end of the tube and fed sticky hemp into the bevel of the rim between the four tack-welds, ramming it home firmly with a wooden spatula. In thirty minutes it would set rock-hard and make a permanent seal.

The job done, he passed down the spatula and the crumpled cellophane. According to instructions, this concluded the first and vital stage of the operation. The rest of it could be completed at leisure.

'Jesus,' Willie thought, shaking sweat from his face. 'At leisure.'

He put a finger to the button of the thin black band around his throat, and pressed it.

'Pumpkin,' he said distinctly. The sensitive throat-mike would pick up the vibration of his vocal chords and relay them to the loudspeaker in Gabriel's radio-room. 'Pumpkin' meant that the first stage, the race against time, had been completed. He wondered if they had taken Modesty with them to the radio-room. He hoped so. This was quite a caper.

The pilot passed him a large pair of fixed compasses, and he inscribed a chalk circle on the steel plates above his head, a circle thirty inches in diameter. Below, the pilot was connecting a cylinder of pure oxygen to the torch, to make it a cutter.

Willie took the torch and adjusted the flame. Then he began to cut a circular hole in the bottom of *The Tyboria*.

'Lotus,' said a croaking voice over the loudspeaker, and there was a sudden stir of excitement in the radio-room.

'He's through,' McWhirter said exultantly, putting a long finger on the plan of the ship. 'And in the right place. He's through the bottom and up in the alley between the water-tanks. Now he has to measure a wee distance along here and cut through the floor of the strongroom.'

Modesty looked across the cabin. Through the open port she could see *The Tyboria* moving steadily along on a parallel course, a mile to starboard. Port Said would be well down beyond the horizon now. She visualised Willie crawling along the dark alley in the bowels of the ship, well below the water-line.

'They must have noticed we're keeping the same course and same speed as they are,' she said. 'What happens if they make a snap inspection of the strongroom?'

'Would *you*?' It was Gabriel, contempt in his voice. 'They're watching us. They're watching us for hidden guns, or an attempt to close and board. But what's so strange about two ships holding the same course for a while? Would *you* think of somebody coming up through the bottom and into the strong-room?'

'Beirut,' said McWhirter gleefully. 'That's when they'll find out. She'll dock during the night, an' they'll lay on half a battalion to see yon diamonds safe to the bank. Then they'll open the strongroom...' He closed his eyes for a moment and suddenly opened them very wide, hands spread in an exaggerated gesture of shock as he gazed at the floor. 'Mice!' he cried in horror.

Mrs. Fothergill stared. Then understanding dawned and she gave a snuffling laugh. 'Mice,' she repeated. 'Here, that's not bad, McWhirter.'

Twenty minutes later there came a hum from the loudspeaker.

'Sunflower,' said Willie Garvin's voice.

He stood in the strongroom, a pair of bolt-cutters in his hands. Behind him, a foot from a large flat wooden crate, there was a ragged circular hole in the floor. The quadrants of the steel disc he had cut out lay in the working alley four feet below. From the inspection-lamp on his brow, a long lead hitched to his waist trailed out through the hole in the floor, along eight feet of the alley, and down through the bell to the batteries in the diving saucer.

The two metal boxes which lay against the strongroom wall were just as Borg had shown him in the photographs; about three feet long by a foot wide and a foot deep. There were two steel hasps and wax-sealed padlocks on each box. Willie cut the padlocks off. He opened each box in turn, lifted the surface padding, and looked at what lay below. They were like small pebbles. He scooped up a handful from each box and inspected them closely. Satisfied, he put the diamonds back and closed both boxes. From the pocket of his coveralls he took two new padlocks and fastened them through the hasps.

Luigi, the pilot, had taken the oxy-acetylene cutter back along the alley. Now he returned, and his head rose through the hole in the floor. Willie dragged the boxes forward one at a time and manoeuvred them down through the hole, Luigi helping from below.

It took ten minutes to get both boxes along the alley, down into the bell, then through the double-hatch to the saucer.

Willie pressed the button of his throat-mike and said: 'Mimosa.'

The pilot lay prone on a foam-rubber mattress, hands on the controls, face close to one of the Plexiglass ports. Willie closed the outer hatch, sealing the base of the bell, and screwed the locks tight with an angled spanner. He closed the inner hatch, in the hull of the saucer, and secured it. Wearily he eased himself on to the engineer's seat, facing the stern of the saucer.

The pilot pumped mercury ballast forward, so that on release the saucer would plunge steeply, bow down. An instrument showed the water-ballast tanks filling to capacity now. At a word from Luigi, Willie spread his fingers along a short bar connecting four small switches. He pressed down. There came a solid metallic sound from the steel collar above the hull as the locks which held saucer and bell together disengaged.

The saucer plunged smoothly, leaving the sealed bell behind, and there came the muffled throb of the ship's propellers passing thirty feet overhead. Gently the pilot brought his craft to an even keel, hanging poised in the water like a great sea-monster.

Willie touched his throat-mike. 'Rendezvous,' he said.

The word came over the loudspeaker in the radio-room of *Andronicus*, and Modesty heard the underlying weariness in Willie's voice. He must have taken a caning; but she knew his resilience. Food and a few hours of sleep would recharge him.

McWhirter was stamping his feet and clapping his hands above his head. Mrs. Fothergill chuckled and scratched her wiry blonde hair aimlessly. Even Gabriel showed emotion, his lips twitching and a dull red tinge creeping into his putty-coloured cheeks.

He picked up the telephone and said: 'Stop engines.' His eyes were on Modesty.

'Now all that's left is for me to sell them,' she said.

He nodded, putting down the phone. 'Sell them for me,' he amended. 'And under supervision. We'll arrange all that later.'

'It's what I meant,' she said with a shrug. 'I've told you, I'm in business for profit, not for lumps, Gabriel.'

'Keep it like that.'

'I will. As long as we don't get lumps anyway. You'll have smoother co-operation if we're fed.'

Gabriel considered her. 'That we can do,' he said at last. 'See to it, McWhirter.'

In a big office overlooking the harbour at Port Said, Tarrant picked up the two messages and read them again.

'It still doesn't make sense,' Hagan said. He stood by the window, his eyes on the yacht *Mandrake*. A motor-boat was puttering away from the yacht, making for the landing jetty.

There was a third man in the office, a major of the Egyptian Army, sitting at a table with three telephones.

'Nothing makes sense,' Tarrant muttered. The messages were from the Captain of *The Tyboria*. The first reported that for over an hour a cargo ship, *Andronicus*, had matched his speed on a parallel course north from Port Said. No suspicious behaviour could be discerned aboard her, but he had put his gun-crews on stand-to.

The second message, timed an hour and a half later, reported that *Andronicus* had hove-to and was being left astern. Apologies for any alarm caused by earlier message.

'It means something,' Tarrant said. 'I can't believe this other ship was just a coincidence.'

'If not, what the hell *does* it mean?' Hagan turned from the window.

Tarrant made no answer. He had asked for a check to be made on Gabriel aboard *Mandrake*, and was waiting for the result. Five minutes later a port official entered the room and gave the major an elaborate salute.

'The man Gabriel is not there,' he reported in English. 'I ask for him on excuse of Customs matters. He is not on *Mandrake*. His captain tells me he has left last night, with other passengers, but cannot say where they go.'

Hagan swore. 'They're on *Andronicus*,' he said to Tarrant. 'So are Modesty and Willie.'

'It seems probable. But why?' Tarrant rubbed an eye wearily. 'Why did they shadow *The Tyboria*? What have they done, or what are they going to do? Have they tried something and failed?'

'Sod the diamonds,' Hagan said distinctly. He waved a hand

at the window. 'Gabriel's disappeared somewhere into the Med. He's got Modesty. If he's failed to snatch the diamonds she's no use to him. *What are we going to do?*'

'Without a full-scale air search before dusk,' said Tarrant, 'which is quite impossible anyway, we haven't a hope of finding *Andronicus.*'

'So?'

'So we sit and wait. And hope that Modesty Blaise and Willie Garvin can play the hard bit by ear.'

Willie Garvin opened his eyes. He was lying on his back on the narrow bunk, his handcuffed hands resting limply on his stomach.

It was six hours since he had climbed from the diving saucer in the airtight hold of *Andronicus*, given Gabriel a verbal report, eaten a big meal, and fallen asleep. He knew it was six hours because he had set his inner mechanism to sleep for just that time.

'Stay there, Willie love.'

Modesty drew up a stool beside him. She held a mug of water, some soap, and an open razor.

Willie stared: 'Gawd,' he said. 'Where d'you get that, Princess?'

'I asked for it. McWhirter was amused but he didn't jib. There's not much we could do with a razor except shave or cut our throats.' She rubbed the wet soap round Willie's chin.

'I'll do it, Princess. I'm a big boy now.'

'Big enough not to argue. Lie still, Willie.'

'Can you manage with the 'andcuffs?'

'No trouble. You'll still know yourself by the time I've finished.'

She was competent with the razor. Years before, when she had first come out of the desert and worked for Louche in Tangier, she had spent part of each day as an assistant in a barber's shop attached to a high-class brothel. It was a place where men talked, and the gossip she picked up had been valuable.

Willie Garvin relaxed and closed his eyes, enjoying the clean cold touch of the razor against the bristle of his cheeks.

'You got to 'and it to Gabriel,' he said indistinctly from the corner of his mouth. 'Some caper, Princess.'

'The biggest.' She touched his ear and pulled the lobe gently. It told him the cabin was probably bugged. This could be part of the reason why she had been allowed in the hold and the radio-room, so that a microphone could be hidden here in the cabin.

Willie opened one eye and shut it again in acknowledgment.

'What 'appens when *The Tyboria* gets to Beirut an' they find the diamonds gone?' he said. 'This ship's going to be 'ot. First port we touch, there'll be an army aboard. They'll find the saucer, the exit-hold, the diamonds—everything.'

'No. I asked about that.' She drew the skin of his cheek tight, and brought the razor skilfully along the jawbone. 'We're leaving the ship tonight, with Gabriel and a few others —and the diamonds. I don't know where. But the ship goes on and the diving-saucer gets dropped off in the Greek Islands with a film unit there.'

'Nice cover. But the ship will still be 'ot. We were running alongside *The Tyboria* for nearly two hours.'

'The ship won't touch any port till Brest. By then the exit-hold will be back to normal. Completely. There'll be nothing for anyone to find.'

'She won't be stopped at sea?'

'Who's going to do it?' Modesty laid down the razor and wiped his face dry with a towel. 'The interested parties are Sheik Abu-Tahir and the British Government. Abu-Tahir hasn't got a gunboat, and the British Government wouldn't use one. Not on the high seas, and on flimsy suspicion.'

Willie ran a hand down his cheek. 'Lovely,' he said. 'Thanks, Princess.' He stretched luxuriously. 'Did I ever tell you about that girl in Santiago?'

'I don't think so. Not in Santiago.' She rinsed the razor under the basin tap and dried it.

'Very good she was,' Willie said reminiscently. ' 'Ighly passionate. But she wasn't interested 'cept when I was bristly. Didn't like a beard, but couldn't stand a clean shave. It 'ad to be bristles.'

'Kinky. But harmless.' Modesty closed the razor, put it on a small shelf, and stretched out on the other bunk. 'What happened, Willie?'

'Well, nothing much. I wasn't there long. And anyway, it's 'ard just to stay bristly. She married a barber. He used to run the 'air-clippers over his chin. That way he was all set, twenty-four hours a day. When I saw 'im again two years later he looked just about ready to go up with the blind.'

Modesty smiled. Picking up a crumpled packet of cigarettes she lit two and passed one across to him. 'It's a pity about Gabriel cutting in front of us,' she said. 'That's a lot of diamonds you brought back, Willie.'

'Can't win all the time. If we'd 'eard Gabriel was after them we might've done a deal on distribution.'

'Too late now.' She exhaled thoughtfully. 'We come out with nothing. If we're lucky.'

He took the cue smoothly and put a tinge of unease into his voice. 'You reckon he might sign us off?'

'There's a chance he's thinking that way. But I don't see how he can make contact in Istanbul without me. He might hold you until that's done.'

'And after?'

'He wouldn't be fool enough to let me go and put you down, Willie. I could talk.'

'Seems a fair chance, then.'

'As long as we don't make trouble. Remember that. We just sweat it out.'

'Right.' Willie stretched and relaxed. After half a minute he said: 'What 'appened about that mare of yours at Benildon that was due to foal?'

SEVENTEEN

IT was eleven o'clock when McWhirter came into Gabriel's cabin. Gabriel sat with fork in hand, eating a large plate of salad, fruit, and nuts. A glass of milk stood near the plate. Mrs. Fothergill lolled on a cushioned seat along one wall, frowning over a crossword puzzle in a magazine. Three words only had been filled in, in a crude childish hand.

'They've been talking,' McWhirter said. 'It's all on tape. For what it's worth.'

Gabriel lifted an eyebrow, and McWhirter gestured.

'Och, just desultory stuff.'

'Like what?'

McWhirter closed his eyes. 'Horses; a girl in Santiago; poems of C. S. Lewis; fixing a quartz-iodine headlamp on her car; Bourdon Street, New Orleans, and Al Hirt's jazz combo; some piece o' de Lamerie silver she bought at a Christie sale; Harold Pinter—Blaise thinks he's great, Garvin thinks he's a theatrical conman; some electronic rubbish about a square-wave generator he was trying to explain to her; Otto Klemperer conducting Beethoven's Ninth; a girl in Singapore——'

'All right.' Gabriel put down the fork. 'You mean they didn't talk about what's going to happen to them?'

'Just for a few minutes. They're ninety per cent sure they'll come out wi' their necks, as long as they behave.'

'Good.' Gabriel drank some milk. Mrs. Fothergill scratched her ribs and watched him with a vaguely anxious expression.

'Seems funny to let them go,' she said.

'It suits me for them to think that—until after Blaise has handled the contact-business in Istanbul.'

Mrs. Fothergill thought for a while. 'You mean you're not going to let them go?' she asked.

'That's what I mean, Mrs. Fothergill.' Gabriel's mouth

stretched briefly. 'Don't worry. They're going to be your perks.'

He drained the glass and pushed his plate aside. For a moment a gleam of anticipation came into the pale eyes. 'Get Canalejas to being the projector and screen,' he said to McWhirter. 'There's plenty of time to run that new cartoon before we dock.'

A wooden landing-platform, built on oak piles, extended from the point of the island. *Andronicus* stopped two hundred yards out, well clear of the shallows. A twenty-two foot single-screw launch was lowered.

The night air was warm; but to Modesty and Willie, brought up from the stuffy cabin below, it seemed cool and refreshing. They stood by the rail, filling their lungs as the two steel boxes of diamonds were carried carefully down the gangway and taken aboard the launch. They did not speak. Their eyes were on the island, absorbing every detail shown by the full clear moon. In the monastery set on the rising hillock of rock at the western end, a few windows gleamed with pale light.

Still handcuffed they were taken down into the launch. Four men were already aboard. Borg and Mrs. Fothergill followed, and finally McWhirter and Gabriel. The launch moved quietly across the short stretch of sea to the landing-stage. As they climbed out, *Andronicus* was already moving away.

It was half-an-hour's slow walk to the foot of the rugged slope where broad, rough-hewn steps wound up to the monastery. Borg, gun in hand, walked behind the two prisoners, Gabriel and McWhirter following him. Ahead, Mrs. Fothergill and the four men rotated in carrying the two boxes of diamonds, a pair to each box.

Throughout the walk, Modesty studied the monastery and its surroundings, fixing every detail in her mind, and visualising what could be deduced of the interior layout. She knew that Willie was doing the same thing.

They entered by heavy wooden doors which led into a huge kitchen. To one side was a range with two large ovens, each six feet long. In a corner, set into the flagged floor of the kitchen, stood the low stone parapet of a well, surmounted by a wind-lass.

Two monks in dark habits were kneading dough on a massive wooden table. A man with a flat, Mongol face lounged in a chair, nursing a sub-machine gun. Wide stone steps led up from the kitchen with a right-angle turn between two flights. At the top was a broad, stone-flagged gallery running along one side of what appeared to be a large chapel undergoing restoration. Here was all the rubble and confusion of building work.

On the open side of the gallery a long section of the wooden balustrade had been removed. Ladders, shovels, picks and crow-bars were stacked against the wall. On simple wooden rollers, on the edge of the thirty-foot drop to the floor below, stood an enormous metal bucket, waist-high to a tall man and three-quarters filled with rubble. From three steel eyes on the rim, short chains converged on a hook. The hook was secured to the end of a single heavy cable which slanted out and up to a pulley-wheel bolted to a massive beam in the shadowy roof. Below, the floor had been cleared of all chapel furniture. On it were piles of sand and ballast, long balks of timber, sacks of cement, and more tools. From the simplicity of the arrangements Modesty judged that the monks themselves were carrying out the work of restoration.

With Borg following, she and Willie picked their way through the clutter of the gallery. Their eyes roved steadily but without obvious intent, photographing every step of their route. At the end of the gallery the procession passed through an open door, along a series of corridors, and came at last to the large room which was the sanctum.

The two boxes of diamonds were heaved up on to the table. The men were breathing heavily from their work. Mrs. Fothergill was unaffected. She looked hopefully at the side-table of drinks, then at Gabriel as he started to unlock the boxes.

'All right,' Gabriel said. 'One all round. Give her a hand, McWhirter.'

'I'll have——' Willie began, then closed his mouth abruptly.

Gabriel nodded. 'You're learning,' he said, and looked at Modesty. 'How do you like our base?'

'It's as good as the rest of the operation,' she acknowledged. 'What happens to the monks afterwards? They may be silent —but not that silent. They can point to your photograph.'

'They won't be able to,' Gabriel said. 'All gone. *Marie Celeste* stuff. A great mystery. But they're useful for the moment.'

'Is a supply ship likely to call? There must be a regular schedule.'

'Every three months. And we took over four weeks after the last call. We'll be gone before the next.'

'Then you've no problems. Except distribution. When do we talk about that?'

'When I'm ready.' He looked at Borg. 'Put them away. Separate cells. Blankets and a mattress apiece, a pail and a basin. Three meals a day. Two hours exercise. A guard in the corridor twenty-four hours a day.'

Modesty stared at him, letting a blend of anger and unease creep into her eyes. 'What the hell do you think we're likely to try?' she asked.

Gabriel opened the two boxes, pulled away the layers of padding, and gazed down at the diamonds.

'You're not likely to try anything,' he said absently. 'I've just made sure of that.'

The cells were at each end of a narrow corridor on the uppermost floor. A winding staircase gave access to the corridor from the floor below. Borg and a thin Spaniard with a scarred face and red-rimmed eyes brought the prisoners up. There was a big metal key in the door of one cell. The door stood ajar and was of solid wood with a small metal grille; it was old, but not as old as the monastery by a full century. Modesty guessed that at some time in its long history the monastery had been taken over for use as a fortress.

Borg pushed the door wide. A straw mattress and two blankets had been dumped on the floor. In one corner stood a pail and a metal bowl. A low-wattage bulb hung from a flex. High in the far wall was a small barred window, unglazed.

Willie looked at Modesty. 'When do you reckon we eat?' he said.

'In half-an-hour, I hope.'

'Good.'

Borg growled: 'You eat tomorrow.' He gave Willie a push that sent him stumbling into the cell. The door closed and the key turned.

The other cell lay thirty paces away at the other end of the corridor. It was exactly the same, except that against the inner wall a broad, sloping chimney-breast jutted out, making the cell a little smaller.

'Gabriel didn't tell you to leave the 'cuffs on,' Modesty said.

Borg shrugged without humour. 'He did not say to take them off.'

She went in, and heard the solid snick of the lock behind her. As she looked round, the Spaniard's face appeared at the grille and she heard Borg's footsteps fading down the winding steps. Kneeling, she began to arrange the mattress and blankets.

Willie Garvin lay with eyes closed for exactly thirty minutes—the half-hour cue Modesty had given him.

He got up quietly and went to the door. Looking obliquely through the grille, he could see the Spanish guard sitting on a chair halfway along the corridor, reading a grubby paperback book in the light of the single lamp that hung above.

Willie lifted his right foot and rested it across his knee. Carefully he picked at the edge of the thin rubber seal which covered the welt. The adhesion was light, and in a few seconds he had peeled the edge clear all round. Inserting his thumb, he pulled off the whole of the rubber covering which enclosed the heel and sole. Still watching the guard, he slipped his thumb-nail into a small screw-head countersunk into the tip of the sole, and turned. The screw moved easily. Seconds later he drew out a slim metal probe with a curiously curved tip.

In the other cell, Modesty clinked her handcuffs softly against the grille. The Spaniard got up and walked towards her. He stood looking at her through the bars of the grille.

'Is there anything to drink?' she said. 'Water?'

'Tomorrow.' He turned away.

'Wait. I'm so hot.'

The broad significance of the word held the Spaniard. He came back to the grille. Now there was a hint of appetite growing in the red-rimmed eyes. His name was Canalejas. His photograph was on her old files, and she knew his reputation well. Before joining Gabriel he had been a hireling of the O.A.S. He had an original talent in the art of interrogation by torture. Working on women pleased him best. She knew of two women who had survived his handling—because they broke early. Even so, if those who died could have seen those who survived they would probably have counted themselves the more fortunate.

'What you hot for?' he said.

'The chimney from the kitchen passes through this cell. It's like an oven. And I can't even get my sweater off.'

He waved her back from the door, and she obeyed. The key turned in the lock and he came in, a heavy single-edged hunting-knife in his hand.

'Pull it up in front,' he said.

She worked the clinging sweater up awkwardly until it was rucked above the slope of her breasts.

'Turn round.'

She obeyed, and felt his hand take the back of the sweater and work it over her head. The fingers of her right hand sought the kongo clamped under her left armpit; only minutes ago she had eased the little weapon out from within the firmly bound chignon which hung at the nape of her neck.

'Turn round.'

She faced him, the bunched sweater drawn tightly across her chest, her shoulders bare. He reached out with his free hand to grip the sweater and pull it down her arms. She felt his finger grope for the edge of her bra, so that it would be ripped away when he jerked. The man was grinning now, and in reaching forward he brought his knife-hand within two feet of her body.

She struck sideways with the kongo, and the jutting hardwood knob drove into the dorsum of his hand. Helpless fingers flew open under the reaction of the savaged nerves, and the knife arced through the air to land on the mattress.

Her feet were already placed for perfect balance as she drove a knee into his groin. He gave a muted, gasping shriek, and doubled up in slow motion, like a bow being bent. With both hands, the left on top of the gripped kongo for extra power, she struck down with all her strength, coldly and deliberately aiming for the killer-point on the temple.

Willie Garvin opened the second 'cuff and withdrew the probe. He stripped off the rubber over-sole of his other boot, got up from the mattress and went to the door. Looking out, he saw that the guard had gone from his chair.

Willie frowned and crouched by the key-hole. This wasn't the probe he would have chosen for the ancient mortice lock, but it was a good all-round instrument. It would do. Gently he twisted it, feeling for the wards. Something moved against the probe from outside, and he froze. The key was being eased into the lock.

Withdrawing the probe he twisted away to stand with his back to the wall beside the door. The key turned and the door opened two inches.

'Don't do anything sudden, Willie,' Modesty's voice said quietly. 'It's me.'

As he moved away from the wall she came in. The sweater was still rucked across her chest. She held out her hands and he began to work with the probe on one of the 'cuffs.

'What about Canalejas?' he said after a few moments.

'I put him down.'

He nodded. 'Good. He'd lived too long.' The first 'cuff sprang open and Willie began on the second. 'What about the rest of 'em, Princess? If we 'ave to play, do we play for sleeps or for keeps?'

'For keeps. The same way they play, Willie.'

He sprang the lock of the second 'cuff. She pulled the sweater down her arms and dropped it to the floor. Willie took off his wind-cheater, threw it on the mattress, then stripped off his dark shirt. He turned his back to her and waited. In the dim light, the skin of his back had a strangely lifeless appearance. Modesty put her fingertips on his shoulders, feeling for the wafer-thin edge of the plastic. She picked the edge free with her nails, gripped it, then suddenly jerked downwards.

There was a sound like plaster being ripped from flesh Willie Garvin winced briefly, then turned round. She was holding a thing of foam rubber with an outer skin of smooth, flesh-coloured plastic. The foam rubber swelled from a fine edge to an inch thickness in the middle. It had been adhered, by the thin plastic edge, to the whole of his back from shoulders to base of spine; and it was so skilfully moulded that the contours were perfect.

Modesty laid the false back down on the mattress. Willie picked up his shirt, drew it vigorously to and fro across his back as if using a towel, and worked his shoulders in relief.

'Was it very bad in the bell with this on?' she said.

'Working was a bit awkward. What scared me, I was sweating like a bull an' wondering if it might break the adhesion.'

He knelt beside her. The foam rubber was in two layers. Together they peeled off the thinner, inside layer. Beneath were recesses cut in the thicker layer, and squeezed into these recesses were several objects, carefully padded. Willie began to ease them out of their beds.

Beside him, Modesty took off her bra and laid it on the mattress. It was of double-thickness elasticised material with a stiffened edging. She ripped away the inner lining. Inside one of the cups, at the base, so that the breast would rest on top and hide any protuberance, lay a coil of very fine black wire and a slender three-inch plastic cylinder, slightly curved, holding anaesthetic nostril-plugs. In the other cup was a large black deflated balloon and another cylinder, a little larger, with a pointed nozzle. She laid the objects down, fastened her bra in place, and put on the sweater.

Willie had laid out the items from the false back. There were two knife-blades, precisely the same as the blades of his throwing-knives, but with long threaded tangs; these screwed into the bases of two thin black hilts of rough-dimpled bone. There were two flat plastic rectangles, each five inches long by three wide and only a quarter of an inch thick; a miniature voltmeter no larger than a lady's watch; two pencil torches; a coil of twin cable with a plug at each end; a small flat screwdriver; a battery; and two eight-inch lengths of what appeared to be stainless steel tubing, the first slender and with a cap at one end, the second as thick as a man's thumb.

He passed the two lengths of tubing to Modesty, and she slipped them into long pockets running down the seam of each thigh.

Willie put on his shirt and jacket, assembled the knife-blades and hilts, and slid the two knives into the empty sheaths inside the left breast of the jacket. He picked up the flat plastic boxes and clipped them together by the spigots and sockets on the two faces. The assembly was a miniature transmitter.

Modesty had worked the neck of the balloon over the nozzle of the cylinder. She said, 'Willie,' and moved to the barred window. He followed her and laid the transmitter on the sill. Putting his arms round her thighs from behind, he lifted her up. She slipped both hands through the bars, held the neck of the balloon firmly in place on the nozzle, and pressed her thumbnail against the base of the cylinder.

There came a hiss of compressed gas, and the balloon in-flated. She worked the neck of it off the nozzle and let the empty cylinder drop on the sill. Her fingers twisted the neck of the balloon and tied it in a knot. She picked up one end of the fine coil of wire, secured it to the knotted neck, then let the balloon go. It rose gently in the still air, the thin wire running out between her fingers. When only three feet were left, she twisted the wire tightly round a bar. The balloon was out of sight now, floating thirty feet above the roof of the monastery and a good two hundred feet above sea-level. She secured the bared end of the wire to an aerial terminal on the transmitter, and said: 'Right.'

Willie lowered her to the floor. 'We won't need the battery,' he said. 'We got power.' He nodded towards the lamp hanging from its flex in the middle of the cell.

They moved back to the mattress. Willie picked up the screwdriver and voltmeter. Modesty took the coil of twin cable. At one end was a tap consisting of two short spikes set in a base of plastic, with a screw-home cap. At the other end was a small two-point plug.

She stood beneath the lamp, legs straddled. Willie ducked,

put his head between her legs from behind, and stood up, lifting her on his shoulders. She separated the wires of the flex serving the lamp, forced the two metal spikes through the insulation, and screwed the cap home.

'Connected,' she said.

Willie plugged his end of the cable into the voltmeter, and took a reading. ''Undred and twenty,' he said. 'Okay.' He unplugged the voltmeter, put it in his pocket, then bent down, lowering her to the floor. Taking the screwdriver he moved to the window and adjusted a tapping on the transmitter. Modesty brought the dangling cable across, and he plugged it into one end of the transmitter. From a small hole in the plastic housing there came the glow of a tiny check-bulb.

'She's going,' Willie said, and glanced out of the window into the darkness. 'With that aerial they ought to pick us up all right.'

EIGHTEEN

MAJOR JAZAIRLI woke from a doze and picked up the phone.

'Yes?' he said in English.

Tarrant stood looking down at the map spread on the table. He had looked at it, with a growing sense of futility, a dozen times in the past hour.

Beside the map was a pad and pencil. Several leaves of the pad lay scattered around. They bore little pencil sketches—a woman's hand holding a cigarette, a dangling foot in a flimsy mule, a bare shoulder and arm. Tarrant knew the sketches were of Modesty Blaise. There were several others, varying slightly, of half the face, just the cheek and the line of the neck from ear to shoulder. It was as if the artist had been groping for a line he could not get to his satisfaction.

Hagan sat straddling a chair, chin resting on folded arms. His eyes stared through the wall to a point a thousand miles away.

Major Jazairli said: 'It is your Embassy calling. Beirut have come through with a bearing.' He was jotting figures on a piece of paper.

Hagan's eyes snapped into focus and he got quietly to his feet. He reminded Tarrant of a time-bomb in which the fuse had suddenly been activated.

'God Almighty,' Hagan said in a low voice. 'They've got the tracer working.'

'Here,' said Major Jazairli without enthusiasm. Hagan snatched the paper and went to the map. Muttering figures, he slid the ruler into place and drew a line from Beirut almost due west. The phone rang again. This time, after the first word, the major spoke in Arabic. Hagan stood over him as he wrote down a new bearing.

'Egyptian Airforce Headquarters,' said the major, and handed the paper to Hagan. The second bearing ran a few

197

degrees west of north from Port Said, and intersected with the first at a point some eighty miles south-west of Cyprus.

'How the devil can they have got the tracer rigged at sea?' Tarrant said.

'Not at sea.' Hagan peered at the map. 'There's a small island here. Kalithos.' He looked up. 'Do you know anything about it?'

'I've never heard of it. We can check with our Embassy.' As Tarrant spoke, the phone rang again.

'It is your Embassy,' Major Jazairli said. 'They have a bearing from Cyprus now.'

'Thank you.' Tarrant took the slip of paper and passed it to Hagan. 'May I speak to them, please?'

Hagan ruled in the third bearing. It checked the other two. On the phone, Tarrant was speaking curtly. 'Yes. Kalithos. I want to know who owns it. Well go and look it up, will you—and quickly.' A long pause of several minutes. Then: 'Yes? I see. Well, that's where our friends are at the moment. No, I don't know what the hell's happening and there's no point in informing London about it yet. Now listen, you'll have to wake up the Ambassador...'

Hagan turned back to the map and began measuring distances. Gabriel was on Kalithos with his prisoners. Kalithos could be reached from the British base in Cyprus within four or five hours by sea. But how long would it take to get the thing organised? He thought of the chain of command involved, and felt a chill of despair.

Tarrant put down the phone. 'Kalithos is a Turkish possession,' he said. 'There's nothing on the island but a three hundred and fifty year old monastery, occupied by a few dozen monks. No airstrip, of course. To get a boat-load of police or troops there, we'd first have to get permission from the Turkish Government. No doubt they'll take action themselves on our behalf when they know the score. Our Ambassador is being got out of bed to deal with that now. With any luck, something might get done in about twenty-four hours.'

'That's no bloody good.' Hagan's face was dark with anger. 'Modesty and Willie have got the tracer going, so they must have started to bust out. They can't just sit and wait. And they'll never make it alone. Goddam it, twenty-four hours will be too late!'

'Now might be too late,' Tarrant said bleakly. 'But let's be optimistic and assume that somehow they can manage to stay alive for a few hours. How can we get help to them?'

'Could Abu-Tahir get Nasser to do something? Send a ship? They haven't refused him anything yet.'

Tarrant looked out over the lights of the harbour. 'There's no government that will put a military or police force on Kalithos without going through diplomatic channels——' he began, then broke off and turned to Hagan with wide, startled eyes. 'I'm wrong, by God,' he said softly. 'There's one government that won't give a damn.'

Hagan stared, uncomprehending, then light flared suddenly in his eyes. He said: 'What about transport?'

'That could be leased, I think. It depends what's available. But I saw something when I was arranging for the D.F. station here...' Tarrant's voice trailed away. He looked at Hagan speculatively for several moments, a hint of excitement creeping into his gaze, then turned to Major Jazairli. 'Would you be so kind as to get the Nile Hilton Hotel for me, please?' he said politely.

McWhirter pushed the cards aside and gathered in the kitty.

'I've observed,' he said severely, 'that the feminine mind has little or no understanding o' mathematical odds. Mrs. Fothergill, dear lady, the odds against drawing one card to make a flush are a little over four to one against. On the other hand, it's only five to two against improving a pair by drawing three cards, d'ye see?'

'I reckon it's cheating when you play like that,' Mrs. Fothergill said sullenly. 'Taking an advantage.'

McWhirter looked up from counting his winnings and beamed at her. 'I'd never cheat a seductive wee bit o' crackling like you,' he said.

Borg gave a grunting laugh. He was refixing one end of a two-foot length of piano wire to a wooden toggle which had come loose.

'Don't you bloody needle me, McWhirter,' Mrs. Fothergill said, a dull red flush touching her cheeks.

'Needle you?' McWhirter looked shocked.

'Yes. You were being sarcastic. I can tell.'

The fourth player lit a cigarette. He was an Englishman called Rudson, with a hard, dissolute face, a bored manner and a public school accent overlaid by a faint American twang. He had once spent two years on the West Coast as hatchet-man for a Sicilian gang-boss. Like Borg, he was an unemotional killer.

'No violence,' he said. 'The angel Gabriel wouldn't like it, Mrs. F. You should close your ears to McWhirter. He's one of those nasty little bastards who can't help needling people.'

'It's true,' McWhirter acknowledged happily. He got up. 'I'm for bed. It's past two. Who's baby-sitting wi' those diamonds?'

'Soulter, Guiseppe and Babur,' said Borg. 'Mrs. Fothergill, Croker and Rudson take over at three.'

The woman was looking at Borg dourly as he jerked the toggles so that the piano wire thrummed. 'Don't you get ideas about Blaise and Garvin,' she said. 'They're mine, Borg. Gabriel said so.'

Borg shrugged indifferently.

'D'ye know,' said McWhirter, 'I'm thinkin' it would be a nice change if we had a hanging wi' one of them. Och, you're a pleasure to watch, dear Mrs. Fothergill, an' so's Borg here wi' his cheese-cutter.' He stretched and yawned. 'But I've never yet seen a hanging. There'd surely be a very fine atmosphere o' ceremonial about it, d'ye no' think?'

Mrs. Fothergill frowned doubtfully.

'I don't know about that,' she said at last. 'It's not...' she groped for the word, 'not *personal* enough for my liking, really.'

Modesty drew out the belt from the loops of her slacks, reversed it, and fastened it on again. Now, on the outside of the belt, there was a loop of soft leather which would hold a gun.

Willie went down on one knee and tapped her leg. One after

the other she put her booted feet up on his knee so that he could strip off the thin waterproof covering adhered over the soles and heels.

He straightened up and looked a query at her.

'We'll make a soft-shoe job of it if we can,' she said. 'Straight for the diamonds. Get them down to that launch at the point, and away. I don't know exactly where we are, but it's not too far south of Cyprus.'

Willie nodded, accepting her statement. This was a gift she had, a compass in her head. Put her blindfold in a closed car and drive her two hundred miles by a roundabout route; without effort she would know due north, could indicate the direction of the starting-point, and give a good estimate of the crow's-flight distance between.

'It'll mean a double-trip,' he said. 'Those diamonds weigh a bit, Princess, and it's a long way to the point.'

'Yes. But I'd say we'll have a full hour before the relief guard takes over here and finds we're gone. Maybe more.' Her eyes were distant as she calculated. 'By then we ought to be well on the last lap of the second trip. It should work, Willie, as long as we keep the sound turned down on this first bit.'

'Right.'

They went silently out into the corridor and down a short, winding flight of stone steps. A broad, dark passage stretched away into total blackness. There was no sound. It seemed that these upper floors were unoccupied; Gabriel's men and the monks slept on the ground and first floors, and there the guards patrolled.

'We'll move to the western end on this floor,' she whispered. 'Better than trying to move where they're thick on the ground.'

She held one of the pencil torches and used it sparingly as they walked along the passage, keeping it partly hooded by her hand. Willie walked a pace behind and slightly to one side. In his right hand he held a knife, the blade between thumb and two fingers.

There were no steps at the western end of the monastery, and they had to turn back to a flight leading down off the middle of the long passage. Three minutes later they stood at the entrance of a long refectory. It was well lit, and at the far end a man sat in a heavy wooden chair with a rifle on his lap. It was a Colt AR-15, a semi-automatic with a five-round box magazine. The man was rubbing the stock with an oily rag and talking softly to the weapon in French, crooning over it, chuckling, whipping it up suddenly to the aim.

Modesty drew Willie back and put her lips close to his ear. 'Got to go through,' she breathed. 'No time to find a way round. Too long-range for a knife?'

Willie spread a hand, palm down, and waggled it in a gesture of doubt. The man was a good ninety feet away. Modesty nodded and drew out the steel tube from her right thigh-pocket. He took it and uncapped the end. Within lay four thin steel rods, less than a quarter of an inch thick. One rod tapered to a needle-point, and all were tapped and threaded. He began to screw them tightly together in one length

The other, thicker length of tubing was in Modesty's hands now. Suddenly it extended telescopically, sections sliding out in both directions, making a four-foot length, thick in the middle and tapering towards each end. The machining was perfect, and in the sliding sections which locked on the overlap there was no whisper of play.

This was the short steel bow which Tarrant had seen in Willie Garvin's combat room.

Bowyers had said it could not be made. They had spoken of mass and energy, of hysteresis loss, of tensile and compressive stresses. Willie had made the bow by trial and error. The eighth model had worked.

Modesty drew out a long piece of gut, looped at each end, which lay piped in the hem of her sweater. Slipping one loop in the nock of the lower limb, she braced the bow against her foot and slid her hand up until the other loop slid into the upper nock.

Willie had completed screwing the sections of the arrow together. From the double-thickness of her soft leather belt she drew out three plastic flights with feathered edges. The butt-section of the arrow was hollowed out for two inches and bore three fine slits into which the flights could be securely wedged.

Willie worked them carefully into place and checked them for symmetry. The whole process of preparing the bow and the shaft had taken just over thirty seconds.

At the far end of the long refectory the man with the Colt rifle was still polishing it, caressing it as a man might fondle a woman. Modesty took up her position, six feet from the open door. She nocked the arrow. Using the secondary draw, with second and third fingers on the string, she drew and sighted carefully.

There came the thrum of the bowstring, the brief hiss of the arrow in flight, and a faint sound of impact. The man in the chair jerked slightly. Modesty lowered the bow. The man was in the same position as before, hands on the rifle as it rested across his lap, head bowed a little. The only difference was that his hands had stopped moving, and that now the small white patch of the flights showed against the darkness of his shirt. Modesty unbraced the bow, collapsed it, and slid it back into the pocket down the seam of her slacks.

Together they walked silently to the far end of the refectory. The arrow had entered just below the breastbone and an inch off-centre. It had driven right through the body and into the solid wooden back of the chair. Willie lifted the semi-automatic from the dead man's lap and glanced at Modesty. She shook her head, and said: 'Too clumsy. See if he's got a hand-gun.'

There was no other gun on the man. Willie gripped the butt of the shaft, put his foot up against the man's chest, and with an effort pulled the arrow free. He wiped it clean on the dead man's shirt, unscrewed the sections and passed them to Modesty.

Beyond the refectory were three small rooms with connecting doors. A tall window opened from the third room on to a long cloister. They moved out into the open. Fifty paces away, the narrow walk swelled into a half-moon terrace with a low stone balustrade. Above the terrace was a long balcony where a bar of light shone from carelessly curtained windows.

'That'll be the room where they put the diamonds,' Modesty said in a whisper. 'I'll take the window, you take the door, Willie. How long will you need to get there?'

He unreeled his mental film of steps and corridors. 'Four minutes.'

'All right. There'll be two men in the sanctum, maybe more. I'll move first to draw them, and I'll make enough noise for you to hear. Come in fast.'

He touched her shoulder in acknowledgment and turned back into the monastery. Modesty began to move along the cloister at a run, her rubber-soled boots making barely a sound.

Ahead, twenty paces away, a man strolled out of a narrow archway. He was in profile to her, moving towards the balustrade, hands in pockets, a cigarette hanging from his lips. On his hip was a Luger in a webbing holster. He caught a whisper of sound, and turned. His reaction marked him as an experienced professional; there was no moment of shock, only a quick narrowing of the eyes. The smooth upward lift of his hand was barely interrupted by the action of drawing the Luger.

She was five paces away and going very fast as the eight-inch barrel cleared the holster. Power exploded through her muscles and she jumped, her legs coming up so that she hurtled at him feet-first, body parallel with the ground. Her crossed feet locked round his neck in the instant that he started to duck, and her extended body twisted fiercely in the air, arms spread to give added torque to her legs.

The man spun sideways in a cartwheel above the low balustrade, his neck the hub of the spin. She dropped face-down towards the coping, forearms spread flat to break the fall, and felt the abrupt cessation of weight-resistance as his somersaulting body broke clear of her feet and plunged down. There came a soft thud from below, and the faint clatter of the gun sliding over rock.

She lay full-length along the coping, gripping the edges of it, her head turned to look down. The drop was almost sheer for the first twenty feet, then sloped outwards in a bulge and fell again. She saw the limp body rolling and slithering towards the curve of the bulge; it disappeared beyond, into the darkness, and she heard no other sound.

The clock in her head told her that she had lost ten seconds.

Quickly she moved on and began to climb the wall to one side of the balcony. The stones were large and rough-hewn; much of the ancient mortar had crumbled, and there were sufficient finger and toe-holds to make an easy climb.

She reached the side rail of the balcony, transferred one hand to it, then the other. As she hung there, preparing to get one foot up on the edge of the thick oak flooring, the curtain was drawn back. A man pushed open the windows and came out. He was dark-skinned, with a thin moustache curving down in a semi-circle to below the ends of his mouth. He yawned and stared blearily out to sea.

Modesty let go with one hand and slid it into her trouser pocket. The man turned his head. Their eyes met at a distance of five feet, through the iron railings round the balcony. She saw the shock in his face. Her hand came up, thumbing the cap off the lipstick-holder. She pushed the button up the curving groove and heard the sudden violent hiss of gas.

The man's shout emerged as a strangled choke and he reeled back blindly, hands clutching at streaming eyes. A pistol swung at the end of a lanyard looped round his shoulder. As Modesty came over the rail in a smooth vault he began to grope for the pistol. One long stride and her foot swung hard, the toe driving squarely into the man's solar plexus. He dropped like a rag doll, and she jumped across him, heading for the window.

A fraction of a second earlier there had been a startled exclamation and the scuffling of a chair from within the sanctum at the dark-skinned man's muffled cry. Enough to bring Willie in.

The kongo was in her hand as she came through the window, swerving to one side as she made a snapshot appreciation of the scene. A man with a stubble of beard was facing her, a Sterling sub-machine gun in his hands. Beyond and to his right, another man, wearing a brown beret, lay on the floor with the black hilt of a knife jutting from the side of his neck. Across the room Willie Garvin stood poised in the open doorway, slightly crouched, his shoulder pointing towards her in the follow-through of a throw. Both his hands were empty now.

The man with the Sterling stared blindly past her. She saw the barrel of the gun dropping slowly, saw him sway forward like a tree about to topple. She moved quickly and caught the gun. His body thudded against her and crumpled to the floor. A black knife-hilt rose from a spreading red stain on the back of his jacket.

For a long moment there was no movement. Modesty stood holding the gun, listening. By the door Willie was still half-crouched, head cocked, ears straining. He relaxed at last and let out his breath. Modesty laid the Sterling down on the floor and straightened up.

'I had a little trouble,' she whispered, jerking her head towards the window. 'There's one out there. But that lipstick gas-gun works fine, Willie.'

'It all came out right,' he said, and collected the knife from the man's throat. 'They were both starting for the window when I came in. It was a pushover.' He jerked the other knife free, wiped them both on the bearded man's jacket, sheathed them, and went out on to the balcony.

Modesty picked up the gun which lay beside the man in the brown beret. It was a Colt Python with a four-inch barrel, loading .38 Special or .357 Magnum. She put on the safety-catch, checked that all cylinders were loaded, and slipped the gun into the leather-loop holster on her belt.

Willie came through the window carrying the dark-skinned man, and dumped the unconscious body on the floor. 'This one's alive,' he said, and looked a question at her.

'I know.' She gave a little shrug. 'Let him keep his luck, Willie. The tabs will hold him.' She took out the small phial of anaesthetic tabs, and slipped one into each of the man's nostrils.

The two long metal boxes of diamonds stood on Gabriel's desk. Willie took the handle of one and tested the weight. 'It's the thick end of a hundredweight,' he said. 'But I could manage one on me own all right.'

'I couldn't manage the other. Not for the best part of two miles. We'll make the double trip, Willie—get one box as near the launch as we can manage in twenty minutes; dump it and come back for the other. Say fifty minutes. With luck we'll at least have them both close to home before the relief guards start coming on and the balloon goes up.'

'Okay. S'pose I 'ump this one till we're clear of the monastery, an' you cover me?'

'Fine.' She drew out the Colt. Willie heaved the box on to his shoulder and followed her to the door. They moved along the broad passage, then through a maze of narrower corridors which they had traversed before as prisoners.

A single lamp burned on the long flagged gallery where restoration and building was in progress. The empty chapel below was a great well of darkness. Carefully they picked their way through scattered rubble and the clutter of building implements. Modesty halted by the massive bucket which stood on rollers where the balustrade had been removed.

'There'll be a guard in the kitchen, Willie,' she whispered. 'When we're nearly there, put down the box and take him your way. I don't want to use the gun, not while there's any chance of keeping this soft-shoe.'

'Right.'

She began to turn, then froze, staring past Willie.

'Well,' said Mrs. Fothergill.

The light gleamed on her bright fuzz of hair. She stood six paces away, thumbs hooked in the belt of her crumpled trousers. The small eyes were bright with an almost feverish excitement, and the lower lip hung slack. She carried no gun.

Willie turned slowly, the box on his shoulder. He swore with silent savagery at himself for having it on the wrong shoulder. Only his left arm was free, and the knives were sheathed under the left breast of the wind-cheater. A quick draw was impossible.

Mrs. Fothergill was looking at Modesty. 'One shot and you're cooked, ducky,' she said with a grin. 'We won't be alone any longer. And don't move. I've got a shout like a bloody ringmaster.'

Slowly Modesty lowered the gun. 'But you're not shouting,' she said in a low voice. 'What do you want?'

Mrs. Fothergill ran the tip of her tongue round wet lips. Her eyes were hot. 'You,' she said suddenly, still grinning. 'You get a chance this way. And I don't get bawled out by Gabriel.'

Modesty touched Willie's arm, keeping her eyes on Mrs. Fothergill. 'Go ahead to the kitchen,' she said.

The woman nodded. 'You do that sonnyboy. I'll be nicely warmed up by the time you get back. Say five minutes, so I can take it nice and slow.' She nodded towards the door fifty paces away at the end of the gallery. 'You show your face there before I'm through, and I'll shout this heap of stones down.'

Willie stood still.

Modesty said: 'Go on.' There was a lash of sharpness in her voice. 'Clean up in the kitchen, Willie.'

He moved away down the long gallery and vanished through the door. Modesty bent, watching Mrs. Fothergill, and sent the gun skidding away along the floor into a heap of rubble.

'That's my baby,' Mrs. Fothergill said approvingly, and moved forward lightly on the balls of her plimsoled feet.

Modesty gripped the kongo. Her feet were apart, knees slightly bent, hands raised to breast-height. She ignored a few preliminary feints, and waited. Against the woman's extra weight and strength it was best to go for counters rather than to attack.

Mrs. Fothergill came into distance with the quick, shuffling footwork of a boxer, then suddenly swung round and lashed out sideways with one foot. It was fast, frighteningly fast. Modesty's side-step barely let the foot carry past her ribs; she darted in and struck with the kongo, aiming for the side of the neck. Her wrist jarred savagely against the hard calloused edge of a swinging hand, and the shock tingled through her arm to the shoulder as she swung away.

The kongo fell, and Modesty backed with small shuffling steps, working the numbed fingers to restore life to them. Mrs. Fothergill followed up swiftly, striking again with a spade-like hand. Modesty ducked, twisted, and caught the wrist, jerking to add momentum to the heavy body. She fell back, her foot shooting up for a stomach-throw, but Mrs. Fothergill went with the jerk, not resisting but throwing herself forward in a high somersault above the reach of Modesty's foot. It was a superbly quick reaction, and a remarkable piece of gymnastic skill.

The grip on the wrist was broken. Mrs. Fothergill landed on her feet and spun round. As she did so, Modesty rolled sideways and came upright. Mrs. Fothergill was grinning and panting, but Modesty knew that the quick breathing was not from exertion. The heavy-jowled face was alight with lust.

Again the woman came in, this time stabbing for the throat with rigid fingers. Modesty swayed and clamped the arm; turned for a throw; realised in a split-second that the weight-and-balance ratio were wrong; jerked a heel backwards against Mrs. Fothergill's knee as a thick arm started to close about her throat, and lunged forward to break clear.

The fight was like a fencing bout. There was no prolonged grappling, only sudden engagements, swift flurries of move and countermove, then a breaking of contact.

Three minutes passed before Modesty tried the drop-kick. It was a dangerous move and a mainly theatrical one, unless performed very very fast indeed. But Modesty knew she had the necessary speed. She also knew that this was the best chance of ending the fight quickly. Mrs. Fothergill had her back to the open section of the balustrade. It was not the best position for drop-kicking her over the edge, for the great metal bucket of rubble was directly behind her. But it would have to do. Any manoeuvring might telegraph the move.

For the first time Modesty went forward. Two quick, short paces and then the jump. On the second pace her right foot came down on the fallen kongo, and the ankle turned as she jumped. Height and distance were halved, and she landed heavily on her back. Her head hit the ground, and the blow was only partly cushioned by her club of hair. Dazedly she heard Mrs. Fothergill chuckle. Instinct tensed her stomach-muscles an instant before the woman dropped on her with both knees.

Her breath hissed out in a tortured wheeze, and she felt strength drain from her body like water running from a bath. Mrs. Fothergill knelt astride her, shuffling forward until her full weight was on the chest. She said: 'Hard luck, ducky. That just might have worked.' Her hands probed for Modesty's throat.

Darkness speckled with bright pinpoints of light swirled

about Modesty's vision. Deep within her, in the dark sealed cave where all emotions of fear were confined, panic hammered wildly for release. But the seals held. With a gigantic effort of will she gathered strength in her neck, holding the chin down hard to block the iron fingers forcing their way to her larynx.

Her right arm swept across the floor, groping for the kongo, a brick, anything to strike with. She felt rough hemp. Rope. Thick rope in a loose coil. Her mind pictured the rope running out and up to the pulley-wheel above the chapel, then slanting back to the great metal bucket. She could feel the side of the bucket against the soles of her boots.

'Chin up, ducky,' said Mrs. Fothergill with a half-hysterical giggle of ecstasy.

Modesty's hand gripped the rope, shook it to test the slack. There was little strength in her arm. Dredging her reserves, she swung her arm up and round. A coil of the rope settled in a half-hitch about Mrs. Fothergill's neck; Modesty jerked hard and the coil tightened.

Mrs. Fothergill laughed deep in her throat. She hunched her shoulders, and the great sinews of her neck hardened, like the neck of a wrestler making a bridge. Her eyes turned to glance along the gallery. There was no sign of Willie Garvin's return yet, and the rope about her neck was harmless. With infinite sensual pleasure she worked her thumbs deeper under Modesty's chin. They touched the rippled cartilage of the larynx, and Mrs. Fothergill began to breathe still more quickly.

Modesty felt the slowly increasing pressure. Her feet were flat against the side of the bucket behind Mrs. Fothergill, her knees bent. She relaxed, letting the woman have her throat, mind closed to everything but the fierce mental concentration on building up energy in her thigh muscles. With every atom of power left to her, she thrust hard with her feet.

The bucket moved on the rollers, and all that happened in the next two or three seconds appeared to her as if in a slow-motion sequence.

She felt the rope twitch free of her feeble grasp, and saw Mrs. Fothergill's head jerk as if struck by a hammer. The hands were torn from her neck. The weight came off her body. There was a faint rumble from the pulley-wheel high above.

Mrs. Fothergill was soaring up, swinging out over the void on the end of the rope, arms and legs jerking like the limbs of a puppet. The half-hitch around her neck held fast under her own weight. Modesty saw a foreshortened view—the soles of Mrs. Fothergill's plimsolls, and between them the twisted head. The figure seemed to shrink as it was whisked upwards. There came a crunch as Mrs. Fothergill's head smashed against the pulley-wheel; then silence. The woman hung limp, her neck twisted at right-angles to her shoulders.

Something nagged in a remote corner of Modesty's mind. The bucket? No noise from its fall? Holding her bruised throat she dragged herself to the edge of the drop and looked down. The bucket stood upright below, buried to half its height in a great mound of sand.

She rested her face sideways on one forearm and let her body go slack, mouth open, sucking in great gulps of air. Later she felt hands touching her, lifting her gently.

Willie Garvin.

She sat up, feeling his arm around her shoulders, and nodded feebly to reassure him. She could not speak yet. Breathing was still an agonising effort. His competent hands felt her throat and neck. He eased her back a little, and one hand moved to her solar plexus, kneading and lifting gently. Her breath began to come a little more easily. He moved behind her, kneeling up straight, put his arms down over her shoulders with fingers curled under her rib-cage, and began to lift and lower in the rhythm of her breathing.

The pain and the effort dwindled. She felt strength creeping back into her muscles, and the muzziness clearing from her head.

After three minutes she spoke, her voice a husky croak. 'All right, Willie love. Help me up.'

She was shaky for a moment, glad of his hands on her shoulders to steady her. She saw the sweat of anxiety on his face, and bewilderment in his eyes.

'What did you do with 'er?' he whispered. She looked up

past his shoulder to the limp shape dangling grotesquely from the pulley-wheel, and he turned to follow her gaze. For five seconds he stared in silence, and when he looked at her again there was an incredulous grin of admiration on his face.

'Well . . .' he said softly. 'It's different, innit?'

NINETEEN

WILLIE collected the second box of diamonds alone. He carried it on his left shoulder, a knife poised in his right hand. When he reached the rubble-strewn gallery Modesty was sitting on a balk of wood, her back against the wall. She had picked up the kongo, and the Colt Python was in her hand. She got up as Willie approached.

'Feeling a bit better?' he whispered.

'A lot.' It was true. Her mind and body were tuned for swift recuperation. 'Did you clean up the kitchen on that first trip?'

'No. I'm sorry, Princess. I'd just got down to the passage an' my ears started to prickle with bad news—so I dumped the box an' came belting back up 'ere like the 'ammers.'

'Your ears weren't fooling,' she said. 'All right. Let's get on with it, Willie.'

She went ahead of him along the gallery and down the steps to the passage which led to the kitchen. The first box of diamonds stood on end against the wall, a few paces from the kitchen door. Willie lowered the second box quietly beside the first.

Through the open door they could see a monk raking out ashes from the big range. Beyond him a man sat on a chair tilted back against the wall, eyes closed, a revolver loosely grasped on his lap. Willie moved into the kitchen quietly, knife in hand. The monk stared. He looked from Willie to the sleeping guard and back again, his eyes resting on the knife. He shook his head in a troubled plea, and his hand moved from side to side making a gesture of negation. Willie winked at him. The monk put his hands together as if in prayer. Willie gave a reluctant nod and moved on. He struck with the butt of the hilt, a sharp blow behind the ear. The guard sagged. Willie eased him to the floor and turned to the monk.

'Just this once,' he whispered severely. 'But he's a very

nasty man. All nasty men 'ere, see? We're trying to get them off your backs.'

The monk nodded vigorously, indicated the guard, made complex signs, and put his palms together in gratitude. Modesty came in, and he looked at her with concern.

'Water?' she said. He hurried to the well in the corner and brought back a full bucket of water which stood beside it. Modesty knelt and plunged her face into the water, scooping handfuls over the back of her neck.

Willie went out and brought in the two long boxes one at a time. He put them on the big table. Modesty was bending over the unconscious guard, slipping anaesthetic tabs into his nostrils. Wisps of wet hair were plastered to her forehead and neck.

' 'Ow you feeling, Princess?'

'As good as new. Just a sore neck, that's all.' She straightened up and looked towards the heavy wooden door which led out of the monastery. 'Let's get moving with the first box.'

Willie went to the door, drew the heavy bolt, and eased the door open. A long oblong of light from the kitchen illumined the smooth-worn surface of the path which led across bare rock to the descending steps of the slope.

The blaring chatter of a sub-machine gun ravaged the silence. Stone chipped from the lintel and a ricochet whined viciously across the kitchen. Willie was flat on the floor, his legs swinging round to kick the door shut. Modesty's shoulder slammed against it and she shot the bolt. The gunfire stopped, and outside a man began to shout.

'Not so good,' Willie said, getting to his feet. 'We'll 'ave our work cut out now without the diamonds.'

'Yes. We'll have to leave them.' She was watching the heavily shuttered window in case of an attempt to break through, but the guard outside was still keeping his distance and shouting.

'Pity,' said Willie. 'Whether we make it or not, Gabriel could be away with the loot in a few hours.'

She nodded, following his unspoken thoughts. Gabriel would find the transmitter and know that his base was blown.

214

Tarrant would be working frantically to get a force here, but who was the authority? It might be a day, two days, before the slow-moving wheels of international liaison brought help. She and Willie might fight their way to the launch and get clear. But Gabriel had enormous resources and a good communications network. In a matter of hours he could call up a fast boat—even a helicopter perhaps.

Faintly she heard a distant but growing clamour throughout the great monastery.

'If Gabriel runs, it won't be with the diamonds,' she said. 'We'll heave them down the well.'

Willie Garvin smiled a happy smile. First Gabriel would have to locate the diamonds, which would be unlikely; then he would need special equipment to bring them up—a diver probably, or large grapnels for dragging.

Together they carried the first box to the well and slid it over the edge. A stream of tiny bubbles broke the surface as the box sank.

A harsh, metallic voice suddenly boomed from high up on the wall. They froze for an instant, then saw the Tannoy speaker there, roughly rigged. There would be others throughout the monastery, no doubt. The voice was Gabriel's, and there was cold murder in it.

'*Attention all men*. Blaise and Garvin are loose. Borg, get your group outside and cover the exits. Santos, Vargel, Rudson—make up three-man search parties and start working through the monastery. All other men to the refectory— NOW!'

Modesty watched the second box vanish into the dark waters. The monk touched her arm. He was pointing to a narrow flight of stairs which wound up from the kitchen behind the angle of the big range. His gestures indicated that this would be a safer way than the main flight.

She nodded and smiled. Putting the Colt Python in her loopholster she picked up the guard's gun. It was a new S&W .41 Magnum, a heavy duty double-action revolver with almost four times the stopping power of a .38 Special. All six cylinders were loaded.

As she moved with Willie across the kitchen, the monk

made a sign of blessing towards them, then went down slowly to his knees and began to pray.

'All you've got, matey,' Willie said soberly, and followed Modesty up the narrow stairs.

Gabriel stood on the edge of the long stone gallery and looked up at Mrs. Fothergill. Light glinted on the bright helmet of her hair as she swayed limply beneath the pulley-wheel.

Gabriel wore slip-on shoes, and a dressing-gown over his pyjamas. McWhirter was beside him, in a striped pyjama jacket and dark worsted trousers.

'God Almighty,' McWhirter muttered in an awed voice. 'An' it's only an hour ago I was saying I'd like to see——' He broke off. 'Och, I must be fey.'

Gabriel turned enormous eyes on him, the pupils tiny black spots in the khaki-coloured irises. 'Find the diamonds,' he said in a voice that cracked. 'Find the diamonds, McWhirter.'

'Aye. They must ha' hidden them somewhere, and they had little enough time.'

From far away on an upper floor there came the sound of shooting.

'*Find the diamonds*,' Gabriel said again, and strode away. At the bottom of some steps beyond the smaller chapel, two men waited with guns.

'What happened?' Gabriel snarled.

One of the men jerked his head upwards and spoke with a strong transatlantic accent. 'Shooting up there. Vargel told us to block this stairway.' He hesitated. 'We checked the cells five minutes ago. Canalejas is dead. And there was a miniature transmitter going, with a bloody great aerial wire hanging from a balloon. We smashed the transmitter, but it must have been pumping out for quite a while.'

Gabriel stared blankly at the man for several seconds, absorbing the shock. Turning, he went on up the stairs, a hand on the Walther in his dressing-gown pocket. He jerked it out as there came a sudden pounding of feet from above, then lowered the gun as two of his men swung round the turn.

They stopped on seeing him. One of them said with a thick accent: 'They come this way, no? You see them, Gabriel?'

'Not this way.' Gabriel shouldered past and they followed him back up the steps. In a long, dimly-lit corridor, three figures lay sprawled on the floor. Two were unmoving. The third lay clutching a shattered knee, breath hissing through his teeth in agony. It was Rudson, the Englishman.

Gabriel bent over the other two. One had a bullet-hole through the neck, exiting through the top of the shattered spinal column. The other lay on his back. He seemed to be balancing a small black oblong on the middle of his chest. It was the hilt of a knife.

Gabriel turned to Rudson, glaring.

'We had them trapped,' Rudson said in a voice shuddering with pain. 'Here. Between us and Vargel's lot. And then ... somehow...' He shook his head dazedly and stiffened in a sudden spasm of agony. 'Ah, Christ, my leg! Do something!'

'All right,' Gabriel said, and shot him through the heart. Lowering the Walther he looked balefully at the two men who stood watching, their eyes wide with shock. 'You want to carry passengers?' he said. 'That transmitter. We've got to get *out*!'

Modesty slid down the low roof which sloped from the monastery window. A flying buttress arched above her, throwing a deep bar of shadow. She eased herself over the stone guttering and hung by her hands. Willie Garvin's fingers gripped her foot and guided it to a toe-hold between the great stones.

Fifteen seconds later they were on the ground, crouched in the shadows. From somewhere on the far side of the monastery came the sound of two shots. The men outside were getting jumpy. There was an exchange of shouting between somebody at a window and the men watching the exits, then silence.

She touched Willie's shoulder and began to wriggle along a shallow gulley in the seamed rock. Fifty yards from the wall of the monastery the ground sloped down. She could see figures in the darkness to her left—men watching a small postern door.

The ground fell away more steeply. They could stand upright now, hidden by the ridge. She touched Willie's arm and made a curving motion with her hand, pointing east. He nodded. The route would bring them out at the foot of the steps which wound up to the monastery.

They moved on steadily, descending the rugged slope. Five minutes later they were on level ground. To the east, the length of the narrow island stretched away from them, bathed in pale moonlight. Scattered boulders and outcrops of rock threw long patches of shadow.

She heard Willie give a faint grunt of satisfaction. The shadows would offer plenty of cover for the journey to the point.

The sound of the shot brought her swinging round by automatic reflex, and in the instant that Willie went down she fired. The crack of the Magnum came so close on the first shot that they sounded almost as one. The man who stood silhouetted on the rounded crest of a hummock thirty paces to their left rear crumpled slowly to the ground. There came a metallic clatter, a clinking and a rattling as something slid erratically down the slope and came to rest within two yards of her feet. It was a rifle, a Lee Enfield .303.

Willie lay on his side, both hands gripping his left thigh close to the groin. She put down the Magnum, snatched up the Lee Enfield, worked the bolt once, and went down on one knee, waiting.

The first rifle she ever handled had been this model, the SMLE. Though the design was decades old, it was still a superb weapon, sturdy and accurate.

A full minute passed. There was no sound of shouting or movement. No sound at all. This did not astonish her, for she knew the oddities of battle. The shots must have been taken for trigger-nerves, as the earlier shots had been.

Willie whispered huskily: 'That ol' monk must be getting through all right.'

She laid down the rifle, took Willie's one remaining knife from its sheath, and slit the leg of his trousers from thigh to ankle. Carefully she cut round the material just below his hands and at the top of the boot, then pulled the whole trouser-leg away. 'Let's see now, Willie love.'

Slowly he released his grip above the wound. The blood flowed fast, but there was no fierce arterial pumping. He tightened his hands again. Modesty felt round the back of his thigh, and sighed inwardly with relief as her fingers found the torn flesh of the exit-hole.

'In and out,' she said. 'Must have missed the bone.'

'Lucky.'

She made a two-inch slit in the right shoulder of his windcheater and took out the sterilised adhesive dressing which formed the padding. When this was in place on the wound, she cut a thick strip from the trouser-leg, twisted it into a rope, and knotted it loosely round his leg above the wound. Taking the eight-inch tube of the collapsed bow from her pocket, she used it to twist the tourniquet tight.

'Hold that a minute, Willie.' She cut two thinner strips of cloth and bound them round the thigh, above and below the tourniquet, to hold the bar firmly in position.

'Thanks, Princess. Let's see 'ow she goes.'

She helped him to his feet, holding him as he gingerly tested his weight on the leg. It gave, and she thrust her shoulder under his arm to support him.

'Sorry. Must 've clobbered a few nerves. I can just about stand, but I can't walk.'

'Never mind. Get your balance while I collect things.'

He steadied himself against a rock. She put the knife back into its sheath, picked up the Magnum and pushed it into the pocket of his wind-cheater. Holding the rifle at its point of balance in her left hand, she moved to Willie's left side and put her free arm round his waist.

'Arm round my shoulders, Willie. All right. Now you set the pace.'

They began to move slowly towards the distant point. Within five minutes her arm was damp with the sweat that poured from him, soaking through his shirt and the light fabric of the wind-cheater. They did not talk. There was nothing to be said; only a slow, hard journey to be made, the mind to be withdrawn, imagination to be starved, and time to be forgotten.

Halfway along the rough track to the point there was a strip of bare ground, a hundred yards wide and stretching right across the narrowing width of the island from beach to beach. It was flat, with no boulders or outcrops to offer cover.

They moved out into the glare of the moonlight. The surface here was soft sand, which slowed their hobbling pace.

'Just this stretch, and then we'll rest,' she panted.

'I'm okay.' Sweat dripped from his chin and she could feel the tremors of pain which racked him.

'I mean *I'll* rest,' she said. 'You're a heavy boy, Willie.'

Something threw up a spurt of sand just ahead and to their right, and a fraction of a second later came the sound of a distant shot.

'Don't rush it,' she said quietly as he struggled to move faster. 'At a thousand yards, they'll have to be lucky.'

Four more shots and a spray of automatic fire came from behind as they stumbled across the last of the sand and into the shelter of the rocks. The shots were well wide, and the automatic fire fell short. She sank to her knees behind a low ridge, easing Willie to the ground as gently as she could. With a grimy handkerchief she wiped the sweat from his face.

To the west, scattered pinpoints of light danced in the darkness as unseen men moved down the slope from the monastery. She picked up the Lee Enfield, took out the magazine, and pressed down on the cartridges to test the tension. There was little give, and she judged that the magazine still held seven rounds at least.

'You'll have to crawl on, Willie,' she said, and clipped the magazine back in place. 'I can hold them on this strip for a good ten minutes. By the time I catch you up you should be pretty close to the launch.'

His face was thoughtful as he calculated the odds. Then he nodded. 'Okay, Princess.'

She watched him go, crawling at a good pace, the wounded leg dragging. The moving lights along the track to the monastery were closer now, and beginning to spread out in a line. Thirty men at least, she thought; Gabriel had built an army for this job. But for a stake of ten million pounds it was worth it. She wondered if Gabriel himself was with the line of men moving towards her.

She lay down behind the low ridge of rock, legs straddled, and brought the rifle up into position. The ridge dipped in a shallow V, giving sufficient traverse and good cover. She checked the backsight, then moistened the foresight with a wet thumb to make it glint. The light was good, with the moon behind her right shoulder. When she closed an eye and looked along the barrel, the sighting was clear.

She lowered the rifle and waited.

TWENTY

IT was five minutes before the first man moved out to cross the bare strip. He was carrying a flashlight and had a sub-machine gun tucked under his arm.

Modesty dropped him with a head-shot before he had taken five paces, and instantly there came the sound of shouting along the line of hunters. The row of lights vanished. There were a few random shots and a burst of automatic fire, but the men were shooting blind and nothing came within yards of her.

She waited, middle finger curled loosely about the trigger, forefinger extended under the bolt-handle, ready to flick it up in a rapid-fire reload. It was not the conventional way of firing, but it was the method by which a contemptible little army of the First War had won an awesome reputation for rapid fire. She had learned it from a grizzled ex-R.S.M. who had married a French girl and settled in Sfax, and it gave her thirty aimed shots a minute.

To the far left a man darted out, running hard to cross the strip and outflank her. She allowed for his speed, and dropped him with a body-shot when he had covered a third of the distance. He went down sprawling and began to scream. Another figure was moving across the soft sand on her far right, crouching and swerving. Her first shot missed; for a moment she thought her second had also missed, but then he plunged face-down into the sand, his legs still trying to run.

She ducked and wriggled to a position fifteen yards along the low ridge, finding good cover in the angle of a rock. Three minutes passed and there came a sudden heavy burst of fire, concentrated on her old position. She heard the thud of bullets flattening against rock, saw spurts of sand along the forward side of the ridge, and heard the long whine of a ricochet.

As the firing stopped abruptly she saw three men on the open strip, strung out over the length of it. The man moving fastest through the soft sand was on her left, and she dropped him first. The figure in the centre hesitated, then turned and raced back to cover. She swung the rifle to the right, sighted and fired. The man flinched, swerving a little, but kept going. She fired again and he went down, rolling. She saw him come to his feet, a hand clutching his shoulder, and start back to safety at a staggering run.

The Lee Enfield was empty. She laid it down quietly and slid back from the ridge. She thought it would be a little while before whoever was in charge of the hunters would be able to arouse any enthusiasm for a fresh attempt. After crawling for a full eighty yards she came to her feet and went on at a crouching run.

On either side the sea was closer now as the island narrowed to an elongated point. Five minutes later she found Willie. He was crawling steadily on, the breath rasping in his throat. Here, the approach to the point was no more than eighty yards across from shore to shore, and the launch lay at the landing jetty the same distance ahead. She could see the top of it over a gentle rise.

Cover was scarce now, with only small scattered rocks and a few low hummocks. Willie was labouring towards a depression in the ground ahead, a shallow basin with an irregularly ridged rim. She thought he was probably too blind with sweat to see it.

'All right, Willie.' She bent to help him to his feet. 'Bear left a bit. We're on the final lap now.'

For the last five minutes a cloud had obscured the moon, and she was grateful for the darkness. Glancing up, she gave the cloud another five minutes. It would be long enough to cloak them as they crossed the final stretch to the launch.

From somewhere behind her there came a soft explosion, and seconds later the whole point was bathed in the brilliance of a Verey light. She went down flat with Willie, and heard him gasp with pain. Two shots sounded, and she heard a bullet spatter on rock nearby. Desperately she heaved Willie forward and down into the shallow basin. Her hand dragged the Magnum from his pocket, and she moved back to the ragged lip of the hollow.

The lights were there again now, as the flare of the Verey light faded. Gabriel's men were still at a distance, in a ragged semi-circle, moving slowly closer. She could see no silhouettes and knew that they must be crawling to take advantage of the scanty cover.

'I'll keep their heads down while you reach the launch and get her started, Willie,' she said. 'Have you got enough juice left to make it alone?'

He did not answer. She turned her head for a moment and saw the flames leaping up from where the launch lay. Willie was propped against the side of the hollow, a little below and to one side of her, watching the flames with quiet disgust on his grimed face.

'Well there's a bloody stroke,' he said hoarsely. 'The cow's on fire from that Verey light.'

Modesty looked to her front again, eyes just above the rim of the basin, head between two jutting pieces of rock. The Magnum was in her hand, but there were only three shots left in it. She drew the Colt Python from her loop-holster and laid it to hand.

The first rush came, four men running hard and firing as they ran. She dropped two, and the other two swerved aside, diving for cover. In the background she could hear Borg's voice shouting orders.

'It's going to cost them, Willie,' she said. 'They've got no cover at all closer than twenty yards.'

'You knocked two off at that?' he said. His breathing had steadied now, and there was professional interest in his voice.

'Yes. This Magnum's a beauty.' She kept her head perfectly still, her eyes roving the area for any shadow that moved. In the distance she saw the beam of a flashlight jogging evenly as a man moved away westward. It grew smaller and more distant as she watched.

'I think Borg's sent back for instructions from Gabriel,' she said in a low voice.

'It's coming expensive for 'em.' Willie eased himself into a more comfortable position and took out his knife. ''Specially now they've lost the launch anyway. I reckon Borg wants to wait for first light.'

'He'll have it by the time his man gets back from asking Gabriel,' she said. 'It's time that tourniquet was loosened, Willie. Can you manage it yourself?'

'Sure.' As he worked slowly at the task, his mind methodically checked over the situation. It seemed likely that as far as he and Modesty were concerned, this was going to be the losing caper at last. The thought did not distress him unduly, though he was glad that the end would be quick when it came. Modesty would so handle it that Borg's men would have to come in blasting on the final rush.

Willie Garvin's long-held view was that in these soft and secure days life was held a lot too sacred, and that the high importance attached to it was no part of natural law. In the natural order of things, life had always been cheap. You came and you went and it didn't much matter. Only cruelty disturbed him.

He let the blood circulate in his leg for two minutes, losing a little, then tightened the tourniquet again.

'Princess,' he said.

'Yes?'

'I think it's time you 'opped it.'

''Opped it where, Willie?' He heard a touch of gentle mockery in her voice.

'The sea. It's only about a forty yard wriggle. You could swim along the coast and find somewhere to lie low. It'll take 'em a good day to comb the island, and ol' Tarrant should be roaring in with a posse before then.'

'Thanks, Willie. But I don't think we'll do it that way.'

'Look,' he persisted, 'you staying won't do me any good in the long run. And we've never gone in for the sink or swim together stuff. It don't make sense. If this was the other way round, you—you wouldn't see me for dust,' he ended lamely.

She turned her head briefly to look down at him, and he saw the trace of a smile on her dirt-smeared face. 'I know, Willie. I know. But just the same, we'll play this Micawber-wise.'

He understood her. It was something they had learned from experience and discussed at leisure; that on a caper you could never tell what was going to turn up. Anything could happen, and it was always worth soldiering on and waiting for it. Great battles had been lost by a sudden and inexplicable weakening of will in one of the protagonists. Gabriel might fall down and break his neck; he might call his men off; a ship might come. And pigs might fly, Willie Garvin thought ruefully.

Fifteen minutes passed, and still there was no move from the men hidden among the rocks.

'How's the leg, Willie?' she asked.

'Fair enough. I feel bloody useless, though, just lying 'ere.'

'You'd be back home if it wasn't for me. Drawing pints.'

'I can think of lots of places I'd be if it wasn't for you, Princess. Some of them under the ground. None of 'em worth a light. It's illegal, anyway.'

'What is?'

'Serving drinks after hours—*'allo*!'

Her head snapped round on his last word, and she saw the man crouched on the far side of the hollow behind her, a Luger in his hand. He was soaked to the armpits from wading through the sea. There was a darting flicker of light, and Willie's knife thudded home in the centre of the man's chest. His legs buckled, and he pitched forward into the shallow basin.

Even as the knife was in flight, Modesty had whipped her head round to face front again, waiting for the rush, but it did not come.

'An individualist,' she said. 'Tried a sneaky one on his own without readying the others.'

'Brought us a Luger, too,' Willie said with pleasure. He dragged himself across the floor of the basin, took the fallen Luger and thumbed the safety-catch on. 'Here, Princess.' She turned and caught it as he tossed the Luger to her. Jerking his knife from the body, he lay back against the slope. 'I'll watch this side in case someone else tries it,' he said.

Half-an-hour later Modesty saw the messenger returning from the monastery. She thought of trying a long shot, but decided against it. Ammunition was too precious.

From behind her, in the east, a thin golden bar of light showed against the horizon.

'Willie,' she said quietly, 'I think Gabriel will have told

them to finish us quickly, and I think they'll try a rush to start with. Come over here and give me the bangers.'

He crawled across the floor of the basin, and she felt his hands working on the heels of her boots. They were deep heels, made of a cast iron fragmentation-casing covered by an eighth of an inch of thick rubber. Each was dove-tailed sideways-on into the base of the boot proper, one with a reverse dove-tail so that the two heels could be locked together. The left heel contained two ounces of compound explosive; the right held a spring-driven striker and detonator-cap, a three-second fuse of channeled gunpowder infiltrating into fulminate of mercury, and a recessed safety pin which swung out from the fore-edge of the heel. A hollow spigot on the dove-tail of the detonator heel fitted into a hole on the other dove-tail to bring the fuse into contact with the main charge.

Willie pushed the safety pin into position, put the grenade in Modesty's hand, and began to force the heels off his own boots.

Five minutes later the rush came. Borg was using a good half of his remaining force. A dozen men rose as one and ran forward, firing. Modesty pulled the safety pin with her teeth, her left arm swung, and she ducked down. The heel-grenade curved through the air in a low arc. It exploded at waist-height and disintegrated in a vicious circle of shrapnel.

Modesty lifted her head. Two men lay sprawled on the ground. Others were getting dazedly to their feet, others running or hobbling frantically back to cover. She fired two carefully aimed shots and brought down two of the running men before a rattle of covering fire made her duck again.

'That'll start a fair amount of cogitation,' Willie said.

'It's all time.' She put down the Magnum and took up the Luger. 'I'll throw a biggish stone next time. There's enough light for them to see, and if they've got any sense they'll go flat. I ought to be able to pick off one or two more. Get your banger ready for the time after that, Willie.'

The attack came, and the stone soaring through the air had its effect. As the halted rush tried to regain momentum she picked off two more men and the rest turned tail. Covering fire from the other side was heavy now but inaccurate. And her position was good on the irregular rim of the basin. Only a lucky or well-aimed shot would be dangerous, and her gun was a lethal deterrent to any man who showed himself long enough to take careful aim.

'Much longer, and Borg will 'ave to stick a gun in their backs to get 'em going,' Willie said. The thought raised another Micawber possibility; that the men themselves would break under the vicious hammering they had taken.

Five minutes later, a sneak attempt to outflank the basin broke up with only one man lost.

'They're liking it less all the time,' Modesty said. She wondered if Borg could keep them going until her remaining few rounds were exhausted. It was a knife-edge question.

A quarter of an hour passed before there came a new mass attack and she threw the second grenade. Three shots as the attackers broke and fled, then silence but for the whimpering groans of a wounded man.

And something else. The drone of a big transport aircraft overhead, flying low along the length of the island. Now that she registered the sound, she knew that she had heard it before, only a few minutes earlier. The noise of the aircraft dwindled and faded. In the growing light a huge shadow swept across the hollow from behind her, and there came the swishing of air from close overhead.

The big military glider was only fifty feet up and losing height fast. It held to the rough track which ran from the point towards the monastery, and she saw it bounce high as the belly touched the ground.

Thirty yards away a man rose from cover, turning to stare after the glider. It was Borg. She hung on her aim for the long range, and shot him through the body.

The glider was skidding along with a splintering and scraping noise. One wing hit a rock and snapped off. The glider spun round and halted.

For seconds nothing happened. Then a door burst open. She saw a man with a long rifle drop to the ground—an Arab, with the skirts of his burnous belted up round his waist. Another followed him, and another, each man vanishing instantly into cover.

'It's Abu-Tahir and his men,' she said, and lowered her head behind the rim, looking at Willie.

He grinned. 'With Mister Hagan on the stick. He said about being in gliders.'

Now there was the rattle of gunfire and confused shouting. The noise was moving away as Gabriel's men tried to break through to the monastery before their new attackers could seal them off on the point.

'Are we okay?' Willie said, propped on an elbow a little below her.

She lifted her head above the rim again. 'Yes. I just killed Borg. They're a rabble now. And there's Paul coming out...' She saw him drop to the ground, then turn to give Tarrant a hand. Two shots smashed into the glider close to them. She saw Paul's arm move, heard the shot, and watched a man half-rise from cover and sprawl limply.

'You were right, he's good,' she said, and slid back down the slope of the basin. Turning on her back beside Willie, she lay with an arm across her eyes.

The gunfire dwindled to a few sporadic shots, and after a little while there came from somewhere in the distance the sound of a voice lifted in a hoarse shout.

'*Modesty!*'

'Our Mister Hagan,' said Willie, and lifted fingers to his lips. 'I'll give 'im a whistle.'

'No. Wait.' Her voice wavered. Turning, she moved closer to him and put her head on his chest. His arm went round her shoulders and he held her while her body shook with silent weeping.

Very content, Willie Garvin lay looking up at the sky. He brought his other hand across and began to pull away the black rubber bands which held her hair bound in a club. He knew that she would want her hair loose now; she would want to feel physically free, to strip off her clothes and cleanse her body in cold, sparkling water.

After two minutes the trembling passed and she lay still. Hagan's voice was still calling, but closer now. With a sigh she knelt up, wiped her face on the sleeve of her sweater, and smiled down at Willie. All tension had gone from her eyes now.

'Why the hell do I do it?' she said helplessly. 'Why do I always have to . . . to snivel once a job's over?'

'Not always, Princess,' he said reasonably. 'Not often. Only after the rough 'uns. And we've been right up the sharp end for a long while this time.' He eased himself to a sitting position. 'I think it's nice meself,' he said simply. 'Honest I do, Princess. It's nice an' sort of . . . womanly.'

She laughed and stood up. 'Maybe. But I wouldn't want anybody to know.'

'Nobody does. Except Mrs. Garvin's little Willie. And you can't count 'im.'

'You can count him,' she said, and went up the slope to look for Paul.

The fighting was over. In the distance she could see Abu-Tahir's men herding prisoners towards the monastery. A small group of three or four Arabs had turned back and were coming towards her. They were several hundred yards away, but she thought she could recognise Abu-Tahir. With them was a tall, grey-haired figure in brown trousers and a dark green jacket. Tarrant.

Paul was quite close, over to the right on a bulging hummock of rock, staring slowly around him. She waved, and saw him slither down from the rock and disappear.

'Back in a minute, Willie,' she said, and moved away. When Paul came into sight he was running, the Colt Cobra swinging in his hand. He slowed to a walk on seeing her, and put the gun away. She saw the two deep grooves on his face, curving down from the nose to the corners of his mouth, and the lines of strain about his eyes.

They stood facing each other. Nearby, two men lay sprawled in death, and there were splashes of blood on the rocky ground.

Hagan shook his head dumbly. This was the end of the long torment. There had been the waiting and the fear; the turmoil of phone-calls and emergency preparations; the race from Port Said to the airfield, the waiting for Abu-Tahir's men to arrive, and the seemingly endless flight over the Mediterranean at the

230

stick of the glider, with the DC-6 roaring ahead and Abu-Tahir's men crammed in the fuselage behind him; Tarrant, incredibly, saying to Abu-Tahir, 'Never mind your bloody diamonds, at least they're indestructible.' Abu-Tahir grinning, patting his rifle, and saying, 'I also think first of Modestee, Sir Tarrant.' And at last the fleeting glimpse of gunfire below before focusing his entire concentration on the landing; the nightmare of those moments, and the doubts that his remembered skill would serve; the sense of wonder when the skidding glider came to a splintering halt and he found himself still alive and unhurt.

Thirty seconds ago, hope had been almost dead in him. He had felt like a walking ghost, a thing without substance as he hunted through the rocks for her body. But now he was aware of flesh and blood again, of limbs and muscle, of bone and marrow, and he was conscious of the warm sun on his face.

She was smiling at him a little uncertainly, as if for a moment he seemed a stranger. Her face was grazed, grimed with dirt and gunsmoke, her hands black. She stood flat-footed, in heel-less boots. The sweater was torn, and a long rip gaped in the knee of her slacks. Her hair was damp and plastered to her head, but hung loose down her neck to just below the shoulders. She looked like an urchin after a morning's play in a wet junk-yard.

'In God's name,' Hagan said slowly, 'how did a scruff like you ever persuade me to take you to bed?'

Her smile sparkled, though weariness hung like a cloak about her. 'You've caught me out,' she said. 'I wasn't expecting you so soon. And it's been one of those mornings.'

He took her by the shoulders and bent to kiss her lips. She smelt of cordite and sweat, and the sharp blend of it stirred him strangely. His hands slid down to her wrists. He stiffened, and lifted one hand to look at the caked blood on the sleeve of the sweater.

'It's not mine, darling. It's Willie's.'

'Bad?'

'Through the thigh. It could have been a lot worse. But we'd better see to him now.'

'*El Sayyide!*' Abu-Tahir came striding towards them with

Tarrant and three men following. The Sheik's dark face was alight with excitement and wonder. 'Here has been great fighting!' he said, and threw powerful arms around her. 'Sir Tarrant has been much troubled for you, Modestee, but all the time I have told him that you would——'

'Please, old friend. Willie Garvin is hurt. We will talk later.'

'Ah?' He looked at her anxiously.

'Over here.' She gave Tarrant a little smile of greeting, and read many unspoken things in his tired eyes. At the lip of the shallow basin they halted and looked down. Willie was propped on an elbow beside the dead body, slowly going through the man's pockets.

Hagan said: 'Hallo, Willie boy.'

Willie lifted his head and peered with eyes that were a little glazed. 'Anyone got a fag,' he said hopefully. 'This bastard seems to 'ave given it up.'

Tarrant sat in a chair under the southern wall of the monastery, looking across the paved courtyard to the expanse of blue sea sparkling under the noonday sun. It was very quiet now. The ache in his bones and in his head had gone, and he felt pleasantly drowsy.

Two Arabs emerged from a door, carrying a body wrapped in a blanket. They passed across the courtyard and laid their burden down in line with a neat row of similarly shrouded forms. Seventeen so far, Tarrant registered automatically, and wondered if they had got the Fothergill woman down yet.

The two Arabs went back into the monastery. There was plenty for them to do. Abu-Tahir and his men were in charge of cleaning up. The monks had set up a make-shift operating theatre.

Tarrant looked at his watch. If the British Ambassador in Cairo and his counterpart in Istanbul had done their jobs, a boat from Turkey should be arriving at the island very soon now. He wondered about repercussions. The Turks were a realistic people; with luck they would accept Abu-Tahir's technical infringement of their territory without complaint under the circumstances. Tarrant decided that he would talk to the old brigand, suggest that he offered to have the monastery repaired and restored. A gesture like that would go a long way.

His own position was interesting. The Ambassador in Cairo had forbidden him to go with the force on the glider. That matter, His Excellency had declared, was the responsibility of Abu-Tahir as ruler of the sovereign state of Malaurak. It was not an affair in which a member of Her Majesty's Civil Service should become involved.

Tarrant had said nothing and disobeyed the instruction, on the grounds that he was covered by orders from the Minister to maintain close liaison in every way with Abu-Tahir. His resignation might be demanded. Or he might get a bouquet. It depended on the Turkish reaction, probably.

Tarrant smiled to himself. Whichever way it went, Jack Fraser was going to be green with envy about all this.

Hagan came out and Tarrant pushed another chair towards him. 'Those monks have had a busy morning,' Hagan said. 'That's quite an operating team they've got.'

'What about Willie?'

'They've just finished fixing him up. Modesty's bringing him along now.' He sat down and looked at Tarrant. 'Too bad about Gabriel—and this other guy, McWhirter or something.'

Tarrant shrugged. 'Modesty wasn't surprised they got away. Apparently Gabriel's the sort of man to have a private bolt-hole. Did you find out what kind of boat he had hidden below the west cliffs?'

'A seventeen-foot two-berth cabin cruiser. With plenty of fuel. If they make the coast of Syria without getting picked up, I wouldn't bet a plugged nickel on taking them.'

Tarrant nodded agreement. 'Does it worry Modesty that Gabriel's loose—I mean, for herself?' he asked.

'No.' Hagan lit a cigarette. 'I figure she doesn't worry too much about tomorrow or the day after. And anyway, she says Gabriel only goes for what pays. That's how he's geared.'

They sat in silence for a while, then Hagan said: 'Do you think she'll let you use her again on another job sometime?'

'Sometime, yes. But not for a while. Modesty isn't my agent, you know. She doesn't belong to anybody.'

'That's right. She doesn't belong to anybody.' Hagan stared at the ground. 'Do you have many women agents on your pay-roll?'

'A few. Some are very good. But they normally operate in less troubled waters than this.' Tarrant's gesture included the island and all that had happened there.

'So I'd hope,' Hagan said in a flat voice. 'This wasn't a job for a woman—or even for a man that I could name.'

'I didn't know that when I put her in, and when I tried to take her out she wouldn't come. She was right, Hagan. It worked in the end.'

'This time. You could kill her next time.'

Tarrant said: 'It's part of my job, risking other people—the hardest part. But I have to use the best instruments available. I'll use her again if she'll let me, because she's unique.' He looked at Hagan. 'You know why. You can take a girl from University or the typing pool; if she's got the right potential you can put her through Intelligence and combat training, and produce a damn good agent. *But you won't produce a Modesty Blaise.* It took a rare potential and twenty-odd years of hard conditioning to do that ... all her life, for as far back as she can remember.'

Modesty came into the courtyard, pushing Willie Garvin in an ancient wheel-chair. Willie was scrubbed clean and wearing a long white shift. A hump of thick bandaging showed under the shift on his wounded thigh. Modesty, too, was clean now. She wore clothes she had found in one of the rooms occupied by Gabriel's men—a yellow shirt, too large for her, grey cotton trousers turned up at the cuffs, and floppy sandals. Her hair was tied loosely back, and she wore no vestige of make-up.

Willie's face was very white beneath a damp tangle of hair, but his eyes were bright. For the moment, recent pain had driven away fatigue.

'Just 'alf-an-hour, Princess,' he was pleading. 'I'd like to sit in the sun for a bit.'

'Well ... just half-an-hour.' She brought the chair to a halt beside Tarrant and Hagan as they rose to their feet. 'But then it's bedtime, Willie.'

'You too, Princess.'

'Me too.' She looked at Tarrant. 'Will you sit with Willie for half-an-hour?'

'I'd be glad to, my dear.' He glanced across the courtyard at the long row of bodies. 'We shall have plenty to talk about. You seem to have had a busy night.'

'It started off quiet,' said Willie, 'but things picked up later.' A touch of anxiety clouded his face. 'I 'ope we didn't upset these ol' monks too much, Sir G.'

'I think not,' Tarrant answered. 'Not under the circumstances. After all "... *they have seen the ungodly in great power; and flourishing like a green bay tree.*" Psalm thirty-seven.'

Willie stared incredulously. 'I never knew you'd been in the coop,' he said, and Hagan laughed.

Modesty looked at Willie and shook her head. 'Your hair,' she said. 'You look like a wet sunflower.' She took out a small pocket-comb and ran it through the tangles. Parting his hair, she combed it neatly into place. 'There. That's much prettier.'

She put the comb away, took out a packet of cigarettes and a box of matches, and laid them on his knee. 'Anything else you might want, Willie love?'

'No. I'm fine thanks, Princess.'

'Sure?'

'Sure. You leave me an' Sir G. to natter about coops we 'ave known.'

She smiled, touched his shoulder, then turned away with Hagan, slipping her arm through his. Tarrant watched them go across the courtyard and out through the arched opening. Later, as they slowly mounted a gentle slope to the edge of the cliffs, he saw them again above the courtyard wall.

He said: 'Does it hurt, Willie?'

'Not too bad. Clever ol' sticks, those monks.'

'I didn't mean the leg.'

Willie followed his gaze to the two figures on the cliff-top, small in perspective, then stared at Tarrant.

'Why should that 'urt?' he said, puzzled. His eyes were becoming a little unfocused now. 'She's entitled, isn't she?'

'Of course. But it seems...' Tarrant gestured vaguely and was silent.

'I'm on a different page of the book to Hagan,' Willie said. Laboriously he lit a cigarette, and exhaled with sleepy contentment. 'But if you come right down to it, I bet he'd rather be where I am than where he is.'

'It's very possible,' Tarrant said slowly. 'You're a fortunate man, Willie.'

'I know it.' Willie inclined his head back towards the monastery. 'What I've got, you couldn't buy with them two crates of diamonds, Sir G.'

They were silent for a while, then Tarrant said: 'Do you think I've lost Hagan?'

'No...' Willie's voice was slurred. 'Not for long. He should 'ave plenty of time to get that portrait finished though.'

'No more than that?'

'She couldn't be tied down...' Willie's voice faded to a mumble and his eyes closed, head drooping. Tarrant leaned forward and gently took the burning cigarette from between his fingers.

On the cliff top Modesty sat propped on one arm beside Paul Hagan. Her eyes, darkly smudged with fatigue, followed a gull circling out over the sea.

'Do you want to smoke?' Hagan asked.

'No, darling. Just to sit.' She looked down at the floppy yellow shirt, the overlarge trousers bunched at her waist, and shook her head resignedly. 'I'll never be able to get you to bed after this.'

'Who knows? I'm very good-natured.'

She flicked a twig at him and looked out to sea again.

'Back in Cairo,' she said dreamily, 'I know a marvellous little hairdresser. And I've got a whole trunk of clothes unopened. There's a dress, Paul. I haven't worn it yet. It's a dark, plushy red, and it's thoroughly wicked. The wickedest thing you ever saw. And there are some long, dangly ear-rings, and shoes with beautiful high heels, and loads of perfume and lipstick and eye-shadow.'

'Sold,' said Hagan. 'Nothing can save you now.'

'I hope not.' A ghost of the urchin grin broke through her weariness. 'We'll find a place where no one can hear my screams.'

'And lay in a week's supply of food.'

She nodded, stretched out her legs and put her head down on his lap. Her eyes closed. 'Shake me if I don't wake up in half-an-hour,' she said. 'I've got to see to Willie.'

Hagan felt her body relax, heard her breathing become slow and deep. Gently his hand moved on her neck, following the line that baffled his brush.

Somewhere in the monastery a bell began to toll. She did not stir. With his hand resting on her waist, he sat watching the gull, marking the freedom of its flight, and listening to the bell.

He knew that it was tolling for him; tolling for him in a time still to come, after unknown days and unknown nights, when she would go and he would die a little.

But not yet. His hand moved to rest quietly on her breast.

Not yet.

Dick Francis
Rat Race £1.75

Top-class novel about a taxi-plane pilot in a fraud scheme . . .
exciting (there is an in-the-air rescue sequence that would
make you really and truly angry if you had to put it down) and a
splendid read' THE TIMES

Banker £1.75

Dick Francis is off at a gallop again! *Banker* is about £5 million
of horseflesh called Sandcastle, a sort of super-Arkle. A young
trainer gets a merchant bank to invest in him, and merchant
banks, like all banks, only invest in sure things . . .' DAILY MAIL

'Strongly told . . . this must be his best yet' THE TIMES
LITERARY SUPPLEMENT

Reflex £1.75

'A tough young steeplechase jockey who's had a rough history
and is nudging success strays upon blackmail and rigged running,
takes on villains with true grit and photographic wizardry'
SCOTSMAN

'A long way ahead of the rest of the field' NEW YORK TIMES

'Dick Francis has excelled himself . . . this is easily his smoothest
and most accomplished novel to date' DAILY TELEGRAPH

Ed Mcbain
Bread £1.50

Elizabeth screamed again, a long blood-curdling scream that
echoed through the squad-room. The horror of it gut-wrenched
even the detectives of 87th Precinct . . . Yet they played the tape
of the mass assault again and again. It could be their best clue
to a mess of arson, dope, homicide and porn.

Heat £1.75

In the heat of the city summer, Jerry Newman, failed painter and
twice-failed husband, died. Suicide they said, but Carella knew
that suicides left notes and didn't turn the air-conditioning off on
the hottest night of the year. Which puts Carella on the trail of a
killer, while Kling's on the trail of a lovely wife he can't trust,
and someone nasty is on Kling's trail.

'Tense, gripping and stylish . . . by the best modern American
crime writer' SUNDAY EXPRESS

Ghosts £1.75

The dead woman on the snowy sidewalk was a little early for a
Christmas Eve suicide. She wasn't a suicide, she was a murder
victim — and so was the ghost-story writer who died of nineteen
stab wounds only minutes later. This Precinct murder hunt,
taking in mediums and haunted houses, was one set to give
Steve Carella the biggest scare of his life.
'In *Ghosts* the maestro is near the top of his form'
CURRENT CRIME

☐	**Travellers' Britain**	} Arthur Eperon	£2.95p
☐	**Travellers' Italy**		£2.95p
☐	**The Complete Calorie Counter**	Eileen Fowler	80p
☐	**The Diary of Anne Frank**	Anne Frank	£1.75p
☐	**And the Walls Came Tumbling Down**	Jack Fishman	£1.95p
☐	**Linda Goodman's Sun Signs**	Linda Goodman	£2.50p
☐	**Scott and Amundsen**	Roland Huntford	£3.95p
☐	**Victoria RI**	Elizabeth Longford	£4.95p
☐	**Symptoms**	Sigmund Stephen Miller	£2.50p
☐	**Book of Worries**	Robert Morley	£1.50p
☐	**Airport International**	Brian Moynahan	£1.75p
☐	**Pan Book of Card Games**	Hubert Phillips	£1.95p
☐	**Keep Taking the Tabloids**	Fritz Spiegl	£1.75p
☐	**An Unfinished History of the World**	Hugh Thomas	£3.95p
☐	**The Baby and Child Book**	Penny and Andrew Stanway	£4.95p
☐	**The Third Wave**	Alvin Toffler	£2.95p
☐	**Pauper's Paris**	Miles Turner	£2.50p
☐	**The Psychic Detectives**	Colin Wilson	£2.50p
☐	**The Flier's Handbook**		£5.95p

All these books are available at your local bookshop or newsagent, or can be ordered direct from the publisher. Indicate the number of copies required and fill in the form below

11

....

Name_____
(Block letters please)

Address_____

_____

Send to CS Department, Pan Books Ltd, PO Box 40, Basingstoke, Hants
Please enclose remittance to the value of the cover price plus:
35p for the first book plus 15p per copy for each additional book ordered
to a maximum charge of £1.25 to cover postage and packing
Applicable only in the UK

While every effort is made to keep prices low, it is sometimes
necessary to increase prices at short notice. Pan Books reserve
the right to show on covers and charge new retail prices which
may differ from those advertised in the text or elsewhere